More praise for
The Monarchies of God Series

**Be sure to discover the first two books of
The Monarchies of God . . .**

HAWKWOOD'S VOYAGE
THE HERETIC KINGS

D0324840

THE IRON
WARS

BOOK THREE OF THE MONARCHIES OF GOD

PAUL KEARNEY

ACE BOOKS, NEW YORK

This book is respectfully dedicated
to the memory of
Richard Evans

This is a work of fiction. Names, characters, places, and incidents either
are the product of the author's imagination or are used fictitiously,
and any resemblance to actual persons, living or dead, business
establishments, events, or locales is entirely coincidental.

THE IRON WARS

An Ace Book / published by arrangement with
Orion Publishing Group

PRINTING HISTORY
Millennium edition / 2000
Ace mass-market edition / March 2002

Visit our website at
www.penguinputnam.com
Check out the ACE Science Fiction & Fantasy newsletter!

ISBN: 0-441-00917-4

ACE®
Ace Books are published by The Berkley Publishing Group,
a division of Penguin Putnam Inc.,
375 Hudson Street, New York, New York 10014.
ACE and the "A" design
are trademarks belonging to Penguin Putnam Inc.

PRINTED IN THE UNITED STATES OF AMERICA

10 9 8 7 6 5 4 3 2

WHAT WENT BEFORE...

FIVE centuries ago two great religious faiths arose which were to dominate the entire known world. They were founded on the teachings of two men. In the west, St Ramusio; in the east, the Prophet Ahrimuz.

The Ramusian faith rose at the same time that the great continent-wide empire of the Fimbrians was coming apart. The greatest soldiers the world had ever seen, the Fimbrians had become embroiled in a vicious civil war which enabled their conquered provinces to break away one by one and become the Seven Kingdoms. Fimbria dwindled to a shadow of her former self, her troops still formidable, but her concerns confined exclusively to the problems within the borders of the homeland. And the Seven Kingdoms went from strength to strength—until that is, the first hosts of the Merduks began pouring over the Jafrar mountains, quickly reducing their numbers to five.

Thus began the great struggle between the Ramusians of the west and the Merduks of the east, a sporadic and brutal war carried on for generations, which, by the sixth century of Ramusian reckoning, was finally reaching its climax.

For Aekir, greatest city of the west and seat of the Ramusian Pontiff, finally fell to the eastern invaders in the year 551. Out of its sack escaped two men whose survival was to have the greatest consequences for future history. One of them was the Pontiff himself, Macrobius—thought dead by the rest of the Ramusian kingdoms and by the remainder of the Church hierarchy. The other was Corfe Cear-Inaf, a lowly ensign of cavalry, who deserted his post in despair after the loss of his wife in the tumult of the city's fall.

But the Ramusian Church had already elected another Pontiff, Himerius, who was set upon purging the Five Kingdoms of any remnant of the Dweomer-folk—the practitioners of magic. The purge caused Hebrion's young king, Abeleyn, to accept a desperate expedition into the uttermost west to seek the fabled Western continent, an expedition led by his ruthlessly ambitious cousin, Lord Murad of Galiapeno. Murad blackmailed a master mariner, one Richard Hawkwood, into navigating the voyage, and as passengers and would-be colonists they took along some of the refugee Dweomer-folk of Hebrion, including one Bardolin of Carreirida. But when they finally reached the fabled west, they found that a colony of lycanthropes and mages had already existed there for centuries under the aegis of an immortal arch-mage, Aruan. Their exploratory party was wiped out, only Murad, Hawkwood and Bardolin surviving.

Back in Normannia, the Ramusian Church was split

down the middle as three of the Five Kingdoms recognized Macrobius as the true Pontiff, while the rest preferred the newly elected Himerius. Religious war eruped as the three so-called Heretic Kings—Abeleyn of Hebrion, Mark of Astarac and Lofantyr of Torunna, fought to retain their thrones. They all succeeded, but Abeleyn had the hardest battle to fight. He was forced to storm his own capital, Abrusio, by land and sea, half-destroying it in the process.

Farther east, the Torunnan fortress of Ormann Dyke became the focus of Merduk assault, and there Corfe distinguished himself in its defence. He was promoted and, catching the eye of Torunna's Queen Dowager, Odelia, was given the mission of bringing to heel the rebellious nobles in the south of the kingdom. This he undertook with a motley, ill-equipped band of ex-galley slaves, which was all the king would allow him. Plagued by the memory of his lost wife, he was, mercifully, unaware that she had in fact survived Aekir's fall, and was now the favourite concubine of the Sultan Aurungzeb himself.

The momentous year 551 drew to a close. In Almark, the dying king Haukir bequeathed his kingdom to the Himerian Church, transforming it into a great temporal power. And in Charibon two humble monks, Albrec and Avila, stumbled upon an ancient document, a biography of St Ramusio which stated that he was one and the same as the Merduk Prophet Ahrimuz. The monks fled Charibon, but not before a macabre encounter with the chief librarian of the monastery city, who turned out to be a werewolf. They ran into the teeth of a midwinter blizzard, collapsing into the snow.

AND now all over the continent of Normannia, the armies are once more on the march.

In thy faint slumbers I by thee have watched,
And heard thee murmur tales of iron wars . . .

Henry IV, Part I

PROLOGUE

IN the sweating nightmare-fever of the dark he felt the beast enter his room and stand over him. But that was impossible. Not from so far, surely—

Oh, swect God in heaven, overlord of earth, be with me now . . .

Prayers, prayers, prayers. The mockery of it, he praying to God, whose soul was black as pitch and already sold. Already lost and consigned to the fires of eons.

Sweet Ramusio, sit with me. Be near me now in this lost hour.

He wept. It was here, of course it was. It was watching, patient as a stone. He belonged to it. He was damned.

Soaked in perspiration, he opened his gummy eyelids to the all-embracing dark of his midnight room. Tears had fled down the sides of his neck as he slept and the heavy furs of his bed were awry. He gave a start at their lumpen, hairy shape. But it was nothing. He was alone after all, thank God. Nothing but the quiet winter night wheeling in its chill immensity beyond the room.

He scratched flint and steel together from the bedside table, and when the tinder caught transferred the seed of sparks to his candle. A light, a point of reference in the looming murk.

Utterly alone. He was without even the God he had once reverenced and to whom he had devoted the best years of his life. Clerics and theologians said that the Creator was everywhere, in every niche and pocket of the world. But He was not here, in this room. Not tonight.

Something else was coming, though. Even now he could sense it hurtling through the dark towards him as unstoppable as the turning sun, its feet hardly setting down upon the dormant world. It could cover continents and oceans in the blink of an eye.

The furs on his bed gave a twitch, and he yelped. He clawed his way to the headboard, eyes starting out of his head, heart hammering behind his ribs.

They gathered themselves into a mound, a hulking mass of hair. And then they began to grow, bulking out in the dimness and the candleflame, the room a sudden playground of moving shadows as the light flickered and swam.

The furs rose and rose in the bed, towering now. And when they loomed over him, tall as some misshapen megalith, two yellow eyes blinked on in their midst, bright-hungry as an arsonist's flame.

It was here. It had come.

He fell on his face amid the damp linen sheets, worshipping. Truly *here*—he could smell the musk of its presence, feel the heat of the enormous form. A drop of spit fell from its maw and as it struck his neck it sizzled there, burning him.

Greetings, Himerius, the beast said.

"Master," the prostrate cleric whispered, grovelling in his soiled bed.

Be not afraid, its voice said without a sound. Himerius's reply was inarticulate, a gargle of terror.

The time is here, my friend, it said. *Look up at me. Sit up and see.*

A huge paw, fingered and taloned like some mockery of man and beast, raised him to his knees. Its pads scorched his skin through the wool of his winter shift.

The face of the winter's wolf, its ears like horns above a massive black-furred skull in which the eyes glared like saffron lamps, black-slitted. A foot-long fanged muzzle from which the saliva dripped in silver strings, the black lips drawn back taut and quivering. And caught in the teeth, some glistening vermilion gobbet.

Eat.

Himerius was weeping, terror flooding his mind. "Please master," he blubbered. "I am not ready. I am not worthy—"

Eat.

The paws clamped on to his biceps and he was lifted off his feet. The bed creaked under them. His face was drawn close to the hot jaws, its breath sickening him, like the wet heat of a jungle heavy with putrefaction. A gateway to a different and unholy world.

He took the gobbet of meat in his mouth, his lips

bruised in a ghastly kiss against the fangs of the wolf. Chewed, swallowed. Fought the instinct to retch as it slid down his gullet as though seeking the blood-dark path to his heart.

Good. Very good. And now for the other.

"No, I beg you!" Himerius wept.

He was thrown to his stomach on the bed and his shift was ripped from his back with a negligent wave of the thing's paw. Then the wolf was atop him, the awesome weight of it pinioning him, driving the air out of his lungs. He felt he was being suffocated, could not even cry out.

I am a man of God. Oh Lord, help me in my torment!

And then the sudden, screaming pain as it mounted him, pushing brutally into his body with a single, rending thrust.

His mind went white and blank with the agony. The beast was panting in his ear, its mouth dripping to scald his neck. The claws scored his shoulders as it violated him and its fur was like the jab of a million needles against his spine.

The beast shuddered into him, some deep snarl of release rising from its throat. The powerful haunches lifted from his buttocks. It withdrew.

You are truly one of us now. I have given you a precious gift, Himerius. We are brethren under the light of the moon.

He felt that he had been torn apart. He could not even lift his head. There were no prayers now, nothing to plead to. Something precious had been wrenched out of his soul, and a foulness bedded there in its place.

The wolf was fading, its stink leaving the room.

Himerius was weeping bitterly into the mattress, blood trickling down his legs.

"Master," he said. "Thank you, master."

And when he raised his head at last he was alone on the great bed, his chamber empty, and the wind picking up to a howl around the deserted cloisters outside.

PART ONE

MIDWINTER

The spirit which knows not how to submit, which retires from no danger because it is formidable, is the soul of a soldier.

Robert Jackson, *A Systematic View on the Formation, Discipline and Economy of Armies,* 1804

ONE

NOTHING Isolla had been told could have prepared her for it. There had been wild rumours, of course, macabre tales of destruction and slaughter. But the scale of the thing still took her by surprise.

She stood on the leeward side of the carrack's quarterdeck, her ladies-in-waiting silent as owls by her side. They had a steady north-wester on the larboard quarter and the ship was plunging along before it like a stag fleeing the hounds, sending a ten-foot bow-wave off to leeward which the weak winter sunlight filled full of rainbows.

She had felt not a smidgen of sickness, which pleased her; it was a long time since she had last been at sea, a long time since she had been anywhere. The breakneck passage of the Fimbrian Gulf had been exhilarating after the sombre gloom of a winter court, a court which had only recently emerged from an attempted coup. Her brother, the King of Astarac, had fought and won half a dozen small battles to keep his throne. But that was nothing compared to what had gone on in the kingdom that was her destination. Nothing at all.

They were sailing steadily up a huge bay, at the end of which the capital of Hebrion, gaudy old Abrusio, squatted like a harlot on a chamberpot. It had been the rowdiest, most raucous, godless port of the western world. And the richest. But now it was a blackened shell.

Civil war had scorched the guts out of Abrusio. For fully three miles, the waterfront was smoking ruin. The hulks of once-great ships stabbed up out of the water along the remnants of the wharves and docks, and extending from the shore was a wasteland hundreds of acres in extent. The still-smoking wreck of the Lower City, its buildings flattened by the inferno which had raged through it. Only Admiral's Tower stood mostly intact, a gaunt sentinel, a gravestone.

There was a powerful fleet anchored in the Outer Roads. Hebrion's navy, depleted by the fierce fighting to retake the city from the Knights Militant and the traitors who had been in league with them, was a force to be reckoned with, even now: tall ships whose yards were a cat's cradle of rigging lines and furiously busy mariners, repairing the damage of war. Abrusio still had teeth in plenty.

Up on the hill above the harbour the Royal palace and the monastary of the Inceptines still stood, though pitted by the naval bombardment which had ended the final assaults. Up there, somewhere, a king awaited them, looking down on the ruins of his capital.

• • •

ISOLLA was sister to a different king. A tall, thin, plain woman with a long nose which seemed to overhang her mouth except when she smiled. A cleft chin, and a large, pale forehead dusted with freckles. She had long ago given up trying for the porcelain purity that was expected of a courtly lady, and had even put aside her powders and creams. And the ideas which had prompted her to don them in the first place.

She was sailing to Hebrion to be married.

Hard to remember the boy who had been Abeleyn, the boy now become a man and a king. In the times they had seen each other as children he had been cruel to her, mocking her ugliness, pulling at the flaming russet hair which was her only glory. But there had been a light about him, even then, something that made it hard to hate him, easy to like. "Issy Long-nose," he had called her as a boy, and she had hated him for it. And yet when the young Prince Lofantyr had tripped her up in the mud one winter's evening in Vol Ephrir, he had ducked the future King of Torunna in a puddle and smeared the Royal nose in the filth Isolla stood covered in. Because she was Mark's sister, and Mark was his best friend, he had said. And he had wiped the tears from her eyes with gruff, boyish tenderness. She had worshipped him for it, only to hate him again a day later when she became the butt of his pranks once more.

He would be her husband very soon, the first man she had ever let into her bed. At twenty-seven she hardly worried about that side of things, though it would of course be her duty to produce a male heir, the quicker the better. A political marriage with no romance about it, only convenient practicalities. Her body was the treaty between two kingdoms, a symbol of their alliance. Outside that, it had no real worth at all.

"By the mark eleven!" the leadsman in the bows called. And then: "Sweet blood of God! Starboard, helmsman! There's a wreck in the fairway!"

The helmsmen swung the ship's wheel and the carrack turned smoothly. Sliding past the port bow the ship's company saw the grounded wreck of a warship, the tips of her yards jutting above the surface of the seas no more than a foot, the shadowed bulk of her hull clearly visible in the lucid water.

The entire ship's company had been staring at the war-wrecked remnants of the city. Many of the sailors were clambering up the shrouds like apes to get a better view. On the sterncastle the quartet of heavily armed Astaran knights had lost their impassive air and were gazing as fixedly as the rest.

"Abrusio, God help us!" the master said, moved beyond his accustomed taciturnity.

"The city is destroyed!" one of the men at the wheel burst out.

"Shut your mouth and keep your course. Leadsman! Sing out there. Pack of witless idiots. You'd run her aground so you could gape at a dancing bear. Braces there! By God, are we to spill our wind with the very harbour in sight, and let Hebrians brand us for mooncalf fools?"

"There ain't no harbour left," one of the more laconic of the master's mates said, spitting over the leeward rail with a quick, hunted look of apology to Isolla a second later. "She's burned to the waterline, skipper.

There's hardly a wharf left we could tie up to. We'll have to anchor in the Inner Roads and send in a long-boat."

"Aye, well," the master muttered, his brow still dark. "Get tackles to the yardarms. It may be you're right."

"One moment, Captain," one of the knights who were Isolla's escort called out. "We don't yet know who is in charge in Abrusio. Perhaps the King could not retake the city. It may be in the hands of the Knights Militant."

"There's the Royal flammifer flying from the palace," the master's mate told him.

"Aye, but it's at half mast," someone added.

There was a pause after that. The crew looked to the master for orders. He opened his mouth, but just as he was about to speak the lookout hailed him.

"Deck there! I see a vessel putting off from the base of Admiral's Tower and it's flying the Royal pennant."

At the same second the ship's company could see puffs of smoke exploding from the battered seawalls of the city, and a heartbeat later came the sound of the retorts, distant staccato thunder.

"A Royal Salute," the leading knight said. His face had brightened considerably. "The Knights Militant and usurpers would never give us a salute—more likely a broadside. The city belongs to the Royalists. Captain, you'd best make ready to receive the Hebrian King's emissaries."

Tension had relaxed along the deck, and the sailors were chattering to each other. Isolla stood on in silence, and it was the observant master's mate who voiced her thought for her.

"Why's the banner at half mast is what I'd like to

know. They only do that when a king is—"

His voice was drowned out by the pummelling of bare feet on the decks as the crew made ready to receive the Hebrian vessel that approached. As it came closer, a twenty-oared Royal barge with a scarlet canopy, Isolla saw that its crew were all dressed in black.

"THE lady has arrived, it would seem," General Mercado said.

He was standing with his hands behind his back, staring out and down upon the world from the King's balcony. The whole circuit of the ruined Lower City was his to contemplate, as well as the great bays which made up Abrusio's harbours and the naval fortifications which peppered them.

"What the hell are we going to do, Golophin?"

There was a rustling in the gloom of the dimly lit room, where the light from the open balcony could not reach. A long shape detached itself soundlessly from the shadows and joined the general. It was leaner than a living man had a right to be, something crafted out of parchment and sticks and gnawed scraps of leather, hairless and bone-white. The long mantle it wore swamped it, but two eyes glittered brightly out of the ravaged face and when it spoke the voice was low and musical, one meant for laughter and song.

"We play for time, what else? A suitable welcome, a suitable place to stay, and absolute silence on anything regarding the King's health."

"The whole damned city is in mourning. I'll wager she thinks him dead already," Mercado snapped. One side of his face was gnarled into a grimace, the other was a serene silver mask which had never changed, not in all the years since Golophin had put it there to save his life. The eyeball on the silver side glared bloodshot and lidless, a fearsome thing which cowed his subordinates. But it could not cow the man who had created it.

"I know Isolla, or did," Golophin riposted, snapping in his turn. "She's a sensible child—a woman now, I suppose. As importantly, she has a mind, and will not fly into hysterics at the drop of a glove. And she will do as she is told, by God."

Mercado seemed mollified. He did not look at the cadaverous old wizard but said: "And you, Golophin, how goes it with you?"

Golophin's face broke into a surprisingly sweet smile. "I am like the old whore who has opened her legs too many times. I am sore and tired, General. Not much use to man nor beast."

Mercado snorted. "That will be the day."

As one, they moved away from the balcony and back into the depths of the room. The Royal bedchamber, hung heavily with half-glimpsed tapestries, carpeted with rugs from Ridawan and Calmar, sweetened with the incense of the Levangore. And on a vast four-poster bed, a wasted shape amid the silken sheets. They stood over him in silence.

Abeleyn, King of Hebrion, or what was left of him. A shell had struck him down in the very instant of his victory, when Abrusio was back in his hands and the kingdom saved from a savage theocracy. Some whim of the elder gods had caused it to happen thus, Golophin thought. Nothing of the Ramusian deity's so-called mercy and compassion. Nothing but bitter-tasting irony to leave him like this, not dead, hardly alive.

The King had lost both his legs, and the trunk above the stumps was lacerated and broken, a mass of wounds and shattered bones. The once boyish face was waxen, the lips blue and the feeble breath whistling in and out over them with laboured regularity. At least his sight had been spared. At least he was alive.

"Sweet Blessed Saint, to think that I should ever have lived to see him come to this," Mercado whispered hoarsely, and Golophin heard something not far from a sob in the grim old soldier's voice. "Is there nothing you can do, Golophin? Nothing?"

The wizard uttered a sigh which seemed to start in the toes of his boots. Some of his very vitality seemed to flicker out of him with it.

"I am keeping him breathing. More, I cannot do. I have not the strength. I must let the Dweomer in me grow again. The death of my familiar, the battles. They leached it out of me. I am sorry, General. So sorry. He is my friend too."

Mercado straightened. "Of course. Your apologies. I am behaving like a maiden aunt. There's no time for hand-wringing, not in days like these. . . . Where have you put his bitch of a mistress?"

"She's accommodated in the guest apartments, forever screaming to see him. I have her under guard—for her own protection, naturally."

"She bears his child," Mercado said with an odd savagery.

"So it would seem. We must watch her closely."

"Fucking women," Mercado went on. "Another one here now for us to coddle and to step around."

"As I said, Isolla is different. And she is Mark's sister. The alliance between Hebrion and Astarac must be sealed by their marriage. For the good of the kingdom."

Mercado snorted. "Marriage! And when will that be, I wonder? Will she marry a—" He stopped and bent his head, and Golophin could hear him swearing under his breath, cursing himself. "I have things I must attend to," he said abruptly. "Enough of them, God knows. Let me know if there is any change, Golophin." And he marched out as if he were about to face a court martial.

Golophin sat on the bed and took the hand of his King. His face became that of a malevolent skull, anger and hatred pursuing each other across it until he blinked, and then a huge weariness settled there in their place.

"Better you had died, Abeleyn," he said softly. "A warrior's end for the last of the warrior kings. When you are gone, all the little men will come out from under the stones."

And he bowed his head and wept.

TWO

BY God, Corfe thought, the man had known how to
breed horses.

The destrier was dark bay, almost black, and a good
seventeen hands and a half high. A deep-chested, thick-
necked beast with a lively eye and clean limbs. A true
warhorse, such as a nobleman alone might ride. And
he'd had hundreds of them, all three years old or more,
all geldings. A fortune in horn and bone and muscle—
but, more importantly, the makings of a cavalry army.

His men were encamped in the pastures of one of
the late Duke Ordinac's stud farms. Three acres of
leather tents—also the property of the late duke—had
been pitched in scattered clumps by the four hundred
tribesmen who remained under Corfe's command. The
makeshift camp was as busy as a broken ants' nest,
with men and horses, the smoke of cookfires, the clinking of hammers on little field-anvils, the vastly intricate

and familiar and to Corfe wholly invigorating stink and clamour of a cavalry bivouac.

The gelding danced under him as it seemed to catch the lift of his spirits and he calmed it with voice and knees. He had mounted pickets half a mile out in every direction, and Andruw was two days gone with twenty men on a reconnaissance towards Staed, where Duke Narfintyr was arming against the King with over three thousand men under his banner already.

Stiff odds. But they would be farmers' sons and lesser nobles, peasants turned into soldiers for the day. They would not be the born warriors that Corfe's savage tribesmen were. And there were very few infantry troops on earth who could stand up to a heavy cavalry charge, if it were well handled. Professional pikemen perhaps, and that was all.

No, Corfe's worst enemy was time. It was trickling through his fingers like sand and he had none to spare if he were to find and defeat Narfintyr before being superseded by the second army that King Lofantyr had sent south.

Today was the third of the five Saint's Days that scholars had tacked on to the last month of the year to keep the calendar in step with the seasons. In two days' time it would be *Sidhaon*, the night of Yearsend, and then the cycle would begin anew, and the season start its slow turn towards the warmth and reawakening of spring.

It seemed long overdue. This had been the longest winter of Corfe's life. He could hardly remember what it was like to feel warm sun on his face, to walk on grass instead of trudging through snow or quagmire. A hellish and unnatural time of the year to be making war, especially with horse-soldiers. But then the world had become a hellish and unnatural place of late, with all of the old certainties overturned.

He considered this second army on its way south to deal with the rebels it was his own mission to destroy. A certain Colonel Aras, one of the King's favourites, had been given a tidy little combined force with which to subdue the southern nobles, as the King had clearly expected Corfe to make a hash of it with his barbaric, ill-equipped command. He had enemies behind as well as in front, more to worry about than tactics and logistics; he had to be something of a politician as well. These things were inevitable as one rose higher in rank, but Corfe had never expected the intricacies and balances to be so murderous. Not in a time of war. Half the officers in Torunn, it had seemed to him, were more intent on winning the King's favour than on throwing the Merduks back from Ormann Dyke. When he thought about it, a black, beating rage seemed to hover over him, an anger which had had its birth in the fall of Aekir, and which had been growing silently and steadily in him ever since without hope of release. Only wanton murder could hope to ease it. The killing of Merduk after Merduk down to the last squalling dark-skinned baby until there were no more of them left to stink out the world. Then perhaps his dreams would cease, and Heria's ghost would sleep at last.

A courier cantered up to him and, without flourish or salute, said: "*Ondrow* come back."

He nodded at the man—his tribesmen were picking up quite a bit of Normannic, but still had little notion of the proper forms of address—and followed him as he cantered easily up the hill that dominated the bivouac. Marsch was there, and Ensign Ebro, with three pickets. Ebro slapped out a salute which Corfe returned absently.

"Where away?"

"Less than a league, on the northern road," Marsch told him. He was rubbing his forehead where the heavy *Ferinai* helm had begun to chafe it. "He's in a hurry, I think. He pushes his horses." Marsch sounded faintly disapproving, as if no emergency were important enough to warrant the maltreatment of horses.

"He's swung round then," Corfe said approvingly. "I'll bet he's been taking a look at our rivals in the game."

They sat there watching the score of horsemen galloping up the muddy northern road with the clods dotting the air behind them like startled birds. In ten minutes the party had reined in, the horses' nostrils flared and red, their necks white with foam. Mud everywhere, the riders' faces splattered with it.

"What's the news, Andruw?" Corfe asked calmly, though his heart had begun to thump faster.

His adjutant tore off his helm, his face a mask of filth.

"Narfintyr sits in Staed like an old woman at the hearth. Farmers' boys, his men are, with a few nobles in fifty-year-old armour. None of the other nobles have risen—they're waiting to see if he can get away with it. They've heard of Ordinac's fate, but no one thinks we are regular Torunnan troops. The gossip has it that Ordinac ran into a war-party of Merduk deserters and scavengers."

Corfe laughed. "Fair enough. Now, what news from the north?"

"Ah, there's the interesting part. Aras and his column are close—less than a day's march behind us. Nigh on three thousand men, five hundred of them mounted—cuirassiers and pistoleers. And six light guns. They have a screen of cavalry out to their front."

"Did they see you?" Corfe demanded.

"Not a chance. We crawled on our bellies and watched them from a ridgeline. They're bound by the speed of the guns and the baggage wagons, and the road is a morass. I'll bet they've cursed those culverins all the way south from Torunn."

Corfe grinned. "You're beginning to talk like a cavalryman, Andruw."

"Aye, well, it's one thing firing them, quite another coaxing them through a swamp. What's to do, Corfe?"

They were all looking at him. Suddenly there was a different feeling in the air, a tenseness which Corfe knew and had come to love.

"We pack and move out at once," he said crisply. "Marsch, see to it. I want one squadron out in front as a screen. You will command it. Another to herd the remounts, and a third as rearguard under Andruw here. The lead squadron moves out as soon as they can saddle up. The rest will follow when they can. Gentlemen, I believe we have work to do."

The little knot of riders split up, Andruw's party heading for the horse herd to procure fresh mounts. Only Ebro remained beside Corfe.

"And what am I to do, sir?" he asked, half resentful and half plaintive.

"Get the baggage mules sorted. I want them ready to move out within two hours. Pack everything you can, but don't overload them. We have to move quickly."

"Sir, Narfintyr has three thousand men; we are less than four hundred. Hadn't we better wait for Aras to come, and combine with him?"

Corfe stared coldly at his subordinate. "Have you no hankering for glory, Ensign? You have your orders."

"Yes, sir."

Ebro galloped off, looking thoroughly discontented.

THE perfect industry of the bivouac was shattered as the officers rode around shouting orders and the tribesmen hurried to don their armour and saddle their horses. Marsch had found a store of lances in the late Duke Ordinac's castle and the troopers ran to collect theirs from the forest of racks that sprouted between the tents. The tents themselves were left behind, as they were too heavy to be carried by the pack mules that comprised Corfe's baggage train. The stubborn, braying beasts had enough to bear: grain for a thousand horses for a week, the field-forges with their small anvils and clanking tools. Pig-iron for spare horseshoes, and extra lances, weapons and armour, to say nothing of the plain but bulky rations that the men themselves would consume on the march. Twice-baked bread, hard as wood, and salt pork for the most part, as well as cauldrons for each squadron in which the pork would be steeped and boiled. A million and one things for an army which was hardly big enough to be an army at all. Ordinarily, a field force would have one heavy double-axled ox-drawn wagon for every fifty men, twice that for cavalry and artillery. Corfe's two-hundred-strong mule train, though it looked impressive en masse, could barely carry anything by regular military standards.

The vanguard moved out within the hour, and the main body an hour after that. By midday, the bivouac they had left behind them was populated only by ghosts and a few mangy dogs who hunted through the abandoned tents for left-behind scraps of food or leather to gnaw on. The race had begun.

WINTER was harsher in the foothills of the northern Cimbrics than it was in the lowlands of Torunna. Here the world was a brutal place of killing grandeur. Twelve thousand feet high and more, the Cimbrics were nevertheless shrinking, their ridges and escarpments less severe than further south. Trees grew on their flanks: a hardy pine and spruce, mountain juniper. In this land the River Torrin had its birthplace. It was already a slashing, foaming torrent two hundred feet wide, an angry spate flushed with the offpourings of the mountains, too violent in its bed to freeze over. It had a hundred and fifty leagues to run before it became the majestic and placid giant which flowed through the city of Torunn and carved out its estuary in the warmer waters of the Kardian Sea beyond.

But here in its millions of millennia of flood it had broken down the very mountains which surrounded it. Here it had carved out a valley amid the peaks. To the north were the last heights of the western Thurians, the rocky barrier which held in the hordes of Ostrabar so that they had been forced in their decades of invasions to take the coastal route in order to break out to the south, and had come up against the walls of Aekir, the guns of Ormann Dyke. To the south-west of the river

were the Cimbrics, Torunna's backbone, home of the
Felimbric tribes and their secret valleys. But this gap,
carved by the course of the Torrin, had for centuries
been the link between Torunna and Charibon, west and
east. It had been a highway of Imperial messengers in
Fimbria's days of empire, when Charibon itself had
been nothing more than a garrison fortress designed to
protect the route to the east from the savages of Almark. It was a conduit of trade and commerce, and in
later days had been fortified by the Torunnans when
the Fimbrian Hegemony came crashing down and men
first began to kill in the name of God. And now there
was an army marching along it, an infantry army
whose soldiers were dressed in black, who carried
twenty-foot pikes or leather-cased arquebuses. A grand
tercio of Fimbrian soldiers, five thousand of the most
feared warriors in the world, tramping through the blizzards and the snow-drifts towards Ormann Dyke.

THAT was the noise he heard and could not account for. It was a sound he had never before heard
in his life, and it carried over the creak of wood and
leather, the clink of metal on metal, even the crunch
of the snow.

Feet. Ten thousand feet marching together in the
snow to produce a low thunder, something felt rather
than heard, a hum in the bones.

Albrec opened his eyes, and found that he was alive.

He was utterly confused for a long minute. Nothing
about him was familiar. He was in something that
swayed and lurched and bumped along. A leather canopy over his head, chinks of unbearably bright light
spearing through gaps here and there. Rich furs encas-

ing him so that he could hardly move. He was bewildered, and could not think of any events which might have added up to the present.

He sat up, and his head exploded into lights and ache, clenching his eyes tight shut for him. He struggled an arm free from his coverings to rub at his face—there was something about it, something strange and whistling in the way he breathed—and the hand appeared bound in clean linen. But it was wrong, it had no shape. It was—

He blinked tears out of his eyes, tried to flex his fingers. But he could not, because they were no longer there. He had a thumb, but beyond his knuckles there was nothing. Nothing.

"Merciful God," he whispered.

He levered free his other hand. It, too, was bound in cloth, but there were fingers there, thank the Blessed Saints. Something to move, to touch with. They tingled as he wiggled them, as though coming to life after a sleep.

He felt his face, absurdly shutting his eyes as if he did not wish to see what his touch might tell him. His lips, his chin, his teeth in place, and his eyes the same. But—

The breath whistled in and out of the hole which had been his nose. He could touch bone. The fleshy part of the feature was gone, the nostrils no longer there. It must look like the hole in the face of a skull.

He lay back again, too shocked to weep, too lost to wonder what had happened. He remembered only shards of horror from a faraway land of dreams. The fanged grin of a werewolf. The dark of subterranean catacombs. The awful blankness of a blizzard, and then nothing at all. Except—

Avila.

And it came back to him with the speed and force of a revelation. They had been fleeing Charibon. The document! He fumbled frantically with his clothes. But his habit was gone. He was dressed in a woollen shift and long stockings, also of wool. He threw aside his furs and crawled over them, lurching as whatever he was inside swayed and bumped along. He scrabbled at the knots which held shut the leather canopy at his feet, the tears finally coming along with the realization of what had happened. He and Avila had been caught by the Inceptines. They must be on their way back to the Monastery City. They would be burnt as heretics. And the document was gone. Gone!

The canopy fell open as he yanked at the drawstrings with his fingered hand, and he fell out and thumped face first into the rutted snow.

He clenched shut his eyes. There was warm breath on his cheek, and something soft as velvet nuzzled his ruined face.

"Get away there, brute!" a voice said, and the snow crunched beside him. Albrec opened his eyes to find a black shape leaning over him, and behind it the agonizing brightness of sunshine on snow, blinding.

Another shadow. The two resolved themselves into men who seized his arms and hauled him to his feet. He stood as confused as an owl in daylight.

"Come, priest. You are holding up the column," one said gruffly. The pair of them tried to stuff him back into the covered cart he saw he had been riding in. Behind them, another such, drawn by an inquisitive mule, and behind that a hundred more, and a thousand men making a dark snake of figures in the snow, all in ranks, pikes at their shoulders. A huge crowd of men standing in the snow waiting for the obstruction ahead to be cleared, the cart to begin moving again.

"Who are you?" Albrec demanded feebly. "What is this?"

They perched him on the back of the two-wheeled cart and one disappeared to take the halter of its mule. They started off again. The column moved once more. There had been no talk, no shouting at the delay, nothing but patience and abrupt efficiency. Albrec saw that the second man who had helped him, like the first, was dressed in knee-high leather boots rimmed with fur and a black cloak which looked almost clerical with its hood and slit sleeves. A plain short sword was hanging from a shoulder baldric. Attached to the harness of the mule he led was an arquebus, its iron barrel winking bright as lightning in the sun, and beside it was a small steel helmet and a pair of black-lacquered metal gauntlets. The man himself was crop-headed, broad and powerfully built under the cloak. He had several days of golden stubble glistening on his chin, and his face was ruddy and reddened, bronzed by days and weeks in the open.

"Who are you?" Albrec asked again.

"My name is Joshelin of Gaderia, twenty-sixth tercio. That's Beltran's."

He did not elaborate, and seemed to think that this should answer Albrec's questions.

"But *what* are you?" Albrec asked plaintively.

The man called Joshelin glared at him. "What is that, a riddle?"

"Forgive me, but are you a soldier of Almark? A—a mercenary?"

The man's eyes lit with anger. "I'm a Fimbrian soldier, priest, and this is a Fimbrian army you're in the midst of, so I'd be watchful of words like 'mercenary' if I were you."

Albrec's astonishment must have showed in his face, because the soldier went on less brusquely: "It's four days since we picked you up—you and the other cleric—and saved you from wolves and frostbite. He's in the cart behind me. He was less beaten up than you. He still has a face, at all events, just lost a few toes and the tips of his ears."

"Avila!" Albrec exclaimed in joy. He began to scramble down from the cart again, but Joshelin's hard palm on his chest halted him.

"He's asleep, like you were. Let him come to himself in his own time."

"Where are we going, if not to Charibon? Why are Fimbrians on the march again?" Albrec had heard rumours in Charibon of such things, but he had dismissed them as novices' fancies.

"We're to relieve Ormann Dyke, it seems," Joshelin said curtly, and spat into the snow. "The fortress we built ourselves. We're to take up the buckler where we set it down all those years ago. And scant gratitude we'll get for it, I shouldn't wonder. We're about as well trusted as Inceptines in this world. Still, it's a chance to fight the heathen again." He clamped his mouth shut, as if he thought he had begun to babble.

"Ormann Dyke," Albrec said aloud. The name was one out of history and legend. The great eastern fortress which had never fallen to assault. It was in

Northern Torunna. They were marching to Torunna.

"I have to speak to someone," he said. "I have to know what was done with our belongings. It's important."

"Lost something, have you, priest?"

"Yes. It's important, I tell you. You can't guess how important."

Joshelin shrugged. "I know nothing about that. Siward and I were told to look after the pair of you, that's all. I think they burned your habits—they weren't worth keeping."

"Oh God," Albrec groaned.

"What is it, a reliquary or something? Were there gems sewn into your robes?"

"It was a story," Albrec said, his eyes stinging and dry. "It was just a story."

He crawled back into the darkness of the shrouded cart.

THE Fimbrians marched far into the night, and when they halted they deployed in a hollow square with the baggage wagons and mules in the middle. Sharpened stakes were hammered into the ground to make a bristling fence about the camp, and details were ordered out of the perimeter to collect firewood. Albrec was given a soldier's cloak and boots—both much too large for him—and was sat in front of a fire. Joshelin threw him cracker-bread, hard cheese and a wineskin, and then went off to do his stint as sentry.

The wind was getting up, flattening the flames of the fire. Around in the darkness other fires stitched a fiery quilt upon the snow-girt earth, and the loom of the mountains could be felt on every horizon, an awesome presence through whose peaks the clouds scudded and ripped like rolling rags. The Fimbrian camp was eerily quiet, save for the occasional bray of a mule. The men at the fires talked in low voices as they passed their rations out, but most of them simply ate, rolled themselves in their heavy cloaks and fell asleep. Albrec wondered how they endured it: the heavy marching, the short commons, the snatches of sleep on the frozen earth with no covering for their heads. Their hardiness half frightened him. He had seen soldiers before, of course, the Almarkan garrison of Charibon, and the Knights Militant. But these Fimbrians were something more. There was almost something monastic in their asceticism. He could not begin to imagine what they would be like in battle.

"Hogging the wineskin as usual, I see," a voice said, and Albrec turned from the fire.

"Avila!"

His friend had once been the most handsome Inceptine in Charibon. There was still a fineness to his features, but his face was gaunt and drawn now, even with a smile upon it. Something had been stripped from him, some flamboyance or facet of youth. He limped forward like an old man and half collapsed beside his friend, wrapped in a soldier's greatcloak like Albrec, his feet swathed in bandages.

"Well met, Albrec." And then as the firelight fell on the little monk's face: "Sweet God in heaven! What happened?"

Albrec shrugged. "Frostbite. You were luckier than I, it seems. Only a few toes."

"My God!"

"It's not important. It's not like we have a wife or

a sweetheart. Avila, do you know where we are and whom we are with?"

Avila was still staring at him. Albrec could not meet his eyes. He felt an overpowering urge to put his hand over his face, but mastered it and instead gave his friend the wineskin. "Here. You look as though you need it."

"I'm sorry, Albrec." Avila took a long swig from the skin, crushing in its sides so that the wine squirted deep down his throat. He drank until the dark liquid brimmed out of his mouth, and then he squirted down more. Finally he wiped his lips.

"Fimbrians. It would seem our saviours are Fimbrians. And they march to Ormann Dyke."

"Yes. But I've lost it, Avila. They took it, the document. Nothing else matters now."

Avila studied his hands where they were gripped about the wine-skin. The flesh on them had peeled in places, and there were sores on the backs of them.

"Cold," he muttered. "I had no idea. It's like what we were told of leprosy."

"Avila!" Albrec hissed at him.

"The document, I know. Well, it's gone. But we are alive, Albrec, and we may yet remain unburned. Give thanks to God for that at least."

"And the truth will remain buried."

"I'd rather it were buried than me, to be frank."

Avila would not meet his friend's glare. Something in him seemed cowed by what they had been through. Albrec felt like shaking him.

"It's all right," the Inceptine said with a crooked smile. "I'm sure I'll get over it, this desire to live."

There were soldiers around them at the fire, ignoring

them as if they did not exist. Most were asleep, but in the next moment those that were awake scrambled to their feet and stood stiff as statues. Albrec and Avila looked up to see a man with a scarlet sash about his middle standing there in a simple soldicr's tunic. He had a moustache which arced around his mouth and glinted red-gold in the firelight.

"At ease," he said to his men, and they collapsed to the ground again. The newcomer then sat himself cross-legged at the fire beside the two monks.

"Might I trouble you for a drink of the wine?" he asked.

They gazed at him at a loss for words. Finally Avila bestirred himself and in his best frosty aristocratic tone said: "By all means, soldier. Perhaps then you will leave us alone. My friend and I have important matters to discuss."

The man drank deeply from the proffered wineskin and pinched the drops from his moustache. "How are you both feeling?"

"We've been better," Avila said, still haughty, every inch the Inceptine addressing a lowly man-at-arms. "Might I ask who you are?"

"You might," the man said, unruffled. "But then again I might not choose to tell you. As it happens, my name is Barbius, Barbius of Neyr."

"Then perchance, Barbius of Neyr, you will leave us, now that you've had your drink of wine." Avila's haughtiness was becoming brittle. He was beginning to sound shrill. The man only looked at him with one eyebrow raised.

"Are you an officer?" Albrec asked, staring at the man's scarlet sash.

"You could say that." Off in the darkness an invisible soldier uttered a half-smothered guffaw.

"Perhaps you would tell us what happened to our belongings then," Avila said. "They seem to have been misplaced."

The man smiled, but his eyes had the glitter of sea ice, no gleam of humour to warm them. "I might have thought some gratitude was in order. My men, after all, saved your lives."

"For which we are duly grateful. Now our things, where are they?"

"Safe in the tent of the army commander, never fear. My turn for questions. Why were you fleeing Charibon?"

"What makes you think we were fleeing the place?" Avila countered.

"You were perhaps taking a constitutional in the blizzard, then?"

"It is none of your business," the young Inceptine snapped.

"Oh, but it is. I saved your lives. You'd be frozen wolf-bait had my men not found you. I believe I am due an answer to whatever questions I have the urge to pose, plus some common courtesy in their answering."

The two monks were silent for a few seconds. It was Albrec who finally spoke.

"We apologize for our lack of manners. We are indeed grateful for our lives, but we have been under some strain of late. Yes, we were fleeing the monastery-city. It was an internal matter, a—a power struggle in which we became embroiled through no

fault of our own. Plus, there was a heretical side to
it . . ."

"I am intrigued," the Fimbrian said. "Go on."

"I saved certain forbidden texts from destruction,"
Albrec said, his mind racing as it concocted the tissue
of half truth and outright lie. "They were discovered,
and we had to flee or be burned as heretics. That is all
there is to it."

Barbius nodded. "I thought as much. The text you
were carrying with you—is it one of these heretical
documents?"

Albrec's heart leapt. "Yes, yes it is. It still exists,
then?"

"The marshal has it in his tent, as I told you." He
seemed to lose interest in them. His gaze flicked out
to the surrounding campfires where his men lay close
to the flames in weary sleep. "I must go. Call by the
marshal's tent in the morning and you shall have your
belongings back. You may stay with the column as
long as you wish, but be warned: we travel to Ormann
Dyke, and the longer you remain with the army the
worse the roads will become, the less easy for you to
make your own way in the wilderness."

"If you could spare us a couple of mules we could
be on our way by tomorrow," Albrec said eagerly.

Barbius's cold eyes sized up the little monk
squarely. "Whither will you go?"

"To Torunn."

"Why?"

Albrec was momentarily confused, sure he had said
too much, given something away. He faltered, and it
was Avila who spoke, his voice dripping with scorn.

"Why, to throw in our lot with Himerius and his

fellow heretics, of course. My enemy's enemy is my friend, as they say. It's a hard world, soldier. Even clerics have to rub along the best they can."

Barbius smiled again. "Indeed they do. I will see you in the morning, then." He rose easily, and it was Avila who called him back as he turned to go.

"Wait! Where is this commander's tent? How shall we find it? This camp is as big as a town."

The Fimbrian shrugged, walking away. "Ask for Barbius of Neyr's headquarters. He commands the army, or so I am told."

THREE

"I don't like it, my lady," Brienne was saying as she fussed with the pins in Isolla's hair. "No one will tell me anything, not even the pageboys."

"If they won't spill their confidences to you, there is truly something wrong with the world," Isolla said wryly. "That's enough, Brienne. I can't bear it when you fuss."

"You've an impression to make," Brienne said stubbornly. "Would you have these Hebrians think you were come from some backwater court where the ladies still wore their hair down on their shoulders?"

Isolla smiled. There was no arguing with her maidservant sometimes. Brienne was a minx of a woman, tiny and slim with raven hair and flashing hazel eyes. Her skin possessed the flawless paleness which Isolla had once yearned for, and with a crook of her little finger she could set men staring and stammering. But

she was no light-headed giggler. She had sense, and
was the closest thing to a friend Isolla had ever had, if
she did not count her brother Mark. Mark the King,
who loved his sister and who had sent her here to wed
a man of whom she knew virtually nothing. A man
who was mysteriously absent.

"You don't think he's dead, do you?" she asked
Brienne.

"No, my lady. Not dead. I ventured to suggest that
to one of the cooks and was almost brained by a ladle
for my pains. They're very touchy, the palace staff. No,
it's my belief something happened to him in the battle
to retake the city. He was wounded, that's plain, but
no one knows or will say how badly. It's unsettling. I
was in Abrusio as a girl—you know my family hailed
from Imerdon—and it was a godless place then, teeming with foreigners and heathens, everything to be had
for a price. It's different now. All that is gone."

"War is apt to put a dampener on things," Isolla said,
studying herself in the dressing mirror. "That will do,
Brienne."

"No powder, my lady?"

"For the fiftieth time, no. I'll not have myself
painted like a mannikin, even for a king."

Brienne pursed her lips in disapproval, but said nothing. She was utterly devoted to her mistress, the
woman who had befriended the kitchen-wench and
raised her to the level of body-servant. And she knew
how conscious Isolla was of her plainness, and suffered
for her when the other ladies at court whispered behind
the backs of their hands. The Princess of Astarac could
sit a horse as well as a man, and she had both a man's
bold way of striding on her long coltish legs and a

man's bluntness in speaking. And she read *books*, books by the hundred it was rumoured. A strange way for a noblewoman to carry on. But Mark the King would have nothing said against his sister and her eccentric ways, and it was even rumoured that he discussed high policy with her in the quiet of her apartments. Discussing politics with a woman! It was unnatural.

Brienne felt the feminine barbs more keenly than her mistress, for they had long ago lost their sting for Isolla. She wanted to see her lady happy, married, with child. All the things that a woman ought to be. But she knew that for Isolla life held more, not merely because she had been born a princess, but simply because of the woman she was.

There was a knock on the door. Isolla rose smoothly from the dressing table and said: "Enter."

A footman stood there in Hebrian scarlet. He bowed. "My lady, the wizard Golophin asks if he might be admitted."

"Golophin?" Isolla's brow creased, then smoothed. "Yes, of course. Show him in." And when the door had closed again: "Quickly, Brienne. He likes wine. And bring some olives."

Her maidservant rushed out to the anteroom whilst Isolla composed herself. Golophin, Abeleyn's mentor and teacher, and, she had heard, his closest friend. Perhaps now she would learn what was ailing the invisible King of Hebrion.

Golophin entered with little ceremony beyond a courtly bow. She was shocked at his appearance, the desiccated look of his flesh. The man was no more than an animated skeleton. The eyes, however, missed nothing.

"My thanks for receiving me so informally, lady," the old wizard said. He had the deep voice of a singer or orator, music all through it.

They sat and looked at one another for a moment whilst Brienne bustled in with the wine and olives. Golophin's gaze was frank and open. He's sizing me up, Isolla thought. He's wondering how much he can tell me.

The old wizard poured for them both, saluted her with a tilt of his glass and then drank his entire gobletfull at a draught and poured himself another. Isolla sipped at hers, suppressing her surprise.

Golophin smiled. "I am trying to regain my lost strength, lady, and perhaps I am trying to forget how I lost it. Pay me no mind."

She liked his frankness, and sat without saying a word. She somehow realized that it would be better if she were not to make small talk.

"Are your apartments to your liking?" Golophin asked absently.

She had been given a vast lonely suite that belonged to some long-dead Hebrian queen—Abeleyn's mother, perhaps. The rooms were hideous with sombre tapestries and hangings and devotional pictures of Saints. The furniture was huge and heavy and dark-wooded. The place felt like a mausoleum. But she nodded and said: "They are very fine."

"Never liked this place myself," the wizard admitted. "Abeleyn's mother Bellona was a fine woman, but a bit austere. I see you've pulled the hangings away from the balconies. That's good. Lets in what sun there is in this black month of the year." He threw back another glass of the wine. Isolla thought privately that it was not the third or even the fourth glass he'd had that morning.

"I remember you as a child," he said. "A patient little creature. Abeleyn liked you, but had the cruelty of all small boys. I hope you do not hold it against him."

"Of course not," she said, rather coldly.

He smiled. "You have a head on your shoulders, lady, or so I am told. That is why I am here. Were you another tinsel-brained princess, you'd be kept in the dark and told whatever we thought you'd believe. But I have a feeling that will not suffice. That is why I am willing to do what I am about to do."

Ah, she thought, and straightened. "Brienne, leave us."

Her maidservant exited the room with a piteous look. Golophin rose from his chair and paced about the floor like some huge cadaverous bat, his mantle billowing out behind him. No—he was more of a raptor, a starved falcon, perhaps. Even his movements were as quick and economical as a bird's, despite the wine he'd quaffed.

He went to the far wall, pulled back the hideous tapestry that hung there and pressed hard on the stone. There was a click, and a gap appeared, rapidly broadening into a low doorway.

Isolla sucked in her breath. "Magic."

He laughed. "No. Engineering. The palace is riddled with hidden doors and secret passageways. Now you must come with me."

She hesitated. She did not like the look of the hole

he was gesturing at. It might lead anywhere. Was there some kind of plot afoot?

"Trust me," Golophin said gently. And then she saw the suffering in his eyes. There was a grief there that he held bottled up as tightly as a genie of eastern myth. Despite herself, she rose and joined him at the secret door.

"I am going to take you to meet your betrothed," the wizard said, and led her into the darkness.

ISOLLA had seen bale-fire before, as a child. A ball of it hovered above Golophin's head in the dark and lit the way for them. But it was a guttering thing, like a candle almost burnt down to the wick. She suddenly realized that the old mage was damaged in some way—something had stolen away his strength and made him into a caricature of what he had once been. It was the war, she guessed. It had drained him somehow.

The passage they trod was smoothly made out of jointed stone, and it rose and wound like the coils of a snake. There were other doors off its sides, leading to other rooms in the palace, Isolla supposed. She knew she, a foreigner, was being trusted with some of the secrets of the palace. But then she'd be Hebrion's queen soon enough anyway.

They halted. The bale-fire went out and there was a grating of stone. She followed the wizard's lean back through another low door like the one in her own chambers, and found herself in a high-ceilinged room that was almost totally dark. A rack of tall candles fluttered by the side of a massively ornate four-poster bed, and she could make out weapons on the walls gleaming in the gloom. Maps and books and more of the dull hangings. A bedstand with jug and ewer of silver. And everywhere engraved or embossed, the Hebrian Royal arms. She was in the King's chambers.

"Speak normally. No whispers," Golophin told her. "He is far away, but not gone, not entirely. It may be that a new voice will reach him as a familiar one might not."

"What—?" But Golophin took her arm and led her to the side of the huge bed.

The King. Her horrified eyes took in what was left of him at a glance, and her hand flew to her mouth. This thing was to be her husband.

Golophin was watching her. She sensed a protective anger in him that was not very far from the surface. She brought her hand down from her face and touched Abeleyn's where it lay on the coverlet.

His features she recognized: the dark hair as thick as ever despite the threads of grey. The face she had known as sun-brown was as pallid as the sheets behind it. She was surprised to feel grief, not for herself who was to be joined to this wreck of a man, but for Abeleyn, the high-spirited boy she had known who had pulled her hair and said cruel things about her nose. He had not deserved to end up like this.

"What was it?" she asked, uncomfortably aware of Golophin's hawk-like scrutiny.

"A shell. One of our own, God help us, in the moment when the battle was won. I was able to seal the stumps, but I had already exhausted myself in the fighting and could do nothing more. It would take a great work of theurgy to heal him completely, something I'm not sure I would be capable of even if I were at my full strength. And so he lies here, his mind in some fathomless limbo I cannot reach. We have made discreet enquiries for Mind-rhymers, but those who were not murdered under Sastro di Carrera's regime fled to the ends of the earth. The Dweomer cannot help Abeleyn. His own will must pull him through, and whatever human warmth we can give." Here he glared at Isolla as if he dared her to contradict him.

But she was not so easily cowed. She released the unconscious King's hand and faced the old mage squarely. "I take it there will be no wedding until the King is brought to himself again."

"Yes. But there *will* be a wedding. The country needs it. We may have slaughtered Carrera's retainers and expelled the surviving Knights Militant, but there are still ambitious men in Hebrion who would stoop to seize a crown if they saw it fall."

"You cannot fool the world for ever, Golophin. The truth will out, in the end."

"I know. But we have to try. This man has greatness in him. I will not abandon him to rot!"

He loves him, she thought. He truly does. And she warmed to the fierce old man. She had always responded to lost causes, had always sided with the underdog. Perhaps because it was how she had always seen herself.

"So you brought me here to join your little conspiracy. Who else knows the true condition of the King?"

"Admiral Rovero, General Mercado, and perhaps three or four of the palace servants whom I trust."

"The whole city is in mourning."

"I had to put out a bulletin on the King's health. He is dangerously ill, but not dying. That is the official line."

"How long do you think you can keep the hounds leashed?"

"A few weeks, maybe a couple of months. Rovero and Mercado have the army and the fleet firmly under control, and in any case Hebrion's soldiers and sailors fairly worship Abeleyn. No, as always, it is the court we must worry about. And that, my dear, is where you come in."

"I see. So I am to make reassuring noises about the palace."

"Yes. Are you willing?"

She looked down at the wrecked King again, and felt an absurd urge to ruffle the dark hair on the pillow. "I am willing. My brother would wish it so anyway."

"Good. I did not read your character wrong."

"If you had, Golophin, what would have become of me?"

The old man grinned wolfishly. "This palace would have become your prison."

FOR the lady Jemilla, the palace had indeed come to seem like a prison. Ever since the retaking of the city she had been shepherded and watched and guarded like some prisoner of war. And she had not seen Abeleyn once in all that time. That old devil Golophin was always there to put her off. The King was too ill to see anyone but his senior ministers, he said. But the rumours were running like wildfire about the palace: that Abeleyn was dead and already buried, that he was too horribly scarred to see the light of day, that his injuries had turned him into an imbecile. In any case, the triumvirate of Rovero, Mercado and Golophin—always Golophin—were running Abrusio as though

they wore crowns themselves. It galled her beyond
measure that she, who bore the King's heir, should be
put off and shuffled about as though she were some
troublesome trull whose swelling belly could be ignored. And then, worst of all, the Princess of Astarac
had arrived with due state to be married to the father
of Jemilla's child. Or to the man everyone thought was
the father, it made no odds—not now.

Things were slipping through her grasp with every
passing day. This wedding must not happen. Her child
must be recognized as the rightful heir. And if Abeleyn
were as near death as everyone supposed, then surely
it made sense to secure the succession. Couldn't they
see that? Or must they be made to see it?

She lay naked on the wide bed in her suite. The short
day was almost over and the room was dark but for
the blaze of a fire in the huge hearth that dominated
one wall. At least they had quartered her in the palace.
That was something. She regarded her body in the firelight, running her hands up and down it as a man might
with a horse he meant to buy. The swelling was visible
now, a bulge that marred the otherwise perfect symmetry of her shape. She frowned at it. Childbirth. Such
a messy, painful affair. Even messier if one sought to
avoid it. She remembered the blood and her own
shrieking the night she rid herself of Richard Hawkwood's first child. Nothing could be worse than that.

Her breasts were filling out. She cupped them, ran
her slender fingers down her abdomen to where the
hair sprang in ebony curls at her crotch. She stroked
herself there absently, thinking. She thought of her
body as an instrument, a tool to be utilized with the

utmost efficiency. It was her key to a better life, this flesh and all that it contained.

She sprang up, pulled round her shoulders a robe of Nalbenic silk and padded barefoot to the door. A moment to gather herself, to rehearse her words, and then she yanked open the heavy portal in a rush.

"Quickly, quickly—you there!"

There were two guards, not one. She must have caught them as they were changing shifts. It made her hesitate, but only for the fraction of a second.

"There's something in my room—a rat. You must come and look!"

The two soldiers were members of the Abrusio garrison, veterans of the battle to retake the city. They were rough, untutored swordsmen who had not been told why they were to guard the lady Jemilla's door, only that her every move was to be reported direct to General Mercado. They hung back, and one said: "I'll get your lady's maidservant."

"No, no, you fools. She can't abide rats any more than I can. Get in there and kill it for me, for God's sake. Are you men at all?"

Jemilla was beautifully unkempt, one shoulder gleaming pale as ivory above the robe she clutched together at her breasts. The two soldiers looked at one another, and one shrugged. They marched into her chambers.

Jemilla followed them, shutting the door behind her. The soldiers poked under the bed, along the wall hangings.

"I believe it's gone, lady," one of them said, and then said no more but simply stared. Jemilla had dropped her robe and was standing incandescently nude before them, touching herself, her body undulating like a willow in a breeze.

"It's been so long," she said. "Won't you please help me?"

"Lady—" one of the men said hoarsely. He held out a hand as if to ward her off.

"Oh, please. Do this thing for me, just this once." She approached them as they stood, thunderstruck. "Please, soldiers. Just this once. It's been so long, and no one will ever know."

The men's eyes met for the briefest moment, and then they moved in on her like wolves on a lamb.

FOUR

THE men were drooping in the saddle when the lead riders of the screen came in sight of Staed. Corfe called a halt—it was by then the middle of the night—and after seeing to their mounts the tribesmen sank to the ground and slept without fires to warm them, pickets out every hundred yards around the bivouac.

Corfe, Marsch and Andruw stole up to the rising ground that hid them from their objective and took a look at the port itself in the starlit night. It was bitterly cold, and flakes of snow were running before the wind like feathers. The ground was frozen stiff as stone, which was all to the good. It would be better for the horses. Nothing worse than a cavalry charge bogged hock-deep in mud.

Staed was a largish port of some ten thousand people, one of the prosperous coastal settlements that the Fimbrians had founded centuries before in their drive to populate what was then a wilderness dominated by the Felimbric tribes. It had done well for itself. Corfe could see the massive breakwaters that protected the harbour and held in their arms over a score of vessels: galleys of the Kardian, probably hailing from one of the Sultanates, and some caravels, the seaworthy little ships that were the lifeblood of trade in the Levangore. Down by the harbour was the old fortress in which Duke Narfintyr had his headquarters no doubt, his ancestral seat. It was tall under the stars, a castle built before artillery. Nowadays walls were squat and thick to resist bombardment. But three hundred men would not fit in that keep, much less three thousand. Where had he them quartered?

They lay on the hard earth with the cold slowly sinking into them, the warmth of their bodies chilled by the metal armour they wore. The world was vast and starlit and bitter with winter. A few lights burned in Staed and in the keep which dominated it, but the rest of the sleeping earth seemed dark as a cave.

This country had been Corfe's home once. He had been born in a farmer's hut not two leagues from where he now lay. He had been a farmer's son for fourteen years, before he followed the tercios north to Torunn to go for a soldier. It was the only profession allowed to the lowest class of commoners in Torunn, those tied to the land by the obligations to their feudal lords. For the poor, it was soldiering, or serfdom. An age ago it seemed, that last morning on the farm, a time back in the youth of the world. There was no familiarity in the dark hills, nothing for him here that he could recall. He remembered only his mother, small and patient, and his father, a broad, taciturn man who had worked harder than any human being he had ever known before or since, who had not stopped his only son from going for a soldier, though it would mean there would be no one around to look after him in his old age.

Old age. They were ten years dead, worn out by a lifetime of backbreaking labour. Dead in their fourth decade so that nobles like Narfintyr might hunt and drink fine wine and foment rebellion. That was the way the world worked. Ironic that the peasant's son would come back with an army intent on destroying the noble. There was a sweetness in that which Corfe savoured.

It was Marsch who discovered the enemy camp, with his eagle sight. A scattering of fires to the south of the town, on a hillside. There was no shape or regularity to them. They might have been sparks fallen from the forge of some skyborne god. Corfe studied them, somewhat puzzled.

"No camp discipline. They're spread over damn near half a mile. What are their officers thinking of?"

"There's folk in the castle," Andruw said quietly. "Lights and such. Do you think Narfintyr is in there, or out in the field with his men?"

"It's a cold night," Corfe said with a smile. "If you were one of the old nobility, where would you be? And if his senior officers are out of the cold with him, then that would explain the slackness of their men's bivouac. But doesn't he know that there's an army approaching him? It's criminally remiss of him to sleep separately from his command, even if he is a bone-headed nobleman."

"We made sixty miles in the last eighteen hours," Andruw reminded Corfe. "It could be we've stolen a march on them. Maybe they're expecting Aras's column and no more, and it's still twenty-five leagues behind us, a week at their pace."

Corfe considered it. The more he thought, the more he was sure that he had to move at once. Now. If he delayed the attack a day there was every chance his men would be discovered, and there went the advantage of surprise, which was vital when he faced the odds he did.

"We attack tonight," he said.

Andruw groaned. "You can't be serious. The men have had no sleep in two days. They've just completed a hellish forced march. For God's sake, Corfe, they're flesh and blood!"

"It's to spare their flesh and blood that I want to hit the enemy tonight. They can sleep all they want once we've broken Narfintyr's men."

"The colonel is right," Marsch said. "We have them where we want them. Such a thing may not happen again. It has to be tonight."

"God's blood, but you're a couple of fire-eaters," Andruw said, resigned. "What's the plan then, Corfe?"

Their colonel was silent for a few seconds, watching the haphazard collection of campfires that was the enemy camp. It was on a slight hill—at least they had had the sense to choose the higher ground—but if he squinted, he could make out a deeper darkness in the night on the far side of the camp. A small forest. Probably they had camped near it for the convenience of the firewood. Something clicked into place in Corfe's head. Finally he said: "Have you ever hunted boar in a wood, Andruw?"

• • •

THE stars wheeled in their courses, the cold deepened. It took two hours to get the squadrons in
position, the men staggering with tiredness, half of
them afoot in accordance with Corfe's plan. It was one
of the most wearing and difficult exercises in the field,
Corfe thought as he sat his horse waiting for his men
to get into position. A night march, when body and
brain are drunk with exhaustion. Men can sleep as they
march, blinking awake as their knees start to buckle.
They begin to see bright lights and hallucinations in
the night. Shadows become living things, trees move
and walk. He had experienced it all himself. He hoped
he had not pushed his willing tribesmen too far.

He had four squadrons about him, two hundred men
mounted and sitting still as graven statues while their
horses breathed pale plumes of smoke into the frigid
night air. Thank God for the surplus horses. Every one
of them was on a relatively fresh mount. Only ten men
remained back at their camp with the rest of the remounts and the baggage. As always, he was staking
everything on one throw of the dice. He had not the
numbers to do otherwise.

His cavalry were deployed in a two-deep line on a
slope to the north of the enemy camp, between it and
the outskirts of Staed itself. From where he was he
could see the sea glittering under the clear night sky
off to his left. Ahead, perhaps half a mile away, the
campfires burned by the hundred, guttering low as
dawn approached.

The rest of his men, on foot, should by now be on
the southern side of the enemy campsite, getting into
position under Marsch and Andruw. Their approach
and deployment would be concealed by the wood

there, and the northern edge of the treeline would be
their start point. They were the beaters, their job to
wreck havoc and flush the enemy in a confused mass
from the camp into the open. Like flushing a boar out
of a hazel brake on to the spears of the hunters. Corfe
had no reserves. Everything depended on speed, darkness, surprise, and the sheer unbridled savagery of his
men.

And there it began. A surf of shouting in the night,
the shrieking war-cry of the Felimbri, a sound to chill
the blood. Corfe's mount twitched and fidgeted under
him at the distant sounds while around him the other
mounted men seemed to straighten in the saddle, their
exhaustion forgotten.

Marsch and Andruw were in the enemy camp. Men
would be stumbling from their tents half awake. They
would be fumbling for weapons in the firelit dark, running from unknown attackers. They would have no
time to don their armour or to form up. Their officers
would not have a chance. If any rallied and got a hold
of themselves, Marsch and Andruw were under orders
to butcher them, to annihilate any sign of organized
resistance. Otherwise, their task was to simply panic
the enemy, make him run north. Into the waiting arms
of Corfe's Cathedraller cavalry.

A few scattered arquebus shots, flashes followed by
bangs. The shouting grew louder. Men screaming and
yelling in fear, pain, anger. Blooming flames startling
bright in the fleeing darkness. Someone was setting the
tents on fire. Shadows and shapes running past the
flames, the campfires blinking on and off as men went
by them. This was the hardest part, judging when the
enemy was in the open, far enough out of the camp so

that Corfe's charge would not carry them back into it.
He could see them now. There was a mass of men in
streaming retreat, a mob rather than an army, hundreds
of them fleeing north towards the town with the tribesmen slashing at their heels, not giving a moment in
which they might reform and dress their ranks. In the
confusion they would not even realize that they outnumbered their attackers.

Now. Corfe hoped his men would recognize the sig-
nals he and Andruw had tried to teach them. He turned
to Cerne, the burly tribesman who was on his right
hand.

"Sound me the advance."

Cerne wet his lips and put a hunting horn to them.
It was an unorthodox kind of cavalry bugle, but it did
the trick and it was somehow fitting that these men
should be summoned to battle with the clear, high call
of the chase, the hunting call of their own mountains.

The first line of heavily armoured horsemen began
to move forward. A walk at first, then a trot. Metal
clanking in the night air, the muffled snorting of
horses. A sound that was almost a deep form of hum:
the thumping of a myriad of hooves on the hard earth.

Corfe moved ahead of his men, lance upraised. He
had to keep them in line, keep the cohesion of the unit
until the last moment, like clenching the fingers into a
fist for the blow. This was new to them, this keeping
of a formation while mounted, and though he had
drummed it into them as far as he could on their journey south he still could not be sure if they would remember the drills in the heat of approaching battle. So
he stayed ahead of the line, something for them to focus on.

A canter. The line was becoming ragged as some men drew ahead, the horses jostling each other. The enemy was a black crowd of faceless shapes two hundred yards ahead. They were still fighting Marsch and Andruw's men to their rear and the fire of the burning camp silhouetted them. They would be blinded by the light of the flames and would not be able to see what was approaching them out of the night. But they would hear the hoof-thunder, and would pause, afraid and uncertain.

"Charge!" Corfe screamed, and levelled his lance. Cerne blew the ringing five-note hunting call of the Cimbric foothills. The horsemen spurred their mounts into a raging flatout gallop, and the lances came down like a wood and iron hedge.

Corfe felt his mount go up and down small dips, rising and falling with the shape of the earth. Someone stumbled—he glimpsed it out of the corner of his eye, and there was the scream as a horse went pinwheeling. A rabbit hole, perhaps. They were blind to whatever was below the hooves of their mounts, an unnerving experience for a horseman, especially when he is encumbered by armour and lance, his vision, such as it is, circumscribed by the weighty bulk of an iron helmet. But the men held together, shrieking their shrill, unearthly battlecry. A hundred armoured troops on a hundred heavy horses, lances out chest-high. They crashed into the enemy at full career, like some ironshod apocalypse come raging out of the dark, and trod them into the ground, impaled them, crushed them, knocked them flying.

Corfe was able to see more clearly. The burning campsite made the night into a chaotic, yellow-lit circus of toiling shadow, the flash of steel, faces half seen and then ridden down, stabbed at with the tall lances or hacked down with swords.

There was no coherent resistance. The enemy could not form ranks, and the cavalry hunted them like animals, spearing them and knocking them off their feet. It was murder, pure and simple. Those who could were running through the gaps in Corfe's first line, now a series of struggling knots of horsemen brought to a standstill by the press of bodies and beasts around them. They ran to what they thought was salvation—northwards towards Staed and the castle of their overlord.

And these staggering survivors who kept running were hit by Corfe's second line which Ensign Ebro now brought screaming out of the night at full gallop. Another thunderous wave of giant shadows which re solved itself into raging eyes and hooves and wicked piercing iron, not horsemen at all but some terrible fusion of beast and man out of nightmare myth. They smashed their way through mobs of men, dropping broken lances and drawing swords to slash and stab whilst under them the trained destriers reared up to bring down shattering hooves and bit and kicked in tune with their riders.

Corfe was not surprised to hear some of his men laughing as they whirled and swung and stabbed relentlessly in that maelstrom of slaughter, their exhaustion forgotten, their blood rising in that strange, reckless exaltation which sometimes comes upon men in combat. They were born horse-soldiers, well-mounted and in the midst of battle. They were doing what nature had created them to do. Corfe realized in that moment that in these few he had the kernel of what could be a great army, a force to rival Fimbrian tercios. With ten thousand of these men he could wipe anyone who opposed him off the face of the earth.

THE sun rose at last in a bloody welter of cloud out of the glittering sea. Shadow lingered in the folds of the hills and there was a ground mist which hid the battlefield like a shroud pulled over for decency's sake. Morning, in all its chill grayness, and the aftermath of the night.

It was *Andaon*, the first day of the Year of the Saint 552.

Over seven hundred corpses littered the field, and of those only thirty were from Corfe's command. Duke Narfintyr's army was a dismembered wreck. More than a thousand prisoners taken, scores more ridden down and killed in the pursuit all the way to the outskirts of Staed. A few hundred had mustered some shreds of discipline and had fought their way clear of the trap. They were in the hills now, their way to the town barred by the heavy cavalry. They could stay there. Corfe's men were hollow-eyed and quaking with tiredness, the adrenalin of the battle dying. And they had lost heavily in horses: the carcasses of more than eighty of the big destriers littered the field.

Corfe stood beside his steaming, quivering horse, grimacing at the flap of flesh some blade had taken out of its shoulder. This was the worst part, the part he hated, when the glory of the fight gave way to maimed men and animals and the trembling aftershock of battle. When one had to look at the contorted and broken faces of the dead, and see that they were one's fellow countrymen, killed because they had been ordered to leave their small farms and do the bidding of their noble masters.

Andruw joined him, bareheaded, his blond hair dark with sweat. His usual jauntiness was subdued.

"Poor bastards," he said, and he nudged the body of a dead boy—not more than thirteen—with his foot.

"I'll hang Narfintyr, when I catch him," Corfe said quietly.

Andruw shook his head. "That bird has flown the coop. He got on a ship when word of the battle reached the town. He's out on the Kardian, probably making for one of the Sultanates, and half his household with him. The piece of shit. But we did our job, at any rate."

"We did our job," Corfe repeated.

"A night cavalry charge," Andruw said. "That's one for the history books."

Corfe wiped his eyes, knuckling his sockets until the lights came. The tiredness was like a sodden blanket which hung from his shoulders. He and his men were shambling ghosts, mere wraiths of the butchering demons they had been during the fight. He had two hundred of them overseeing the slow, limping progress of the prisoners back to town, whilst the rest looked after their wounded comrades and scoured the battlefield for anyone who might have been overlooked and who was lying still alive under the sky. Others under Ebro were commandeering Narfintyr's castle and all it contained, setting up a crude field hospital and collecting anything in the way of provisions that Staed had to offer. So many things to do. Clearing up after a battle was always much worse than the preparation for one. So many things to do . . . but they had won. They had defeated a force many times their own, and at such slight cost to themselves that it seemed almost obscene. Not a battle, but a massacre.

"Have you ever seen men such as these?" Andruw asked him wonderingly. He was staring at the Cathedrallers who shambled about the field leading their worn-out horses, their armour cast in the strange and barbaric style of the east. They looked like beings from another world in the morning light.

"On horseback? Never. They make Torunnan cuirassiers look like boys. There is some . . . energy to them. Something I have never seen before."

"You have made a discovery here, Corfe," Andruw said. "No—you are creating something. You have added discipline to savagery, and the sum of the two is something awesome. Something new."

They were both drunk. Drunk with fatigue and with killing. And perhaps with more than that.

"A few of the surviving local notables are waiting for us in the town," Andruw said more briskly. "They want to treat for peace and hand in the arms of their retainers. They have no stomach for fighting, not after this."

"Do they know how few we are, the shape we're in?" Corfe asked.

Andruw grinned evilly. "They think we've two thousand men out here, everyone a howling fiend. They don't even know which country we hail from."

"Let's keep them in ignorance. By God, Andruw, I'm as feeble as a kitten, and I feel like lord of the world."

"Victory will do that," Andruw said, smiling. "Me, I just want a bath and a corner to pitch myself in."

"It'll be a while before you have either. We have a busy day ahead of us."

ALBREC had never known any soldiers before, not even the Almarkan troops of the Charibon garrison. He had assumed that men of war were necessarily crude, rough, loud and overbearing. But these men, these Fimbrians, were different.

A blinding white snowscape that reared up in savage, dazzling mountains on both sides. Snow blew in flags and banners off the topmost peaks of the Cimbrics to his right and the Thurians to his left. This was the Torrin Gap, the place where west met east, an ancient conduit, the highway of armies for centuries.

Fimbrians had marched here before, back in the early days of the empire when they had been a restless, eternally curious folk. They had sent expeditions northeast into the vast emptiness of the Torian plains where now Almark's horse-herds grazed. They had been the first civilized men to cross the Searil River into what was now Northern Torunna, and their parties of surveyors and botanists had crossed the southern Thurians into what was now Ostrabar. They had been a nation full of questions once, and sure of their own place in the world. Albrec knew his history; he had pored over untold volumes relating to the Fimbrian Hegemony when he had been assistant librarian in Charibon. He knew that the western world as it presently existed had largely been created by the Fimbrians. The Ramusian kingdoms had each been provinces of their empire. The capitals of the western kings had been built by Fimbrian engineers, and the great highways of Normannia had been constructed to speed the passage of their tercios.

So he felt strangely as though he were back in time, lost in some earlier century when the black-clad pikemen of the electorates had reigned supreme across the west. He was in the company of a Fimbrian army marching east, something which had not been seen in four hundred years. He felt oddly privileged, as if he had been given a glimpse of a larger world, one in which the rituals of Charibon were archaic irrelevancies.

But he was not sure what to make of these hard-faced men who were, for the moment, his travelling companions. They were sombre as monks, laconic to the point of taciturnity, and yet generous to a fault. He and Avila had been completely outfitted with cold-weather clothing and all forms of travelling gear. They had been given mules from the baggage train to ride when every man in the army marched on foot, even its commander, Barbius. Their hurts had been doctored by army physicians with terse gentleness, and as they were completely inept their rations were cooked for them at night by Joshelin and Siward, the two soldiers who seemed to have been assigned to look after them: two older men who had been relegated from the front rank of fighting infantry to look after the baggage train, and who accepted their extra duties without a murmur.

"An incredible society, it must be, in Fimbria," Avila said to his friend as they rode along near the back of the mile-long column.

"How is that?" Albrec asked him.

"Well, so far as I can make out, there is no nobility. That's why their leaders are called electors. They have a series of assemblies at which names are put forward, and the male population *vote* for their leaders, with each man's vote counting for the same as the next, whether he be a blacksmith or a landowner. It's the merest anarchy."

"Strange," Albrec said. "Equality among all men. Have you noticed how free and easy the men are with our friend the marshal, Barbius? He has no household worth speaking of, no bodyguards or retainers. And he keeps no state, except for a tent where the senior officers meet. But for the fact that they do as he says, there's no difference between him and the lowliest foot-soldier."

"It is incredible," Avila agreed. "How they ever conquered the world I'll never know. Were they always like this, Albrec?"

"They had emperors once, and it was the choosing of the last one that sent the electorates into civil war and provided the opportunity for the provinces to break away and become the Seven Kingdoms."

"What happened?"

"Arbius Menin, the emperor, was dying, and wanted his son to succeed him even though he was a boy of eight. Sons had succeeded fathers before, but they had been men of maturity and ability, not children. The other electors wouldn't stand for it, and there was war. The empire crumbled around their ears while Fimbrian battled Fimbrian. Narbosk broke away from Fimbria entirely and became the separate state it is today. The other electorates finally patched up their differences and tried to win the provinces back, but they had bled the country white and no longer had the strength. The Seven Kingdoms arose in place of the empire. The world had changed, and there was no going back. Fimbria retreated in on itself and no longer took an interest in anything outside its own borders."

"Until now. This time," Avila said grimly.

"Yes. Until this day."

"What changed their minds, I wonder?"

"Who can say? Lucky for us something did."

Joshelin came alongside them leading his train of mules, his weathered face aflame with the cold and the pace of the march.

"You sound like a student of history," he said to Albrec. "I thought you were a monk."

"I used to read a lot."

"Aye? What about that book you were so keen to get back from the marshal's tent? Is it worth reading?"

"Whatever it is, it doesn't concern you," Avila said tartly.

Joshelin merely looked at him. "Only the ignorant are too poor to afford courtesy," he said. "Inceptine." He slowed his paced so that the two monks drew ahead of him again.

Albrec touched the ancient document that was once more hidden in the folds of his cloak. Barbius had given it over with not even a question as to its content. The little monk had received the impression that the Fimbrian marshal had a lot on his mind. There were couriers—the only Fimbrians who ever went mounted—coming and going every day, and camp rumour had it that they were in contact with General Martellus of Ormann Dyke, and that the news they bore was not good.

Soon the time would come when the two monks would have to break away from the army and strike

out on their own towards Torunn, whilst the column
continued to follow the eastern road to the Searil River
and the frontier. Already, Albrec was rehearsing in his
head what he would tell Macrobius the High Pontiff.
The document he bore seemed like a millstone of responsibility. He was only a humble Antillian monk. He
wanted to turn it over to someone else, one of the great
people of the world, and let them bear the burden. It
was too heavy for him alone.

The two clerics rode south-east in this manner with
an army as escort. Three more days of sitting foul-
tempered mules, sharing the nightly campfires with the
soldiers, having their slow-to-heal injuries dressed by
army physicians. The Fimbrians were all but quit of
the Torrin Gap by that time, and were setting foot in
Torunna itself, the wide, hilly land bisected by the Torrin River that rolled for a hundred leagues down to the
Kardian Sea. It was largely unsettled, this region, too
close to the blizzards that came ravening out of the
mountains and the Felimbric raiders that sometimes
came galloping down in their wake, even in this day
and age. The most populous towns and settlements of
Torunna were on the coast. Staed, Gebrar, Rone, even
Torunn itself, were ports, their eastern sides flanked by
the surf of the Kardian. The interior of the kingdom
still had great swathes of wilderness leading up to the
mountains where none went but hunters and Royal
prospectors and engineers, seeking out deposits of ore
for the military foundries to plunder and turn into
weapons, armour, cannon.

The Fimbrians left the snow behind at last, and
found themselves marching through a country of pine-
clad bluffs which teemed with game. Antelope, wild

oxen and wild horses abounded, and Barbius allowed hunting parties to leave the column and pot some meat to eke out the plain army rations. But of the natives of the kingdom, the Torunnans themselves, they saw no sign. The land was as deserted as an untouched wilderness. Only the ancient highway their feet followed gave any sign that men had ever been here at all.

But the highway forked, one branch heading off east, the other almost due south. The eastern road forded the Torrin River and disappeared over the horizon. Some sixty leagues farther, and it would end at the fortress of Ormann Dyke, the destination of this marching army. The southern way had three hundred winding and weary miles to go before it too ended, at the gates of Torunna's capital.

The army camped that night at the fork and Albrec and Avila were invited to the marshal's tent. They ducked under the leather flap and found Barbius awaiting them, but he was not alone. Also there were Joshelin and Siward, and a young officer they did not recognize.

"Take a seat, Fathers," Barbius said with what passed for affability with him. "We soldiers will stand. Joshelin and Siward you know. They have been your . . . guardian angels for some time now. This is Formio, my adjutant." Formio was a tall, slim man of about thirty. He seemed almost boyish compared to his comrades, though perhaps this was because he lacked the traditional bull-like build of most Fimbrians.

"We have come to the parting of the ways," Barbius went on. "In the morning the column will continue toward Ormann Dyke, and you will go south to Torunn. Joshelin and Siward will go with you. There are all manner of brigands in these hills, more now since Aekir's fall and the war in the east. They will be your guards and will remain with you as long as you need them."

Albrec chanced a look at Joshelin, that grizzled campaigner, and was rewarded with a glare. Clearly, the old soldier was not enamoured of the idea. He remained silent, however.

"Thank you," the little monk said to Barbius.

The marshal poured some wine into the tin cups that were all to be had in camp. He and the two monks sipped at it, while Formio, Joshelin and Siward sat staring into space with the peculiar vacancy of soldiers awaiting orders. There was a long, awkward silence. Clearly, Marshal Barbius was not a believer in small-talk. He seemed preoccupied, as if half his mind were elsewhere. His adjutant, too, seemed subdued, even for a Fimbrian. It was as if the two of them were burdened with some secret knowledge they dare not share.

"It only remains for me then to wish you Godspeed and good travelling," Barbius said finally. "I rejoice to see you both in such good health, after your travails. I hope you find journey's end what you wish it to be. I hope we all do . . ." He stared into his cup. In the dim tent the wine within seemed black as old blood.

"I will not keep you from your sleep then, Fathers. That is all." And he turned from them to the table, dismissing them from his mind. Joshelin and Siward filed out silently. Avila looked furious at the curt dismissal but he drained his wine, muttered something about *manners* and followed the two soldiers outside. Albrec lingered a moment, though he was not sure why he did.

"Is the news from the dyke bad, Marshal?" he asked.

Barbius turned as though surprised to find him still there. "That is a matter for the military authorities of the world," he said wryly.

"What should I say to the Torunnan authorities if they ask me about it?" Albrec persisted.

"The Torunnan authorities are no doubt well enough informed without seeking the opinion of a refugee monk, Father," the younger adjutant, Formio, said, but he smiled to take the sting out of his words, un-Fimbrian in that also.

"The dispatches I send out daily will have kept them up to date," Barbius said gruffly. He hesitated. There was some enormous pressure on him; Albrec could sense it.

"What has happened, Marshal?" the little monk asked in a low voice.

"The dyke is already lost," Barbius said at last. "The Torunnan commander Martellus has ordered its evacuation."

Albrec was thunderstruck. "But why? Has it been attacked?"

"Not as such. But a large Merduk army has arrived on the Torunnan coast south of the mouth of the Searil River. The dyke has been outflanked. Martellus is trying to extricate his men—some twelve thousand of them, all told—and lead them back to Torunn, but he is being caught between the two sides of a vice. He is conducting a fighting withdrawal from the Searil, pressed by the army that was before the dyke, whilst the new enemy force comes marching up from the coast to cut him off." Barbius paused. "My mission as I see it has changed. I am no longer to reinforce the dyke because the dyke no longer exists. I must attack this second Merduk army and try to hold it off long enough for Martellus's men to escape to the capital."

"What is the strength of this second army?" Albrec asked.

"Perhaps a hundred thousand men," Barbius said tonelessly.

"But that's preposterous!" Albrec protested. "You have only a twentieth of that here. It's suicide."

"We are Fimbrian soldiers," Formio said, as if that explained everything.

"You'll be massacred!"

"Perhaps. Perhaps not," Barbius said. "In any case, my orders are clear. My superiors approve. The army will move south-east to block the Merduk advance from the coast. Mayhap we will remind the west how Fimbrians conduct themselves on the battlefield."

He turned away. Albrec realized he knew he was ordering his men to their deaths.

"I will pray for you," the little monk said haltingly.

"Thank you. Now, Father, I wish to be alone with my adjutant. We have a lot to do before morning."

Albrec left the tent without another word.

FIVE

POWER is a strange thing, the lady Jemilla thought. It is intangible, invisible. It can sometimes be bought and sold like grain, at other times no amount of money on earth can purchase it.

She had some power now, some small store of it to wield as she saw fit. For a woman in the world she had been born into, it was impossible to possess the trappings of power as men possessed them. Armies, fleets, cannon. The impedimenta of war. It was said that the most powerful woman in the world was the Queen Dowager of Torunna, Odelia, but even she had to hide behind her son the King, Lofantyr. No Ramusian nation would ever tolerate a queen who ruled alone, without apology for her sex. Or they had not thus far at least. Women who possessed ambition had to use other means to gain their ends. Jemilla had realized that while she was still a child.

She held the lives of two men in the palm of her hand, and that power had gained her her freedom. Allowing herself to be taken by the two guards had been unpleasant but necessary. She blocked out of her mind the acts she had performed for them in the dark firelight of her chambers, and reminded herself instead that with one word she could have them hung. It was not permitted for palace guards to couple with noble ladies in their care. They knew it—they had done so as soon as their lust was spent and she had risen from the bed still shining with their effluent, laughing at them. Which was why she was free to wander the palace whenever one of them was on duty outside her door.

Such a simple thing. It worked with common soldiers as easily as it worked with kings.

It was well after midnight, and she was prowling the palace corridors like a wraith wrapped in hooded silk. She was looking for Abeleyn.

The Royal chambers were guarded, of course, but there were untold numbers of secret passageways and tunnels and alcoves in the palace, some of which predated Abrusio itself, and it was in search of these that she was out here creeping in the echoing dark. Abeleyn had told her of them months ago, one airless night in the Lower City when they were both spent and sweat-soaked with the late summer stars glittering beyond the window and two of the King's bodyguards discreet as shadows in the courtyard of the inn below. He used the secret ways of the palace to come and go as he pleased, without fanfare or remark, and take his pleasure in the riotous night life of Old Abrusio below, as free and easy as any young man with a pocketful of gold and a nose for mischief. It was—had been—a glorious game to him to roam the backstreets and alleys of the teeming city, to wear a disguise and drink beer and wine in filthy but lively taverns, to feel the buttocks of some Lower City slut wriggling in his lap. And to be their king, and they not know it. Perhaps to forget it himself for a while, to be a young man with nothing tripping at his heels, a high-living gentleman and no more.

There had been a light to him, Jemilla thought, not without regret. Something that had nothing to do with being a king but was part of the man himself. He had been easy to like, pleasant to bed, the boy in him counting for more than the monarch. But then the summer had ended, and this winter had come hurtling down upon the world full of blood and fire and powdersmoke. And Abeleyn had changed, had grown. There were times after that when he frightened her, not with any threat or violence, but simply with the steady stare of his dark eyes. He had become a king indeed, much good it had done him.

Her feet were bare, slapping slightly on the floors. She carried her slippers under her mantle; they slipped and slid on the cold marble and were no good for speed. It was cold in the slumbering palace, and only a few oil-fed lamps burned in cressets up on the walls, throwing a serried garden of light and dark about her and making of her hooded shape a cowled giant down the passageways. One hand for her slippers, the other curved protectively about her swelling belly. One good thing about the nausea that overwhelmed her most mornings—it kept her thin. Her face was unchanged. Only her breasts had grown, the nipples often stiff and sore. Apart from her belly and breasts, the rest of her was as lithe as it had always been.

Except . . . oh, no. Not now.

Except for this thing. She appropriated a vase and ducked behind a curtain with it, then pulled her silks aside and squatted over it and sighed in relief as liquid gushed out of her. Oh, such a God that visited such indignities upon women.

She left the vase behind and pattered along as fast as she might. Abeleyn had told her how to come and go from his chamber to other rooms in the palace when he had been drunk, and she had been pretending to be. But it had been a long time ago, or seemed so. She was not sure if she could remember the exact places, the things to do. And thus here she was in the moonless chilly night, running along palace corridors in her bare feet, dodging sentries and yawning servants running midnight errands, and, absurdly, pushing at walls and feeling behind hangings and pressing loose stone flags. But it was somewhere here, in the guest wing of the palace. Some secret entrance which would admit her to the hidden labyrinth of passages and, finally, to the King's presence. If the King still breathed and they had not had his corpse spirited away and secretly buried days ago. She would not put anything past the wizard, Golophin. But she had to know if Abeleyn were truly alive, if he were too maimed ever to recover—there were terrible rumours flying about the palace. Only then would she be able to decide what her own course of action might be.

Movement in the passageway ahead. She shrank into the shadows, heart beating wildly, bladder suddenly ready to burst again. Thank God for the darkness of her mantle.

"—no change, none at all. But I have seen this kind of thing before. We need not despair, not just yet."

It was the wizard's voice, that skeletal fiend Golophin. But who was with him? Jemilla edged farther down into the dark. There was a cold, bobbing light approaching which she knew was unnatural: the wizard's unholy lantern. She found a heavy tapestry at her back, an alcove where the palace servants had stowed brushes and brooms away from the genteel eye, and she slipped in there gratefully, peering out through a chink she left for herself, watching the cold light approach.

Yes—Golophin. The werelight gleamed off his glabrous pate. But there was a woman with him in rich robes, a hooded mantle much like Jemilla's own. Two pale hands threw back the hood and Jemilla saw a white face, the coppery glint of hair. An ugly woman, a face with little harmony to recommend it, but there was strength in it. And she carried herself like a queen.

"I'll keep visiting him, then," the woman said in a voice as low and rich as a bass lute. "Mercado's men are still looking, I suppose?"

"Yes." The wizard's voice was musical also. A pair of beautiful voices, oddly matched. And at strange odds with the features of their owners. Who might this aristocratic but plain woman be? Her accent was strange, not of Hebrion, but it was cultured. It was of some court of other.

They were three yards away. Jemilla put her hand over her mouth. Her heart was thumping so loudly she could hear the rush and ebb of her blood in her throat.

"No luck, I am afraid," the wizard went on. "The kingdom has been scoured clean of the Dweomer-folk. I doubt Hebrion will ever be host to them in any numbers again. We are a dwindling people, we practitioners of the Seven Disciplines. One day we will be only a rumour, a lost tale of ancient marvels. No, there will be no mighty mage uncovered in time to heal Abeleyn. They are all fled or dead, or lost in the uttermost west . . . And I am a broken reed at best. No, we must continue to do what we can with what we have."

"Which is precious little," the woman said.

They were moving past her. Jemilla caught a hint of the woman's expensive scent, saw the hair piled up on her head in great coils of copper fire, the only thing of beauty about her other than her voice. They then had turned the corner and were gone.

She waited a while, and then left her hiding place, her breath coming fast. As silently as a cat she retraced their steps, and came up against a dead end. The corridor ended with an ornate leaded window through which she could see the lights of the city below, the mast lanterns of ships in the ruined harbour, the glimmer of the cold stars.

She began investigating every inch of stone in the walls, tapping, pressing, poking. Perhaps half an hour she was there, her heart beating wildly, bladder painfully full again. And then she felt a click under her fingers and a section of the wall, perhaps a yard square, moved in with a suddenness that almost made her fall. She staggered as the grave-cold air came whispering out of a lightless hole in the wall. A glimpse of steps leading down, and then nothing but the blackness.

She shivered, her toes growing numb with the wintry

blast. It looked an awful place to go in the dark hour of the night.

She padded quickly back up the corridor and took a lamp down from its cresset. Then she put her slippers over her frigid feet and, shielding the flame from the cold draught, she entered the passageway.

A metal lever here, on the inside. She pulled it down and the door shut behind her, almost panicking her for a second. But she cursed herself for a fool and went on, angry with herself, hating the composure of the plain woman who had been with Golophin, hating them both for being privy to the secrets of the palace, for being so close to the hub of power. Hating everyone and everything indiscriminately because she, Jemilla, must lurk and creep in cold passages like a thief though she bore the King's heir. By the blood of the martyred saints, they would pay for making her do this. One day she would serve them all out. Before she died, she would call this palace her own.

Doors and levers like the one she had entered by on both sides. She itched to try every one, but knew somehow that they would not take her where she wanted to go. The door to the King's chambers would be marked, she felt. It would be different.

And it was. The passage wound for hundreds of yards in the bowels of the palace, but at its end there was a door taller than the rest, and set in the door was an eye.

She almost dropped the lamp. It blinked at her, meeting her own horrified gaze. A human eye set in a wooden door, watching her.

"Sweet lord of heaven!" she gasped. It was an abomination, set here by that bastard wizard. She was discovered. She almost turned tail and ran, but the harder Jemilla, the one who had aborted Hawkwood's first child, who had coldly set out to seduce the youthful King, made her stand still, and think. She had come this far. She would not turn back.

It made her insides squirm even to approach the thing. How it stared! She shut her own eyes, and jabbed it as hard as she could with her thumb.

Again, harder. It gave like a ripe plum, and burst. Her thumb went in to the first joint, and she was spattered with warm liquid. When she opened her eyes there was a smeared, bloody hole in the door and her mantle was streaked with clear and crimson gore. She turned away, bent and vomited on the stone floor, dappling her slippers.

"Lord God." She wiped her mouth, straightened and pushed at the door.

It gave easily, and she was in the King's bedroom, a place she knew well.

She paused, wondering if the alarm would be raised quickly, if Golophin the demon was even now raging towards her with terrible spells on his lips to blast her out of existence. Well, she was where she had wanted to be.

She approached the great ornate bed in which she and Abeleyn had cavorted in the humid nights of late summer, the balcony screens flung wide to let in a breath of air off the sea. Candles burning now, as there had been then, and Abeleyn's head on the pillows.

She stood over the prostrate King like a dark, bloody angel come to fetch his soul away. And realized why they hid him here, why there was nothing but rumour about his condition.

She touched the dark curls, for a moment feeling something akin to pity; and then wrenched away the covers with one violent tug.

A tattered fragment of a man below them, naked to her gaze, his stumps muzzled in linen wraps. His chest moved as he breathed, but the pallor of death was about him, his lips blue in the candlelight, the eyes sunken in their sockets. He could not be long for this world, the King of Hebrion.

"Abeleyn," she whispered. And then louder, more confidently: *"Abeleyn!"*

"He cannot hear you," a voice said.

She spun around, the lamp-flame guttering wildly. Golophin was standing behind her as silently as an apparition. She could not speak: the terror closed her throat on a scream.

The old mage looked like something unholy made incarnate by night shadow and candle-flame. His eyes glittered with an inhuman light, and one of them was weeping tears of black blood down his cheek.

"My lady Jemilla," he said, and glided forward across the stone with never the sound of a footfall. "It is late for you to be up. In your condition."

She was more afraid than she had ever been in her life, but she fought a swift, soundless battle with her terror, mastered herself, composed her face.

"I wanted to see him," she said hoarsely.

"Now you have seen him. Are you happy?"

"He's dead, Golophin. He is not a man any more." Her voice grew calmer by the second, though she was calculating furiously, wondering if a scream would be heard if uttered here. Wondering if anyone would come to investigate it. The old mage looked like some night-dark prowling fiend with his bright eyes and skull-like countenance.

"I bear the King's heir," she said as he approached her.

"I know." He was only pulling the covers back up over the King's exposed body. She could almost smell the fury in him, but his actions were gentle, his voice controlled.

"You cannot touch me, Golophin."

"I know."

"You had no right to keep me from him."

"Do not talk to me of *rights*, lady," the wizard said, and his voice made her hair stand on end. "I serve the King, and I will do so to the last breath in my body or his. If you do anything to injure him, I will kill you."

Said so quietly, so calmly. It was not a threat, it was a statement of fact.

"You cannot touch me. I bear the King's heir," she said, her voice a squeak.

"Get out." Venom dripped from the words. Hatred hung heavy in the air of the room between them. She felt that violence was not far off. She retreated from the bed, one shaking hand still holding the lamp, the other cradling her abdomen.

"I will be treated according to my station," she insisted. "I will not be shut away, or be forgotten. You will not muzzle me, Golophin. I will tell the world what I bear. You cannot stop me."

The old mage merely stared at her.

"I will have my due," she hissed at him suddenly, venom for venom.

She could not bear his eyes any longer. She turned and left the room without looking back, aware that he watched her all the way, never blinking.

SIX

"HERE he comes," Andruw said. "Full of piss and vinegar."

They watched as the knot of horsemen drew near, pennons billowing in a breeze off the grey sea. And behind them nearly three thousand men in full battle array waited in formation, the field guns out to their front, cavalry in reserve at the rear. Classic Torunnan battle formation. Classic, and unimaginative.

"Do you know this Colonel Aras?" Corfe asked his adjutant.

"Only by reputation. He's young for the job, a favourite of the King's. Thinks he's John Mogen come again, and is too easy on his men. He's had a few skirmishes with the tribes, but hasn't seen any real fighting."

Real fighting. Corfe was still amazed at how much of the Torunnan army had not seen any *real* fighting.

Torunnan military reputation had been built up by the men of the Aekir garrison, once considered the best troops in the world outside Fimbria. But the Aekir garrison were all dead, or slaves in Ostrabar. What was left were second-line troops, except for Martellus's tercios at the dyke. And now it was these second-line troops that would have to take on the Merduk invasion, and beat the armies which had taken Aekir. It was a chilling prospect.

The rest of his own men, the Cathedrallers, were drawn up behind him in two ranks. Scarcely three hundred of them able to mount a horse out of the five hundred he had started south with. His command was being inexorably worn down, despite the victories he had won. The men needed a rest, a refit, fresh horses. And reinforcements.

Aras's party reined to a halt in front of Corfe and Andruw. Their armour was shining, their horses well-fed. They wore the standard Torunnan cavalry armour, much lighter than the Merduk gear Corfe's men had. Corfe was keenly aware that he and his men looked like a horde of barbaric scare-crows, clad in scarlet-daubed Merduk war harness, eyes hollow with weariness, their mounts scarred and exhausted.

"Greetings, Colonel Cear-Inaf," the lead rider opposite said. A young man, red-haired and pale, his freckles so dense as to make him look suntanned. He had the big hands of a horseman and he sat his mount well, but compared to Corfe's troopers he seemed a mere boy.

"Colonel Aras." Corfe nodded. "You have a fine command."

Aras sat visibly straighter in the saddle. "Yes. Good

men. Now that we have arrived, we can get on with the business at hand. I take it Narfintyr and his army have decamped from the vicinity, else you would not be here." And he smiled. Corfe heard some of the tribesmen muttering angrily behind him. They understood enough Normannic to grasp what was being said.

"Indeed," Corfe answered civilly. "I fear Narfintyr is far away by now. But you're welcome to try and catch him if you like."

Aras's smile grew brittle. "That is why I am here. I am sure your men have striven nobly under you, but you must now leave it to me and my command to get the job done."

Corfe was very tired. He had almost forgotten what it was like not to be tired. He was too tired even to be angry. Or to boast.

"Narfintyr has fled across the Kardian," he said. "My men and I have destroyed his army. There are over a thousand prisoners locked in the halls of his castle as I speak. I leave the last of the mopping up to you, Colonel. I am taking my command north again."

There was a pause. "I don't understand," Aras said, still struggling to smile.

"We've done your job for you, it seems, sir," Andruw said, grinning. "If you doubt us, there's a pyre to the south of the town with seven hundred corpses on it, still smouldering. Narfintyr's finest."

Aras blinked rapidly. "But you . . . I mean, where are the rest of your men? I thought you had only a few tercios."

"We're all here, Colonel," Corfe told him wearily. "There were enough of us to do what was needed. You can stand down your own men. As I said, we leave for the north at once. I must get back to the capital."

"You can't!" Aras blustered. "You must stay here and help me. You must attach your men to my command."

"God's eyes—have you been listening?" Corfe barked. "Narfintyr is gone, his army destroyed. You cannot give me orders—you are not my superior. Now get out of my way!"

The two groups of riders remained opposite each other, the horses beginning to dance as they picked up the tension from their masters. Corfe had intended to have a civilized meeting, a military conclave of sorts where he would fill Aras in on the current situation. They were, after all, on the same side. But instead he found he could not bear the thought of trying to brief this arrogant puppy. His unravelling patience had finally frayed entirely. He wanted only to be on the move again, to get his men some well-earned rest. And to go north, where the real battlefields were. There was no time for bitching and moaning.

One thing, though, that he could not forget.

"Before we depart, Colonel, I must inform you that I must leave behind some score or so of my wounded who are too badly injured to travel. They're billeted in the upper levels of the keep. Those men are to be looked after as though they were of your own command. I will hold you accountable for the well-being of each and every one of them. Is that clear?"

Aras opened and shut his mouth, his pale face flushed. Behind him, one of his aides muttered audibly: "Playing nursemaid to savages now, are we?"

It was Andruw who nudged his mount forward until it was shoulder to shoulder with the speaker's.

"I know you, Harmion Cear-Adhur. We went to gunnery school together. Remember?"

The man Harmion shrugged. Andruw grinned that infectious grin of his.

"One of these savages behind me is worth any ten of your parade-ground heroes. And you—you only got those haptman bars by kissing the arse of every officer you were ever placed under. What have you to say to that?" Andruw's grin had become wild, giving his grimed face a slightly demented aspect. He had his right hand on his sabre.

"Enough," Corfe said. "Andruw, get back in ranks. You are out of order. Colonel Aras, I apologize for my subordinate's behaviour."

Aras got hold of himself. He cleared his throat, nodded to Corfe and finally asked in a civil tone: "Is it actually true? These men of yours have defeated Narfintyr?"

"I do not make a habit of lying, Colonel."

"You are the same Colonel Cear-Inaf who was at Aekir and Ormann Dyke, are you not?"

"I am."

Aras's face changed. He cleared his throat again. "Then might I shake your hand, Colonel, and congratulate you and your men on a great victory? And perhaps I can prevail upon you to stay here for one more night and partake of my headquarters' hospitality. I can also have some equipment and spare mounts sent over to your men. If you do not mind my saying so, they look as though they need it."

Corfe rode forward and took the younger man's hand. "Courteously put. All right, Aras, we'll remain another night. My senior ensign, Ebro, will acquaint your quartermaster's department of our needs."

AND so they remained, the two little armies encamped upon the muddy plain north of Staed. Aras had wanted to billet his men with the townspeople, but Corfe talked him out of the idea. The local people had suffered enough lately, and they were Torunnans, after all, not some conquered nation. It was enough that they went hungry to provision the soldiers who had lately swamped their countryside, and that their sons had died by the hundred whilst fighting those soldiers.

The camps of the Cathedrallers and Torunnan regulars were kept separate, and between them were Aras's headquarters tents. The Torunnans seemed at first dubious, then curious, and small parties of men from both camps met at the stream where the horses were watered, and there took wary stock of each other, like two dogs sniffing and circling, unable to decide whether to go for each other's throats.

Aras's column was remarkably well stocked with all manner of military supplies. He sent over to the Cathedraller lines wagons full of new lances, pig-iron, charcoal for the field forges, fresh rations, forage and sixty fresh horses.

Corfe, Andruw and Marsch watched them come in. Big-boned bay geldings with matted manes and wild eyes.

"They're only half broken," Andruw pointed out.

"What did you expect—the best of his destriers?" Corfe asked him. "If they had three legs apiece I'd still

take them. What think you, Marsch? Do they amount
to much?"

The big tribesman was looking over the snorting,
prancing new arrivals with a practised eye.

"Three-year-olds," he said. "Only just lost their
stones, and still feeling the loss. They'll quiet down in
time. My men will soon break them in."

"Why is this Aras suddenly kissing your backside,
Corfe?" Andruw asked thoughtfully.

"It's obvious. We head for Torunn tomorrow, back
to the court. He wants us to give a good account of
him, maybe even let him share in some of the glory."

Andruw snorted. "Fat chance."

"Oh, I'm not going to disparage him before the
King. I won't make any friends that way either. But
he won't steal the glory my men bled for."

THERE was a feast that night in Aras's conference
tent, a huge flapping structure thirty feet long and
high enough to stand upright in. All his officers were
there, dressed, to Corfe's astonishment, in court uniforms, complete with lace cuffs and buckled shoes.
There was a Torunnan soldier acting as waiter behind
every one of the folding canvas chairs which seated
the diners, and the long board table blazed with silver
cutlery and tableware. As Corfe, Andruw and Ebro
walked in, Andruw laughed aloud.

"We must be lost, Corfe," he muttered. "I thought
we were supposed to be on campaign."

Corfe was seated at Aras's right hand at the head of
the table, Andruw farther down and Ebro near the bottom. Marsch had declined to come. He had to see to
the settling in of the new horses, he said, though Corfe

privately thought that the prospect of using a knife and fork terrified him as no battle ever could.

"Some of my staff brought down several deer last week in the march south," Aras told Corfe. "They're tolerably well hung by now. I hope you like venison, Colonel."

"By all means," Corfe said absently. He sipped wine—good Candelarian, the wine of ships—from a silver goblet, and wondered how large Aras's baggage train had to be to sustain a headquarters of this magnificence. For an army of under three thousand it was ridiculous.

As the wine flowed and the courses came and went, the table set up a respectable din of talk. Ensign Ebro, Corfe saw, was in his element, regaling the other junior officers with war stories. Andruw was eating and drinking steadily, like a man making up for lost time. He was seated beside an officer in the blue livery of the artillery, and the two were engaged in a lively discussion between wolfed-down bites of food and gulps of wine. Corfe shook his head slightly. The field army of Aekir, John Mogen's command, had never done things thus. Where had the pomp and ceremony which permeated the entire Torunnan army come from? Perhaps it had to do with soldiering to the rear of an impregnable frontier. Apart from himself and Andruw, no man here had ever fought in a large-scale pitched battle. And with the fall of Aekir, the frontier was no longer impregnable. An entire army, over thirty thousand men, had been destroyed in the city's fall. The only truly experienced soldiers left in the kingdom were those at the dyke with Martellus. Once again, Corfe felt a thrill of uneasiness at the thought. Had he been Lofantyr, he would be conscripting and drilling men by the thousand, and marching them off to Ormann Dyke. There was a leisurely nature to the High Command's strategy that was downright alarming.

Aras was talking to him. Corfe collected his thoughts quickly, mustering his civility. He had precious little of it to spare these days.

"I suppose you have heard the rumours, Colonel, you having been at the court for the arrival of the Pontiff."

"No. Tell me," Corfe said.

"It seems hard to credit it, but it would seem that our liege lord has hired Fimbrian mercenaries to reinforce Ormann Dyke."

Corfe had heard as much in the war councils of the King, but his face betrayed nothing. "How very singular," he said, and sipped at his wine.

"Yes—though there's other words I'd rather use. Imagine! Hiring our ancient overlords to fight our wars for us. It's an insult to every officer in the army. The King has never been greatly loved by the rank and file, but this has enraged them as nothing else ever could. It makes it look as though he does not trust his own countrymen to fight his battles for him."

Corfe privately thought that in this at least the King was showing some shred of wisdom, but he said nothing.

"So now we have a grand tercio of them marching across Torunna as if they owned it. Fimbrians! I wonder they can still fight at all after having locked themselves behind their borders for four hundred years."

"I am sure that Martellus will know what to do with them," Corfe said mildly.

"Martellus—yes—a good man. You know him, I suppose, having served at the dyke."

"I know him."

"He's not a gentleman, they say—a rough-and-ready kind of character, but a good general."

"John Mogen was no gentleman either, but he could fight battles well enough," Corfe said.

"Of course, of course," Aras said hastily. "It is just that I think it is time the new generation of officers was given a chance to prove their mettle. The older men are too set in their ways, and the world is changing around them. Now give me a couple of grand tercios, and I'll tell you how I'd relieve the dyke . . ." and he launched into a detailed description of how Colonel Aras would outdo Martellus and even Mogen, and send the Merduks reeling back across the Ostian River.

He was drunk, Corfe realized. Many of the officers there were by now, having thrown back decanter after decanter of the ruby Candelarian, their glasses blood-glows brimming in the candlelight. Outside, Marsch and the Cathedrallers would be making their cold beds in Torunnan mud, and up along the Ostian River, a hundred and thirty leagues away, the bones of the men who had once been Corfe's comrades in arms would be lying still unburied.

I'm drunk myself, he thought, though the wine had curdled in his mouth. He hated the black mood that settled upon him with ever increasing frequency these days. He wanted to be like Andruw or Ebro, able to enjoy himself and laugh with his fellow officers. But he could not. Aekir had set him apart. Aekir, and Heria. He wondered if he would ever know a moment's true peace again, except for those wild, murderous times in battle when all that existed was the present. No past, no thought of the future, only the vivid, terrifying and exhilarating experience of killing. Only that.

He thought of the night he had bedded the Queen Dowager of Torunna, his patron. That had been like battle, a losing of oneself in the sensations of the moment. But there was always the aftermath, the emptiness of awakening. No—there was nothing to fill the void in him except the roar of war, and perhaps the comradeship of a few men he trusted and esteemed. No room for softness there, no place for it any more. He had his wife's face and her memories stored away in that inaccessible corner of his mind, and nothing else would ever touch him there.

"—but of course we need men, more men," Aras was saying. "Too many troops are tied down in Torunna itself, and more will be sent south to guard against any fresh uprising. I suppose I can see the King's reasoning. Why not let foreigners bleed for us at the dyke, and harbour our own kind until they are truly needed? But it leaves a bad taste in one's mouth, I must say. In any case, the dyke will not fall—you should know that better than anyone, Colonel. No, we have fought the Merduks to a standstill, and should be thinking about taking the offensive. And I am not the only officer in the army who thinks this way. When I left the court, the talk centred around how we might strike back along the Western Road from the dyke and make a stab at regaining the Holy City."

"If all campaigns needed were bold words, then no war would ever be lost," Corfe said irritably. "There are two hundred thousand Merduks encamped before the dyke—"

"Not any more," Aras said, pleased to have caught him out. "Reports say that half the enemy have left the winter camps along the Searil. Less than ninety thousand remain before the dyke."

Corfe tried to blink away the wine fumes, suddenly aware that he had been told something of the greatest importance.

"Where have they gone?" he asked.

"Who knows? Back to their dank motherland perhaps, or perhaps they are in Aekir, helping with the rebuilding. The fact remains—"

Corfe was no longer listening. His mind had begun to turn furiously. Why move a hundred thousand men out of their winter camps at the darkest time of the year, when the roads were virtual quagmires and forage for the baggage and transport animals would be nonexistent? For a good reason, obviously, not mere administration. There had to be a strategic motive behind the move. Could it be that the main Merduk effort was no longer to be made at Ormann Dyke, but somewhere else? Impossible, surely—but that was what this news suggested. The question, however: if not at Ormann Dyke, then where? There was nowhere else to go.

A sense of foreboding as powerful as any he had ever known suddenly came upon him. He sobered in a second. They had found some way to bypass the dyke. They were about to make their main thrust somewhere else—and soon, in winter, when Torunnan military intelligence said they would not.

"Excuse me," he said to a startled Aras, rising from his chair. "I thank you for a hospitable evening, but I and my officers must depart at once."

"But . . . what?" Aras said.

Corfe beckoned to Andruw and Ebro, who were staring at him, bowed to the assembled Torunnan officers
and left the tent. His two subordinates hurried to keep
up with him as he squelched through the mud outside.
Andruw saved the bewildered and drunken Ebro from
a slippery fall. A fine drizzle was drifting down, and
the night was somewhat warmer.

"Corfe—" Andruw began.

"Have the men stand to," Corfe snapped. "I want
everything packed and ready to move within the hour.
We move out at once."

"What's afoot? For God's sake, Corfe!" Andruw
protested.

"That is an order, Haptman," Corfe said coldly.

His tone sobered Andruw in an instant. "Yes, sir.
Might I ask where we are going?"

"North, Andruw. Back to Torunn." His voice soft-
ened.

"We're going to be needed there," he said.

TORUNNA seemed the hub of the world that winter, a place where the fate of the continent would
be decided. Around the capital, Torunn, the hordes of
unfortunates from Aekir were still squatting in sprawl-
ing refugee camps beyond the suburbs of the city. They
were foreigners, bred to the cosmopolitan immensity
of a great city which was now gone. And yet at day's
end they were Torunnan also, and thus the responsibility of the crown. They were fed at public expense,
and materials for a vast tented metropolis were carted
out to them by the wagonload, so it seemed to an ob-
server that there was a mighty army encamped about
the capital, with the smoke and mist and reek and clam-

our of a teeming multitude rising from it. And also the stench, the disease, and the disorder of a people who had lost everything and did not know where to go.

The nobility of Normannia were fond of heights. Perhaps it was because they liked to see a stretch of the land they ruled, perhaps it was for defensive purposes, or perhaps it was merely so they were set apart from the mass of the population who were their subjects. There were no hills in Torunn to build palaces on, as there were in Abrusio and Cartigella, so the engineers who had reared up the Torunnan palace had made it a towering edifice of wide towers interconnected with bridges and aerial walkways. Not a thing of beauty, such as the Peridrainian King inhabited in Vol Ephrir, but a solid, impressive presence that frowned down over the city like a stooped titan. From the topmost of its apartments and suites one might on a clear day see the glint of white on the western horizon that was the Cimbric Mountains. And on a still spring morning it was possible to see fifty miles out to sea, and watch the ships sail in from the Kardian Gulf like dark-bellied swans.

But now the mist that arose from the camps walled in the city like a fog, and even from the highest towers it was impossible to look beyond the suburbs of Torunn.

ODELIA, the Queen Dowager, sighed and rubbed her hands together. Slim fingers, impeccable nails—the hands of a young woman but for the liver spots which dotted them and reminded her of her age. The cold seemed to have settled in her very marrow this winter—this endless winter. She had fought

against time for so very long now that it was with
instant resentment she noted every fresh signal of her
body's decay, every new ache and pain, every subtle
lessening of her strength. She would repair the waning
theurgy of her maintenance spells tonight—but oh how
she so wanted that young man in her bed again, to feed
on his vitality, to feel his strength. To feel like a
woman, damn it. Not a queen slipping into the twilight
of old age.

No one knew for sure how old she was. She had
been married to Lofantyr's father King Vanatyr at the
age of fifteen, but the first three children they had conceived together in their joyless fashion had died before
they could talk. Lofantyr had survived, and her womb
was barren now. And Vanatyr was dead these fifteen
years, having choked on something he ate. She smiled
at the memory.

There had been three lovers in her life in the decade
and a half since her husband's death. The first had been
Duke Errigal, the regent appointed to advise, guide and
educate the thirteen-year-old King Lofantyr upon his
coronation. Errigal had been her creature, body and
soul. She had ruled through him and her son for five
years, until Lofantyr attained his majority, and then she
had ruled through Lofantyr. But her son the King was
rising thirty now, and more and more often he brushed
her advice aside and made decisions without consulting
her. In short, he was learning to rule in his own right.

Odelia hated that.

Her second lover had been John Mogen, the general
who had been Aekir's military commander, one of the
greatest leaders the west had ever seen. And she had
truly loved him. Because he had been a *man*. A great

man, devoid of manners, culture or breeding, but with
a roaring humour and an art of remembering everything he was ever told, everyone he ever met. His men
had loved him too: that was why they had died for him
in their tens of thousands. She had helped along his
career, and it was she who had procured for him the
military governorship of the Holy City. She had never
dreamed it could fall with him in command. And she
had grieved for him, weeping her tears into her pillow
at night, furious with her lack of self-control. It had
been six years since she had last exchanged so much
as a word with him.

And now there was this new lover, this embittered
young man who had served under her beloved Mogen,
who had seen him die. She knew full well that in advancing him she was indulging in a form of nostalgia,
perhaps trying to recapture the magic of those years
when she had ruled Torunna in all but name, and Mogen had been her knight, her champion. But she would
allow sentiment to take her only so far, and the darkness of these times was something different, something
new. She believed she could smell out greatness as
surely as a hound scenting a hare. Mogen had possessed it, and so did this Corfe Cear-Inaf. In her own
son, the King, there was no vestige of it at all.

As if summoned by her musings, her maid entered
the chamber behind her and curtsied. "Lady, His Majesty—"

"Let him in," she snapped, and she closed the balcony screens on the rawness of the day, the reek of the
refugee camps and the roaring bustle of the city below.

"A little short of late, aren't you, mother?" Lofantyr
said as he came in. He had a heavy fur-lined cloak

about him; he hated the cold as much as she did.

"The old are permitted impatience," she retorted. "They have less time to waste than the young."

The King seated himself comfortably on one of the divans that sat around the walls and warmed his hands at the saffron glow of a brazier. He looked around.

"Where's your playmate?"

"Asleep. He caught a kitten, and he is so decrepit now he needs to gather his strength before tackling it." She nodded towards the ceiling.

Lofantyr followed her eyes and saw up in the shadowed rafters a spiderweb fully twelve feet across. At its centre his mother's familiar crouched, and twitching in a corner was a small web-wrapped bundle that uttered a faint, pathetic mewing. Lofantyr shuddered.

"To what do I owe the honour of this visit?" the Queen Dowager asked, gliding across the floor to her embroidery stand and seating herself before it. She began selecting a needle and a bright silken spool of thread.

"I have some news—more of a rumour, actually— that I thought might interest you. It is from the south."

She threaded the needle, frowning with concentration. "Well?"

"The rumours have it that our rebellious subjects in the south have been subdued with unwonted speed and ease."

"Your Colonel Aras made good time then," she said, baiting him.

"The rumours say that the rebels were beaten by a motley group of strangely armoured savages under a Torunnan officer."

She kept her face impassive, though her heart leapt

within her. The needle stabbed through the embroidery board and into her finger, drawing a globule of blood, but she gave no sign.

"How very intriguing."

"Isn't it? And I will tell you something else intriguing. As well as the refugees from Aekir, we have encamped at our gates almost a thousand tribesmen from the mountains *with* their mounts and weapons. Cimbriani. Felimbri, Feldari. A veritable melting-pot of savages. They have sent a delegation to the garrison authorities saying that they wish to enlist under the command of one Colonel Corfe, as they call him, and that they will not leave the vicinity of the city until they have seen him."

"How very curious," she said. "And how have you dealt with them?"

"I do not want a horde of armed barbarians at my gates. I sent a few tercios to disarm them."

"You did what?" Odelia asked, very softly.

"There was an unfortunate incident, and blood was shed. Finally I surrounded their camp with artillery and forced them to give up their arms. They are now in chains awaiting transfer to the Royal galleys to serve as oarsmen." Lofantyr smiled.

Odelia looked at her son. "Why?" she asked.

"I don't know what you mean, mother."

"Don't seek to play games with me, Lofantyr."

"What has irked you? That I made a decision without first running to your chambers to consult? I am King. I do not have to answer to you, whether you be my mother or not," the King said, his pale face flushing pink.

"You are a damned fool," the Queen Dowager told

her son, her voice still soft. "Like a child who destroys
something precious in a fit of pique and cannot have
it mended afterwards. Look beyond your own injured
pride for a moment, Lofantyr, and consider the good
of the kingdom."

"I never consider anything else," the King said, at
once angry and sullen.

"This man I have sponsored, this young officer—he
has ability beyond any of your court favourites and you
know it. We need men like him, Lofantyr. Why do you
seek to destroy him?"

"I will promote my own war leaders. I will not have
them chosen for me!" the King exclaimed, and he
stood up, his fur cloak billowing around him.

"Perhaps you will be allowed to choose your own
when you have learned to choose wisely," Odelia told
him. Her skin seemed almost to glow and her eyes
were alight, like emeralds with the sun refracted
through them.

"By God, I do not have to listen to this!"

"No, you do not. A fool never likes to listen to wisdom when it crosses his own desires. Think, Lofantyr!
Think not of your own pride but of the kingdom! A
king who is not master of himself is master of nothing."

"How can I be master of anything when you are
always there in the shadow, spinning your webs, whispering into the ears of my advisors? You have had your
day in the sun, mother, now it is my turn. I am the
King, damn it all!"

"Then learn to behave like one," Odelia said. "Your
antics are more those of a spoilt child. You surround
yourself with creatures whose only goal in life is to

tell you what you want to hear. You place your own absurd pride above the good of the country itself, and you refuse to listen to any news which conflicts with your own ideas of how the world should work. The men bleeding on the battlefields are the glue which keeps this kingdom together, Lofantyr, not the fawning office-seekers of the court. Never forget where the true power lies, what the true nature of power is."

"What is this, a lesson in kingship?"

"By the blood of the Saint, were I a man I'd thrash you until you shrieked. You're so blinded by protocol and finery you cannot hear the very footfalls of doom come striding across the world."

"Don't become apocalyptic on me, mother," her son told her, scorn in his own voice now. "We all know the witchery you practise—it is common knowledge at court—but it cannot help you predict the future. Your gifts do not lie that way."

"It does not take a soothsayer to predict the way the world is going."

"Nor does it take a genius to understand your sudden interest in this upstart colonel from Aekir. Does it help you to forget your age to take a man young enough to be your son to bed?"

They stared at each other.

Finally Odelia said: "Tread carefully, Lofantyr."

"Or what? It is all over the court—the Queen Dowager bedding the ragged deserter from John Mogen's vanished army. You talk to me of my behaviour. How do you think yours reflects upon the dignity of the Crown? My own mother, and a ragged-arsed junior officer!"

"I ruled this country when you were a snotty-faced child!" she cried shrilly.

"Aye, and we know how you managed that. Errigal you bedded too. You would prostitute yourself a thousand times over if it would seat you any nearer the throne. Well, I am a grown man, mother, my own man. You are not needed any more."

"You think so?" Odelia asked. "You really think so?"

They were both standing now, with the hellish radiance of the brazier between them, illuminating their faces from below so that they were transformed into masks of flame and shadow. Above them, the giant spider that was Arach had awoken and its legs were gently tapping the web it clung to, as though readying itself for a spring. Lofantyr peered up at the thing; it was uttering a low keening, something like an anguished cat's purr.

"Stop meddling in the affairs of state," Lofantyr said more calmly to the Queen Dowager. "You must give me a chance to rule, mother. You cannot hang on for ever."

Odelia inclined her head a trifle, as if in gracious agreement. Her eyes were two viridian flickers mingled with the yellow flame-light.

"Release the tribesmen," she said in a reasonable tone. "Let him have them. It can do no harm."

"Arm the Felimbri? Is that what you want? And you were the one who cautioned me about hiring the Fimbrians!"

"They will obey him. I know it."

"They are savages."

"Maybe if you had given him a command of regulars

at the beginning this problem would never have arisen," she said, her voice cutting.

"Maybe if you had not—" he began, and stopped. "This bickering does neither of us any good."

"Agreed."

"All right, I will release them. Your protégé can have his savages. But they will receive no assistance from the military authorities. He is on his own, this Aekirian colonel."

Odelia bowed her head in acceptance.

"Let us not fight, mother," Lofantyr said. He moved around the brazier and held out his hands.

"Of course," his mother said. She took his hands and kissed his cheek.

The king smiled, then turned away. "There are couriers from Martellus on their way in from the gates. I must see them. Will you come with me?"

"No," she said to his retreating back. "No, see them alone. I have my work to do here."

He smiled at her, and left the room.

Odelia sat a moment in the quiet he had left behind, her eyes hooded, their fire veiled. Finally she picked up the embroidery board and hurled it across the room. It cracked against the far wall in a tangled mess of snapped wood and fabric and thread. The maid peeped in at the door, saw her mistress's face, and fled.

THE black-burnt stone of Admiral's Tower seemed somehow in keeping with the tone of Abrusio in these times. Jaime Rovero, admiral of Hebrion's fleets, had his halls and offices near the summit of the fortress. In a tall chamber there he paced by his desk while the smell of seawater and ashes came sidling in from the docks below, and he could hear the gulls screaming madly. A winter fishing yawl must be putting in. All his life he had been a seaman, having risen from master's mate aboard a caravel to command of his own vessel, then of a squadron, then a fleet, and finally the very pinnacle of his career—First Lord of the Navy. He could go no higher. And yet he would look down on the trefoil of harbours that the city of Abrusio encircled and, seeing the ships there, the hiving life of the port, the hordes of dock hands and mariners, he would sometimes wish he were a mere master's mate again with hardly two coppers to rub together in his pocket, and the promise of a fresh horizon with the next sunrise.

The door was knocked and he barked: "Enter!" and straightened, blinking away the memories and the absurd regrets. One of his secretaries announced: "Galliardo Ponera, Third Port Captain of the Outer Roads, my lord."

"Yes, yes. Send him in."

In came a short, dark-skinned man with an air of the sea about him despite some fine clothes and an over-feathered hat. Ponero made his bow, the feathers describing an arc as he swung his headgear in a gesture he imagined was elegance itself.

"Oh, stow that courtly rubbish," Rovero grated. "This isn't the palace. Take a seat, Ponero. I have some questions for you."

Galliardo was sweating. He sat in front of the massive dark wood of the admiral's desk and soothed down his ruffled feathers.

Rovero stared at his visitor silently for a second. He had a small sheaf of papers on his desk which bore the

Royal seal. Galliardo glimpsed them and swallowed.

"Calm down," Rovero told him. "You're not here on corruption charges, if that's what you're thinking. Half the port captains in the city turn a blind eye now and again. It's the grease that turns the wheels. No, Ponero, I want you to have a look at these." He tossed the papers across the desk at his trembling guest.

"They're victualling warrants, Royal ones," Galliardo said after a moment's perusal.

"Bravo. Now explain."

"I don't understand, your excellency."

"Those two ships, outfitted and victualled at Royal expense and carrying Hebrian military personnel, were readied for sea in your section of the yards. I want to know where they were headed, and why the King sponsored their voyage."

"Why not ask him?" Galliardo said.

Rovero frowned, an awful sight.

"I beg your pardon, your excellency. The fact is the ships were owned by one Richard Hawkwood, and the leader of the expedition and commander of the soldiers was Lord Murad of Galiapeno."

Rovero's frown deepened. "*Expedition*? Explain."

Galliardo shrugged. "They were carrying stores for many months, horses for breeding—not geldings, you understand—and sheep, chickens. And there were the passengers, of course . . ."

"What about them?"

"Some hundred and forty of the Dweomer-folk of the city."

Rovero whistled softly. "I see. And what of their destination, Ponero?"

Galliardo thought back, back to the tail end of a

summer that now seemed years ago. He remembered clinking a last glass of wine with Richard Hawkwood in the portside tavern by his offices which had seen so many partings, the backs of so many men who went into tall ships and sailed towards the horizon, never to return. Where was Richard Hawkwood now, and his ships, his companies? Rotting in the deep perhaps, or wrecked on some cragged rock out in the unmapped ocean. One thing Galliardo knew: Hawkwood had been meaning to sail west—not to the Brenn Isles or the Hebrionese, but west as far as his ships would take him, farther perhaps than anyone had ever sailed before. What had become of him? Had he found at last the limits of the turning world and set his foot on some untrodden strand? Galliardo would probably never know, and so he deemed it safe to tell the admiral what he knew of the Hawkwood expedition despite the fact that Richard had enjoined him to secrecy. Richard was probably dead, and beyond the consequence of anything Galliardo might do. The Hawkwood line had ended: his wife, Estrella, had died in the howling inferno that had been Abrusio scant weeks ago.

"West, you say?" Rovero rumbled thoughtfully when Galliardo had told him.

"Yes, excellency. It's my belief they were trying to discover the legendary Western Continent."

"That's a fable, surely."

"I think Hawkwood had some document or chart which suggested differently. In any case, he has been gone for months with no word sent back. I do not think he survived."

"I see." Rovero seemed strangely troubled.

"Is there anything else, excellency?" Galliardo asked timidly.

The admiral stared at him. "No. Thank you, Ponero. You may go."

Galliardo rose and bowed. As he left the room and negotiated his way through the dark maze that was the interior of Admiral's Tower, sharply lit memories came to his mind, pictures from what seemed another age. A hot, vibrant Abrusio with a thousand ships at her wharves and the men of a hundred different countries mixed in her streets. The *Gabrian Osprey* and the *Grace of God* sailing out of the bay on the ebb tide, proud ships plunging into the unknown.

As he came out into the cold grey day of the winter city, Galliardo whispered a swift prayer to Ran the God of Storms, the old deity many seamen sought to placate when they were a thousand miles from land or priest or hope of harbour. He prayed briefly for the souls of Richard Hawkwood and his crews, surely gone to their long wave-tossed rest at last.

SEVEN

YEAR OF THE SAINT 552

DIM though the winter afternoon was, it was darker yet in the King's chambers. It seemed to Isolla that lately she had been living her life by candlelight and firelight. She sat by Abeleyn's bedside reading aloud from an old historical commentary on the naval history of Hebrion, glancing every so often at the King's inert form in the great postered bed. In the first days she had been here she had constantly been prepared for some sudden show of life, some twitch or opening of an eyelid, but Abeleyn lay as still as a graven statue, if a statue could occasionally break into loud, stertorous breathing.

She stroked his hand as she read, the book propped on her knees. It was dry stuff, but it gave her a reason to be here, and Golophin believed that Abeleyn might yet be recalled to himself by the sound of a voice, a touch, some external stimulus which none of them had yet discovered.

It never for an instant occurred to her to wonder what she was doing here, by the bedside—or perhaps the deathbed—of a man she scarcely knew, sitting reading aloud to a man beyond hearing, in a country that was not her own, in a city half ruined by fire and the sword. Her sense of duty was too deeply ingrained for that. And there was an innate stubbornness too which her maid Brienne could have vouched for. A willingness to see something through to the end, once it was undertaken. She had never run away from anything in her life, had braved the snide asides of the Astaran court ladies for so long that it slipped like water from the feathers of a duck. She knew her brother the King loved her, also. That was one of the unshakable pillars of her life.

And he wanted her here with this man, or what was left of him. Isolla could no more have shirked this task than she could have grown wings and flown back to Astarac. Life was not to be enjoyed, it was a thing to work at, to be carved and polished and sanded down until at its end some form of beauty and symmetry might be left behind for others to see. Happiness was rarely a factor to be considered in that process, not when one was born to royalty.

The door opened softly behind her. One of the palace servants, an old man who was one of the few entrusted with the reality of the King's condition. He stood unsure and silent behind her, coughed quietly.

"What is it, Bion?" She knew all their names.

"My lady, the King has a . . . a visitor, who insists on being admitted. A noblewoman."

"No visitors," Isolla said.

"Lady, she says that my lord Golophin expressly gave her permission to see the King."

Isolla put away her book, intrigued but wary. Half the nobility of Hebrion had blustered or wheedled at the door at some point, eager for a look at Hebrion's invisible monarch. Golophin had turned them away, but he was indisposed. Something had happened to his eye—he was wearing a black patch over it—and even his febrile energy seemed to be fading.

"Her name?"

"The lady Jemilla." Bion seemed ill at ease, perturbed even. He could not meet her eyes.

"I'll see her in the anteroom," Isolla said briskly, unwilling to admit even to herself that she was glad of the interruption.

The lady was pale-skinned, raven dark-haired and assured: a doppelganger of half a dozen who had made Isolla's childhood a misery. But things were different now.

The lady paused a moment as Isolla entered, black eyes watchful, gauging. Then she swept into an elegant curtsey. Isolla acknowledged this with a slight bow of her head. "Please, be seated."

They took up positions on small, uncomfortable chairs with their robes spread out around them like the plumage of two competing birds.

"I hope I see you well, lady," Jemilla said pleasantly.

A series of vapid exchanges essential to courtly conversation, all of which were meaningless, a convention. How had the lady Isolla found Hebrion? Cold, was it

not, at this time of year, but more pleasant in the
spring, surely. The summer far too hot—best to retreat
to a lodge in the mountains until the turning of the
leaves. And Astarac! A fine kingdom. Her brother the
very model of a Ramusian monarch (his current heresy
and excommunication blithely passed over). The lady
Jemilla held a roll of parchment in one fine-fingered
hand. It stirred Isolla's curiosity, and pricked her into
a fine-tuned wariness even as the empty talk slid from
her mouth.

"So Golophin agreed that you be admitted to see the
King," Isolla said at last when the polite phrases had
run their course.

"Yes, indeed. He and I are old acquaintances. The
palace is like a village really. One cannot help but get
to know everyone—even the King himself."

"Oh, indeed?" Isolla's face gave nothing away, but
there was an apprehension growing in her.

"Such a man! Such a monarch! He is greatly loved,
lady, as I am sure you are aware. The kingdom is riddled with worry for him. But the dearth of news as to
his progress has been quite worrying." She put out a
hand as Isolla stirred. "Not that I mean any reflection
on Golophin or the worthy Admiral Rovero, you understand, or General Mercado either. But the people
who bled for Abeleyn have a right to know, as do the
great men of the kingdom. After all, if the King's con-
valescence is to be a long one, then it is only proper
that some other personage of fitting rank be nominated
to help steer the course of the kingdom. These . . . *professionals* are very well in their way, but the common
folk like to see good blood at the head of the government. Do you not agree?"

There it was, the gleam of steel through the velvet. Jemilla smiled. Her teeth were small, fine, and very white. Like those of a cat, Isolla thought. Could Golophin actually have given this creature leave to see the King? No, of course not. But what was she to do, tell this lady she lied, to her face? And what was in that damned parchment?

Isolla's face, unknown to her, grew severe, forbidding almost. It was what her brother Mark called privately her "beat to quarters expression."

"I will not speculate on the policies of the man who is soon to be my husband, nor on those of his closest and most trusted advisors. It would not be fitting, you understand," Isolla shot back, watching the little barb slide home. "And unfortunately, the King is very fatigued today, and unable to receive anyone. But be assured, lady, I will convey to him your best wishes and hopes for his recovery. I am sure they will hearten him mightily. And now, alas, I too am not mistress of my own time. I am afraid I must bring this delightful interview to a close." She paused, expecting the lady Jemilla to get up, to curtsey and to leave. But Jemilla did not move.

"Forgive me," she said, purring, "but I am afraid I must beg your indulgence for a few moments more. I have here"—the parchment at last—"a document of sorts which I have been charged to deliver to you, as the King's betrothed. Little do I, a mere woman, understand of these things, but I believe it to be a petition signed by many of the heads of Hebrion's noble families. May I leave it in your hands? It would be a weight off my mind. Thank you, gracious lady. And now I must bid you farewell." A curtsey, only just as deep as custom demanded, and a swift exit, the triumph flashing in her eye.

The bitch, Isolla thought. The scheming, insolent bitch. She cracked open the seal—it was the house seal of some high born princeling or other—and scanned the long scroll which fell open in her hands.

A petition all right, and the names on it made Isolla purse her lips in a silent, unladylike whistle. The Duke of Imerdon, no less. The Lords of Feramuno, Hebrero and Sequero. Two thirds of the highest aristocrats in Hebrion must have their signatures here—if the document were genuine. She would have to check that, although did not doubt that it would be genuine. Who was this Lady Jemilla anyway? She was not married to anyone of rank, or she would have taken his name instead of parading around under her own. A husband's name was the label of a woman's stature in this world.

And what did this petition request? That the King reveal himself to his anxious subjects and prove that he was the ruler of Hebrion, not the triumvirate of Golophin, Mercado and Rovero. Or, if he were too ill to do so, that a suitable nobleman, one whose bloodline was closest to the King, be named regent of Hebrion until such time as the King himself was capable of ruling again. Second, that access to the King's person be granted for the signatories, his noble cousins, whose concern for him was overwhelming. Third, that the aforementioned triumvirate of Golophin, Rovero and Mercado be broken up, these gentlemen to resume their proper duties and station and allow the kingdom to be ruled by whomsoever the Council of Nobles decreed regent. And, by the way, the Council of Nobles—an institution that Isolla, for all her reading on Hebrian history, had never heard of—would be convening in two sennights in the city of Abrusio to debate these matters, and to call on the King to marry his betrothed Astaran princess and give the kingdom the joyous spectacle of a Royal wedding, and perhaps, within due time, an heir.

There it was, the gauntlet tossed down before her. Marry him or go home. Produce him, upright and breathing, or let the nobles squabble over his successor. It was what it amounted to, for all the flowery language. Isolla wondered how deeply Jemilla was buried in this thing. She was more than a mere errand-runner, that was plain.

"Bion!" Her voice snapped like a whip.

"My lady?"

"Ask the mage Golophin if he will receive me at once. Tell him it is a matter of the direst urgency. And be quick about it."

"Yes, my lady."

Hebrion had just gone through one war, now it was to suffer another; but this one would be played out in the corridors of the palace itself. Strangely enough, Isolla was almost looking forward to the prospect.

EIGHT

IT depressed Corfe to see Torunn again in the numbing drizzle of the new year, the smoke of the refugee camps hanging about it like a shroud and the land for miles around churned into a quagmire by the displaced thousands of Aekir. They were still squatting in the hide tents provided by the Torunnan authorities, and seemed no nearer than before to dispersing and rebuilding their lives.

"Our glorious capital," Andruw murmured, his usual good cheer dampened by the sight, and by the swift miles they had put behind them in the last week. They had killed twenty-three horses in the retracing of their steps north, and even the tribesmen of the command were sullen and stupid with exhaustion. They had had enough, for the present. Corfe knew he could push them no further. Perhaps that depressed him too. He was as tired as any of them, but still all he could think of was getting out of here, up to the battlefields of the north. Nothing else held any attraction for him.

This, he thought, is what my life has become. There is nothing else.

The long column of filthy, yawning cavalry and silent mules wound down from the higher land overlooking the capital and came to a halt outside the city walls amid the tented streets of the shanty town. The folk of Aekir stared at the hollow-eyed barbarians on the tall warhorses as if they were creatures from another world. Corfe stared back at them, the white lightning-fury searing up in him at the sight of the muddy children, their ragged parents. These had once been the proud citizens of the greatest city in the world. Now they were beggars, and the Torunnan government seemed content to let them stay that way. He felt like dragging King Lofantyr out here and grinding his face into the liquid filth of the open sewers. When the warmer weather came, disease would sweep through these camps like wildfire.

He turned to Andruw and Marsch. "This is no damned good. Get the men bedded down beyond the camps, away from this."

"We've no bedding, no food—not even for the horses," Andruw reminded him. As if he needed reminding.

"I'm aware of that, Haptman. I'm going into the city to see what can be done. In the meantime, you have your orders." He paused, and then added reluctantly. "You might want to slaughter a couple of the pack mules. The men need meat in their bellies."

"God's blood, Corfe!" Andruw protested quietly.

"I know. But we can't expect too much. Best to prepare for the worst. I'll be back as soon as I can."

He turned his horse away, unable to meet Andruw's eyes. He felt as though the anger in him could set the world alight and take grim satisfaction in its burning, but it left him feeling empty and cold. His men depended on him. If needs be he would lick the King's boots to see them provided for.

The sentries at the main gate forgot to salute, so outlandish did he appear in his crimson Merduk armour. He turned over the options in his mind and finally pointed his horse's nose towards the courtyards and towers of the Royal palace. His patron would, perhaps, be able to do something for him. He had passed the first test she had set him, at any rate.

"COLONEL Corfe Cear-Inaf," the chamberlain announced, a little wide-eyed.

The Queen Dowager turned from the window. Her hands fluttered up over her face and hair. "Show him in, Chares."

Her chamber was warm with braziers and blood-coloured tapestries. A pair of maids sat quiet as mice in a corner. At a look from her they rose and left by a concealed door. She awaited him with regal poise, though her heart thumped faster in her breast, and she felt a winged lightness there she had not known in many years. It both cheered and irritated her.

He clumped in. He seemed to love that outlandish armour of his, but at least he had doffed the barbaric helm that went with it. He was a mud-stained, bloody harbinger of war, out of place, uncomfortable-looking. His face had aged ten years in the few weeks since she had seen him last. The light in his eyes actually unnerved her for a moment, she who had faced down kings. There was a strength and violence there she had not noted before, a reined-in savagery.

"So," she said quietly. "You are back."

"So it would seem." Then he collected himself, and went down stiffly on one knee, clods of dirt falling from his boots. "Your majesty."

"I told you before, I am 'lady' to you. Get up. You look tired."

"Indeed, lady." He rose as slowly as an old man. There was blood on him, she noted, and he stank of old sweat and horse and burning.

"For God's sake," she snapped, "couldn't you have bathed at least?"

"No," he said simply. "There was nowhere else to go. We have only just got in." He swayed as he stood, and she saw the deep bone-weariness in him. Her lips thinned, and she clapped her hands. Chares entered at the main door, bowing. "Your highness?"

"Have a bath brought here at once, a fresh uniform for the Colonel and a couple of valets who know their job."

"At once, highness." Chares withdrew hurriedly.

"I haven't the time," Corfe said. "My men—"

"What do you need?" she demanded.

He blinked stupidly, as if the question had caught him unawares.

"Quarters for three hundred men, and food. Stabling for nearly eight hundred horses and two hundred mules. Fodder for them, too."

It was her turn to be taken aback. "Horses?"

The shadow of a smile. "Spoils of war."

"I'll see to it. You have been busy, it seems, Colonel."

"I did what was expected of me, I believe." Again, that ghost smile. This time she returned it.

His armour was rusted to his back. The buckles had to be cut free by two owl-eyed palace valets while a flurry of others brought in a bronze hip-bath and filled it full of steaming water, kettle upon kettle of it until there was a mist hanging in the room. Others carried in fresh clothing and footwear. The Queen Dowager withdrew behind a screen, stifling a laugh when she heard Corfe curse away the flunkeys who fussed over him. She sat herself at her writing desk and in her swift, stabbing hand drew up the necessary orders, sealing them with her signet. It was the twin of her son the King's. That much authority she retained. She snapped her fingers for a servant.

"Give this to the Quartermaster-General," she told him, "and be quick, too." She raised her voice. "Colonel, where are your men?"

A grunt, the clump of a boot hitting the floor. "By the southern gate, outside the camps. Haptman Andruw Cear-Adurhal commands at the moment. You'll find them by the smell of roasting mule."

THE attendants left at last, and she heard him splashing in the bath beyond the screen. It would be over the palace in minutes, that the Queen Dowager had a muddy colonel of cavalry bathing in her private chambers. It was a signal she sent out quite deliberately. People would tread more warily around her protégé as a result. It was his reward for the passing of the first test.

And besides, she liked having him here.

The splashing had stopped. "Corfe?"

She peered round the screen. He was asleep in the bath, arms dangling over its sides, mouth open.

She rose and approached him, silent as a spider in her court shoes. The floor around him was a mess of mud and water. As she crouched by his side it soaked the bottom of her skirts.

Some of the lines faded when he slept. He seemed younger. His forearms were scarred with old wounds, and the bathwater was bloody where a more recent one in his thigh had reopened. She touched the wound, running her hand over him under the water. She closed her eyes and the gash healed under her fingers. The bleeding stopped.

He came awake with a violent start that sent the bathwater spraying. His hand gripped her wrist. "What are you doing?"

"Nothing," she said softly. "Nothing at all." She leaned over and kissed his bare shoulder and felt him tremble under her lips.

"You don't fear scandal much, do you?" he remarked.

"As much as you."

His hand, calloused from rein and sword-hilt, caressed her cheek gently. For a second he seemed almost a boy. But the second passed. The lines settled in his face again. He hauled himself out of the bath and reached for a towel to cover himself. He seemed almost bewildered.

"I must get back to my men."

"Not yet," she told him, her voice becoming harder

as she rose with him. "Your men are being looked after. You, I need here for now."

"For what, payment?"

"Don't be a fool," she snapped. "Get dressed. We have much to discuss."

He held her eyes for a moment, and she was sure her need for him would betray her, spill out of her and plead with him. She turned away. The attendants had left decanters of Gaderian, a joint of venison, apples, cheese, fresh bread. She poured herself some of the blood-red wine whilst he towelled himself dry and pulled on the black Torunnan infantry uniform which had been left for him. As a cavalryman, he should have been in burgundy, and she thought it would suit him, but she knew also that he would prefer black.

"Eat something, for God's sake," she ordered. He was standing motionless as though on parade, obviously hating the court version of the uniform, the lace cuffs, tight collar and buckled shoes.

He seemed to experience some kind of inner struggle. It flitted across his face.

"Your men are being fed as we speak," she said. "Stop playing the noble leader and get something into your own stomach. You look half-starved."

At last, he unbent. She saw it was all he could do not to wolf down the food like an animal. He made himself chew it slowly, and sipped at the wine. Again, the tiredness in his face making him look so much older. How old was he? Thirty? Not much more, perhaps even less. He took a seat by one of the glowing braziers with a brimming wine glass in one fist and a chunk of bread in the other, taking alternate bites and sips. Finally he paused, conscious of her eyes on him, and said, "Thank you" in a low voice.

She sat down opposite him wishing she'd had time to ready a few rejuvenating spells. She was very aware of the liver spots on the backs of her hands. She hated herself for feeling so absurdly self-conscious.

"You are your own courier, it seems," she said. "I take it the business in the south was concluded satisfactorily?"

He nodded. "Aras is still down there. I left him the last of the mopping up."

"Your tribesmen did well."

"Amazingly well." For the first time some real warmth came into his voice, and his face became more animated. He gave her a brief outline of the short campaign, neither boasting nor deprecating. When he was done she looked at him in some wonder.

"So the Felimbri make soldiers. If we'd known that twenty years ago it would have saved the country some grief. You are down to three hundred now, you say."

"Yes, plus some two dozen wounded I had to leave with Aras."

She smiled, glad to be able to give him the news. "It's lucky your savages acquitted themselves so well. There are a thousand more of them currently awaiting you at the North Gate. News travels fast in the mountains, it appears." Better not to tell him that these men had almost been sent to the galleys by the King. He would find out soon enough.

His eyes were glittering, fingers whitening around the wine glass. "By the Saints—" He bowed his head and for an astonished instant she thought he might weep, but she heard him give a strangled laugh instead.

When he looked up the relief was engraved in his features like the words on a tombtop. She saw then how tautly strung he was, and had some inkling of the strain that bent him.

The wine glass shattered in a spray of scarlet.

"Forgive me." He shook the liquid from his fingers, grimacing. His palm was gashed and trickling blood.

"Corfe . . ." she said, and took his bloody hand, pulled him across to her. It was like tugging on the branch of an unyielding tree for a moment, before he gave in. He knelt on the floor and buried his face in her lap with a sigh. Summoning the Dweomer, she smoothed away the slash in his palm, restoring the skin as though she were shaping warm wax. As the spell worked the energy in her flickered. She felt her years dragging at her limbs, age baying for her life.

He would have risen, but she held him there, suddenly needing his youth close to her.

"You can rest a while. The Merduks have drawn half their army off from the dyke. Campaigning has finished for the winter. I will see to it that your men have all they need." *Stay with me.*

"No." He raised his head. His eyes were dry. "It's just begun. I believe they've outflanked the dyke somehow. Martellus is in trouble, I know it."

The soldier again. He had retreated from her. She let him go, and he rose to pace about the room, pausing to stare at his healed hand and then at her.

"You *are* a witch then."

"Indeed," she said wearily. "What nonsense are you talking about the dyke?"

"It's a feeling, nothing more. Has Martellus sent any dispatches lately?"

"Not for ten days. But the roads are bad."

"He's cut off already then."

"Oh, for God's sake! Are you an oracle, who knows this through intuition alone?"

He shrugged. "I know it. For what purpose would the Merduks mobilize a great army in the depths of winter? They are making another assault, that's clear—but not a head-on one this time. They're doing something else, something we have no idea of. And time is not on our side. I must go north."

She saw she could not move him. "You need rest, you and your men. I'll have couriers sent to the dyke. We'll find out the truth of it."

He hesitated. "All right."

Their eyes locked. Odelia knew there was greatness in him, something she had glimpsed before with John Mogen. But there was something else, too. An injury that refused to heal, old agony which racked him yet. She thought it might be that pain which drove him on, which had changed him from the lowly ensign of Aekir to the man who stood here now, his star on the rise. But still, the pain was always there.

She rose in her turn and padded over to him, wrapped her arms about him and kissed him on the lips, crushing her mouth against his.

"You will come to bed now."

He was still tense, resisting her. "I have not yet reported to the King. And I must see these new recruits . . ." He faltered. "Why?" he asked. There was genuine puzzlement in his voice.

She grinned fiercely. "I want you there, and you need to be there too."

At last he smiled back.

• • •

FIFTY leagues, a crow might fly, nor-nor-east from the room where Corfe and the Queen Dowager shared a bed. Across the empty hills which bordered the Western Road, itself a brown swampish gash across the earth with old corpses littering its length. Thousands had died along that road, lying down in the mud and rain in the retreat from Aekir and the trek from Ormann Dyke, relinquishing their grip on a life which had become a waking nightmare.

But now Ormann Dyke was burning.

The smoke could be seen for miles, a black, thunderous reek of destruction. Men were fighting in the midst of it. A thousand Torunnans, valiant with despair, struggled vainly to stem the onslaught of the Merduk army. The enemy had already crossed the Searil in force and was overrunning the three-mile length of the Long Walls, which for the first time in their proud history were about to fall to an assault.

The rest of the dyke's garrison was in full retreat, its artillery spiked and left behind to burn, its stores destroyed, the men marching with nothing more than the armour on their backs and the weapons in their hands. Their comrades left behind at the dyke were buying time with their lives, precious hours of marching which might yet save what was left of Martellus's army.

The army moved in a vacuum. Around it, the countryside was alive with harassing clouds of enemy light cavalry which severed communications with Torunn and the south. No one in the capital even suspected that Ormann Dyke had fallen. The Merduk light horse had already slain half a dozen couriers which Martellus, in desperation, had sent south.

THIRTY leagues away, another column of troops, this time black-clad Fimbrians, their pikes resting on their shoulders, their fast pace eating up the miles in a deadly race. They were coming in from the northwest, the last direction the Merduk High Command was looking. Their mule-mounted scouts ranged far ahead of the main body, seeking out the whereabouts of the third army in the region, striving to come to grips with it before it might descend upon Martellus's flank and complete the destruction of the dyke's garrison.

AND the third army, the largest of the three, had left behind the ships which had transported it across the Kardian Sea and was steadily making its way north-west to cut off Martellus's retreat. In its van rode the elite Merduk cavalry, the *Ferinai*, and behind them the shock troops of the *Hraibadar*, armed now with arquebuses instead of the spears and tulwars with which they had assaulted Aekir. War elephants by the score marched like mobile towers in their midst, and others in the rear hauled huge-bored siege guns through the mud whilst alongside strode the men of the *Minhraib*, the feudal levy of Ostrabar, and regiments of horse-archers from Ostrabar's new ally the Sultanate of Nalbeni. A hundred thousand men moving in four columns, each several miles long. And in the middle of this moving multitude trundled the chariot of Ostrabar's Sultan, Aurungzeb the Golden; to its rear were the eighty heavily laden wagons which transported the

Sultan's household, his campaigning gear and his concubines. Aurungzeb liked to go to war in style.

"THEY'VE gone," Joshelin said with low harshness. "You can get up off your bellies, priests."

Albrec and Avila rose out of the tall grass they had been skulking in. Behind them Siward stood and slapped out the burning end of his slow-match, then replaced the end in the wheel lock of his arquebus.

"What were they?" he asked his fellow Fimbrian. "Foragers, or scouts?"

"Scouts. Merduk light horse, a half-troop. A long way from the main body, I'm thinking. Where are the Torunnans? Looks like they've given over the whole damn country to the enemy."

Albrec and Avila listened to the exchange in shivering silence. They were wet through, mud-stained and hungry and their legs wobbled under them, but the two old soldiers seemed to be built out of some other substance than mere human flesh. Twenty years older than either of the two monks, and they were as fit and hardy as youths.

"Must we go farther today?" Avila asked.

"Yes, priest," Joshelin told him curtly. "We've done scarcely eight leagues today by my pacings. Another two or three before dark, then we can lie up for the night. No fire, though. The hills are crawling with Merduks."

Avila slumped. He rubbed a hand over his face and said nothing.

"Do you think the capital is safe yet?" Albrec asked.

"Oh, yes. These are merely part of the enemy screen. He sends out light cavalry so that we can learn nothing of his movements, while he learns all about ours. Basic tactics."

"How ignorant we are, not to know such things," Avila said caustically. "Can we ride now?"

"Yes. The mules have had a good rest these last three leagues."

Avila muttered something venomous none of them could catch.

They had been four days travelling, the two monks and the two Fimbrians. During that time they had marched and ridden harder than Albrec had ever thought it possible for the human frame to bear. They had spent fireless nights shivering against the mules for warmth, and had eaten salt beef and army biscuit through which the weevils squirmed. Joshelin reckoned that another three days would see them in Torunn, if they continued to elude the Merduk patrols. Those three days loomed ahead of them like a long period of penance. Albrec found it easier to think only about putting one foot in front of the next, or getting to the next rise on the horizon. He had not even had the energy to pray. It was only the crinkling bulk of the ancient document he carried which kept him on his feet at all. When it was safe with Macrobius in Torunn, his mind as well as his body might know some peace at last.

At day's end Albrec and Avila were numb and swaying on the backs of the two mules. Nothing in their lives had prepared them for this unbelievably swift, unencumbered travel across a wilderness. Their feet were blistered, the stumps of Avila's lost toes weeping blood and fluid, and their rumps were rubbed almost raw by the crude pack-saddles. When the little party finally stopped for the night the two monks were too far gone to care. They had not even the energy to dismount. Their companions looked at each other wordlessly for a long moment, and then Siward began to lift the monks down off their steeds whilst Joshelin unpacked an entrenching tool and began to dig a hole.

They had halted in the eaves of a small wood, mostly spruce and pine with beech and pale-trunked birch on the outskirts. Farther in, the coniferous trees grew closer together, and their needles carpeted the ground making the travellers' footfalls soundless as a cat's. Night was fast setting in, and it was black in the wood already. Beyond it, the wind had picked up into a whine which roamed across the Torunnan hills like winter's courier. Albrec thought that never had he felt himself so lost, or in such a place of desolation. During the day they had passed abandoned farms and had helped themselves to food from their larders. They had even sighted a roadside inn, as deserted as a mountaintop. The entire population of Northern Torunna, it seemed, had fled at the coming of the Merduks. Would the Torunnans ever make a stand and fight?

When Joshelin had dug his hole to the depth of his knees, he threw aside his entrenching tool and began gathering wood from under the deciduous trees at the outskirts of the forest. Siward threw the two shuddering monks a couple of greasy, damp blankets, and then unsaddled and rubbed down the mules before fitting them with bulging nosebags. The animals were so tired he did not even hobble them, but merely tied their picket ropes to a nearby tree.

An owl hooted in the ghost-dark of the wood, and something—a fox, perhaps—yipped and barked far off, the sounds adding to the emptiness rather than subtracting.

There was a flash, a jump of sparks which revealed the face of Joshelin bent and puff-cheeked as he blew on tinder. A tiny flame, smaller than that of a candle. He fed it as delicately as if he were tending a sick baby, and when it had grown a hand's breadth, he lifted the small pile of twigs and needles into the trench he had dug and began feeding it with larger limbs. He looked as though he were peering into some crack in the earth which led to hell, Albrec thought, and then dismissed the image as unlucky.

The fire grew, and the two monks crawled over to its warmth.

"Keep it going," Joshelin told them. "I have things to do."

"I thought we were to have no fire," Avila said, holding his hands out greedily to the flames. His blanket stank as it began to warm.

"You looked as though you needed it," the Fimbrian said, and then strode off into the darkness with his sword drawn.

"Ignorant fellows," Avila muttered. His eyes were sunken, and the firelight writhed in them like two worms of yellow light.

"Their bite may not be quite so bad as their bark, I'm thinking," said Albrec, blessing the warmth and the gruff thoughtfulness of their companions.

Chopping sounds, breaking wood, and then the two soldiers returned to the firelight holding a rough screen-like structure they had created out of interlaced branches stuffed with sods of turf. They planted it in the ground on the side of the fire trench that faced the border of the wood, and at last sat down themselves, pulling their black military cloaks about them.

"Thank you," Albrec said.

They did not look at him, but threw over a wineskin and the provisions bag. "You'll eat well tonight, at any rate," Joshelin said. "That's dainty fare we picked out of that farm."

They had a chicken, already plucked and gutted, bread which was several days old but which nonetheless seemed like ambrosia after Fimbrian hardtack, and some apples and onions. The chicken they spitted over the fire, the rest they wolfed down along with swallows of rough wine which in Charibon they would have turned their noses up at. Tonight it slid down their throats like the finest of Gaderian vintages.

Siward produced a short black pipe from the breast of his tunic, filled it from a pouch at his waist and he and Joshelin smoked it in turns. The pipe smoke was heavy and strong and acrid. There was some tang in it that Albrec could not quite identify.

"Might I try it?" he asked the soldiers.

Siward shrugged, his face a crannied maze of light and dark in the fire-laced blackness. "If you have a strong head. It is *kobhang*, from the east."

"The herb the Merduks smoke? I thought it was a poison."

"Only if you take too much of it. It helps keep you awake and sharpens the senses, so long as you do not abuse it."

"How do you obtain it?" Albrec's curiosity awoke, taking his mind off his exhaustion.

"It is army issue. We get it along with the bread and

salt horse. When there is no food to be had, a man can keep going for weeks by smoking it."

"And can he then stop smoking it if he has a mind to?" Avila drawled.

Joshelin stared at him. "If he has the will."

Albrec took the pipe Siward proffered rather gingerly and sucked a draught of the bitter smoke deep into his lungs. Nothing happened. He returned the pipe to its owner, rather relieved.

But then his aches and pains dimmed to a comfortable glow. He felt a new strength seeping through his muscles and his body became as light as a child's. He blinked in wonder. The firelight seemed a beautiful, entrancing thing of bright twisting loveliness. He put out his hand towards it, only to have his wrist grasped by the hard fist of Joshelin.

"One must be careful, priest."

He nodded, feeling foolish and exhilarated in the same moment.

"I haven't seen you smoke it before," Avila said to the Fimbrians.

Siward shrugged. "We are getting tired. We are men also, Inceptine."

"Well, bless my soul," Avila retorted, and wrapped himself in his evil-smelling blanket.

They took the chicken off the spit and ripped it into four pieces. Albrec was no longer hungry, but he ate the scorched meat anyway, no longer able to taste it. His mind felt clear as ice. His worries had vanished. He began to chuckle, and then stopped himself as he found his three companions were watching him.

"Marvellous stuff. Marvellous," he muttered, and

fell back into the soft pine needles, snoring as soon as he was horizontal.

Avila threw a blanket over him. It had holes in it from other nights spent lying close to campfires.

"I will dress your feet in the morning," Joshelin told him.

The young Inceptine nodded distantly and took a huge swallow of the wine. "What will you do when you have escorted us safely to Torunn?" he asked.

The two Fimbrians glanced at each other and then into the fire. "We will await further orders from the marshal," Siward said at last.

"You don't believe you'll get any further orders, though. Albrec told me his intentions. Your marshal is leading his men to their deaths."

"Mind your own matters, priest," Joshelin hissed with sudden passion.

"It is no matter to me," Avila said. "I only wonder that you had not thought out what will become of you when you have run this errand for him."

"As you say," Joshelin grated. "It is no matter to you. Now get you to sleep. You need a lot of rest if you are to keep up today's volume of whining on the morrow."

Avila looked at him for a long minute, and finally his face broke out into a smile.

"Quite right. I would hate to let my standards slip."

NINE

HE thought she looked younger in the morning light than she had the night before. He lay propped up on one elbow watching her quiet sleep, and in him a storm of feelings and memories fought for the forefront of his mind. He wrestled them back brutally, slammed a door in their faces, and was able for some few precious seconds to lie there and watch her, and be almost content.

Her eyes opened. No morning bleariness or process of awakening. She was instantly alert, aware, knowing. Her eyes were green as the shallows of the Kardian Sea in high summer, a bewitching, arresting green. His wife's eyes had been grey, quick to humour, and holding less knowledge in their depths. But then his wife had died still a young woman.

"No grief," Odelia said quietly. "Not on this morning. I will not permit it." Her words were imperious but their tone was almost pleading. He smiled, kissed her unlined forehead, and sat up. His moment of peace had passed, but that was to be expected. He did not wish for more.

"I must away, lady," he said, feeling like some swain in a romantic ballad. To connect himself back to reality, he swung his feet off the bed and on to the stone floor. "I have a thousand men waiting for me."

"What is one woman, set against a thousand barbarians?" she asked archly, and rose herself, naked and superb. He watched her as she slipped a silk robe about her shoulders, her hair spilling gold down her back. He was glad she was not dark. That would have been too much.

He pulled on the court uniform he hated, stamping his feet into the absurd buckled shoes. They seemed as insubstantial as cotton after the weeks in long cavalry boots.

A discreet knock at the door.

"Yes," Odelia said, never taking her eyes off Corfe.

A maid. "Highness, the King is in the antechamber. He wishes to see you at once."

"Tell him I am dressing."

"Highness, he will not wait. He insists on entering immediately."

Odelia met Corfe's eyes, and smiled. "Find yourself a corner, Colonel." Then she turned to the maid. "Tell him I will see him now, in here."

The maid scurried out. Corfe cursed venomously. "Are you out of your Royal mind?"

"There's a tapestry behind the headboard which will serve admirably. Make sure your toes do not stick out below it."

"Saint's blood!" Swallowing other oaths, Corfe dashed across the room and concealed himself there. The tapestry was loose-woven. He could see through it as though through a heavy fog. His heart hammered as cruelly as if he were going into battle, but he found time to wonder if he were not the first man ever to hide in that spot.

The King of Torunna entered the Queen Dowager's bedchamber seconds later.

Odelia sat down at her dressing table with her back to her son and began brushing her golden hair.

"An urgent matter indeed, if you must burst in on me before I am even dressed," she said tartly.

Lofantyr's eyes swept the chamber. He was sweating, and looked like nothing so much as a frightened boy in the schoolmaster's study.

"Mother, Ormann Dyke has fallen."

The brush stopped halfway through the gleaming tresses. Corfe thought that his heart had stopped with it. Almost he stepped out from behind the tapestry.

"Are you sure?"

"Merduk light cavalry have been sighted scarcely ten miles from the city walls. General Menin sent out a sortie which destroyed or captured an enemy patrol. One of the enemy was found to have this on him."

Lofantyr proffered his mother a small leather cylinder, much scuffed and stained.

"A dispatch case," Odelia said mechanically. She snatched it out of her son's hands and ripped it open, tapping out the scroll of parchment within. She unrolled and read it, the sheet quivering like a captured lark in her hand.

"Martellus's seal—it's genuine enough. Dated the

day before yesterday. The courier must have made good time ere they caught him. Blood of the merciful Saint, he's on the march, trying for the capital. Ten thousand men, Lofantyr. We must send out a host to meet him."

"Are you mad, mother? The countryside is swarming with the enemy. General Menin's sortie barely made it back to the walls alive. We must ready ourselves for a siege here, and Martellus must fend for himself. I cannot spare the men."

Odelia raised her head. "Do you jest with me?"

"It is the considered advice of the General Staff," the King said defensively. "I concur. I have already given orders that the Aekirian refugee camps be broken up and their occupants shipped south. The fleet is at anchor in the estuary. We will bleed the Merduks white before the walls."

"As they were bled at Aekir and Ormann Dyke, no doubt," the Queen Dowager said. "My God, Lofantyr, think about what you are doing. You are abandoning a quarter of the country and its people to the enemy. You are throwing away Martellus and his army—the best troops we have. Son, you cannot do this."

"The necessary orders are being written out as we speak," the King snapped. "I'll thank you to remember who is monarch of this kingdom, mother." His voice had grown shrill. Perspiration glittered on his temples. He snatched Martellus's dispatch out of her hand. "From now on, the affairs of state are no business of yours." His eyes swept the chamber, passing over the two wine glasses, the rumpled clothing. "I see you have other things to keep you occupied, at any rate. I shall send a clerk round for the seal you still possess this afternoon. Good day." He bowed, wild-eyed, turned, and spun out of the room, wiping the sweat from his forehead as he left.

There was a moment of silence, and then Corfe came out of his hiding place. The Queen Dowager was sitting at her dressing table, chin sunk on breast. She looked up at him as he emerged from behind the tapestry and he saw to his shock that there were tears in her eyes, though her face was set as hard as that of a statue.

"God knows how I ever gave birth to that," she said, and something in her voice made the hairs on Corfe's nape stand up.

She rose. "The fool had not the courage to take the seal outright—he must send a lackey to do it for him. Well, I am forewarned, which is something. You must have a set of orders, Colonel, something suitably vague so that you may not be accused of overreaching yourself. I shall see to it at once."

Corfe was already at the door, his arms full of his old uniform, rusting Merduk armour, the sabre baldric over one shoulder. "What would you have me do?" he asked harshly, pausing.

"Save Martellus, if you can. Use the tribesmen awaiting you at the gates. You can have nothing else. If I read this dispatch correctly, Martellus is still at least a week's march away."

"An infantry march," Corfe told her. "My men will do it in half the time." He hesitated. "Do you really think my tribesmen can make a difference?"

"I would not be sending you else. How soon can you move?"

He turned it over in his mind. His men were exhausted, as were his horses. He had a thousand new recruits, who had to be integrated into his command.

"I need at least a day. Two, probably," he replied.

"Very well."

Corfe turned to go, but she called him back.

"One more thing, Colonel—two more, in fact. For the first, there is a Fimbrian grand tercio on the march out there, trying to intercept the southern Merduk army. It may well be closer to you than Martellus is. I shall not presume to teach you tactics, but it might be best to combine with it ere you launch into the enemy."

Corfe nodded. His mind was racing, juggling the information, trying to make a plan, a sense of it.

"And the other," the Queen Dowager went on. "I shall write out a commission for you which will await your return. If you can save Martellus and the Fimbrians, you shall be a general, Corfe."

He looked at her unsmilingly. I am tasting the carrot, he thought. When shall I feel the stick? But all he said was "Goodbye, lady," before striding out the door.

HIS men had been billeted in an empty warehouse down by the river. They were lying there with nothing to cover them, on a stone floor which was inadequately strewn with straw. Heaped around their sleeping bodies were opened barrels of salt pork and hardtack and kegs of the weak beer which the Torunnan military quaffed daily. They had torn down some of the timber sidings of the building's interior to make smoky fires. In the collective fug of the warehouse, the tribesmen stank and the smoke smarted Corfe's eyes. He roused Andruw, Marsch and Ebro, and the trio

stared at him as though he were a ghost, their eyes red-
rimmed pits, the filth of the march north still slobbering
their clothing.

"What ho, the popinjay," Andruw said, rubbing his
eyes, managing a tired grin.

Corfe began removing the court uniform and don-
ning his old one. He felt furiously ashamed to be clean
and well dressed while his men lay like forsaken vagabonds upon the straw-strewn stone. "I thought you
would be billeted in regular barracks," he said, savagely angry.

"It's all they could find, apparently," Andruw told
him. "I don't give a damn. I'd have slept in a ditch,
the men too. The horses are being well looked after,
though. I made sure of that. They too have straw to lie
on."

"Let the men sleep. You three come with me. We
have work to do."

His three officers obeyed him like laboured old men.
The expression on Corfe's face quelled any questions
they might have had.

Torunn in winter, like all the northern cities, was a
choked quagmire, the streets running with liquid mud,
commoners splashing through it ankle-deep, their bet-
ters on horseback or carried in sedan chairs or sitting
in carriages. It was a weary trek through the crowds
under a thin drizzle, but the rain woke them up. Corfe
was glad of it. He could still catch the scent of Odelia
on his skin, even over the stink of his scarlet armour.

Companies of Torunnan regulars elbowed aside the
crowds of civilians at frequent intervals, all heading
towards the city walls. The capital was crawling with
activity, but there seemed to be no panic, or even un-

ease as yet. The news of Ormann Dyke's fall was not yet common knowledge, though it was known that the refugee camps about the city walls were about to be broken up. As the foursome made their way to the northern gate, Corfe filled in his subordinates on the situation. Andruw became silent and glum. Like Corfe, he had served at the dyke, but for longer. He had friends with Martellus. The dyke had been his home. Marsch, by contrast, seemed uplifted, almost merry at the thought of meeting a thousand more of his fellow tribesmen.

The prospective recruits were encamped a mile from the walls, out of the swamp of the refugees. They had posted sentries, Corfe was gratified to see, and as he and his three comrades puffed up the slope to meet them a knot of riders thundered out of their lines, coming to a mud-splattering halt ten yards away. The lead rider, a young, raven-dark man as slender as a girl, called out in the language of the tribes, and Marsch called back. Corfe heard his own name mentioned, and the dark rider's eyes bored into him.

"I hope they don't put too much store by appearances," Andruw muttered. "We should have ridden."

The dark rider dismounted in one fluid movement, and came forward. He was shorter even than Corfe, and he wore old-fashioned chainmail of exquisite workmanship. A long, wickedly curved sabre hung at his side, and Corfe noted the light lance dangling from the pommel of his horse's saddle.

"This is Morin," Marsch said. "He is of the Cimbriani. He has six hundred of his people here. The rest are Feldari, and a few of my own people, the Felimbri. He has been elected warleader by the host."

Corfe nodded.

The dark tribesman, Morin, launched into a long and passionate speech in his own language.

"He wishes to know if it is true that his men are to fight the Merduks only," Marsch translated.

"Tell him it's true."

"But he also says that he will fight the Torunnans too if you wish. They tried to enslave his men when first they arrived, and had them disarmed. Three were killed. But then they were released again. He"—here Marsch sounded apologetic—"he does not trust Torunnans, but he hears you were an officer under John Mogen, and so you must be an honourable man."

Corfe and Andruw looked at each other. "Torunnan military courtesy is as famed as ever, I see," Andruw murmured. "I'm surprised they didn't bugger off back to the mountains."

"They want to fight," Marsch said simply, whilst beside him Ensign Ebro, a prime example of Torunnan military courtesy, glowered at the ground.

"Tell Morin," Corfe said, holding the eyes of the dark tribesman, "that as long as his people serve under me, they shall be treated like men, and I shall speak for them in everything. If I break faith with them, then may the seas rise up and drown me, may the green hills open up and swallow me, may the stars of heaven fall on me and crush me out of life for ever."

It was the ancient oath of the mountain tribes which Marsch and the rest of the Cathedrallers had once sworn to him. When Marsch had finished translating it to Morin, the dark tribesman instantly fell on one knee and offered Corfe the hilt of his sabre—and Corfe heard the same words coming back at him in the rolling tongue of the Cimbriani.

His little army had just grown by a thousand men.

TEN

IT would take not two days but three to get the command ready for the road north. Thirteen hundred men
and almost two thousand horses, plus a baggage train
of some two hundred mules. The entire column had
been fitted out in the discarded Merduk armour which
lay mouldering in a quartermaster's warehouse, and the
new men's gear was lathered in red paint, just as that
of the original Cathedrallers had been. They had
looked somewhat askance at the Merduk equipment at
first. Unlike Marsch and his five hundred, they possessed their own weapons and wore finely wrought
mail hauberks, but Corfe had insisted that they don the
same armour his original command had fought in down
south. Also, he wanted heavy cavalry, the shattering
impact of an armoured charge. Half of the newcomers
had powerful recurved compound bows of horn and
mountain yew and bristling quivers hung from their

cantles, but they were now outfitted with the lances of the Merduk heavy horse. They were to be shock troops, pure and simple.

Thirteen hundred men, a thousand of whom had never been part of a regimented military command before. Corfe organized them into twenty-six troops, fifty strong each, and sprinkled the three hundred survivors of his original command throughout the new units as NCOs. Two troops made up a squadron, and four squadrons a wing: thus three wings, plus a squadron in reserve to guard the baggage and spare horses. Corfe made Andruw, Ebro and Marsch wing commanders, Ebro almost speechless with gratitude at being given a real command at last.

All very well on paper, but the reality was infinitely more complex. It took a day and a half to equip the new men and reorganize the command. Morin, it turned out, spoke good Normannic and Corfe detailed him as his adjutant and interpreter. The tribesman was none too pleased at not having command of a wing, but he knew nothing of the tactics that Corfe meant to employ, and had to be content with the promise of a field command at a later date. As it was, his pride was satisfied with relaying Corfe's orders as though he had given them himself.

The command was heterogenous to an extreme, liable to sub-divide along the lines of tribe. The new men saw themselves as Cimbriani or Feldari rather than Cathedrallers, but once they had a few battles under their belt, Corfe knew that would change.

Their camp was a buzzing maelstrom of activity, night and day. Andruw and a couple of squadrons busied themselves with the collection of stores from a reluc-

tant and somewhat outraged Torunnan quartermaster's
department, and had it not been for the goodwill of
Quartermaster Passifal his men would never have been
issued a single piece of hardtack. Others were occupied
having the horses shod and the armour reconditioned,
while Corfe conducted formation drill on the blasted
plain north of the capital and the battlements of the city
were lined with fascinated and in some cases derisive
spectators.

He worked his men hard, but no harder than he
worked himself. By the third day the three wings were
able, with a certain amount of cursing and jostling, to
move from road column to line of battle at a single
trumpet call from Cerne, Corfe's bugler. Their efforts
would have made a Torunnan drill-master stare, but the
end result was well enough, Corfe thought. There was
no time to teach them any of the niceties. The image
which chiefly disturbed him was that of his men breaking formation and reverting to some tribal warband,
especially if they happened to push an enemy into
flight. He impressed upon them, at campfire gatherings
interpreted by Morin, that they were not to break from
the line or advance without direct orders from their
wing commanders. There was some muttering at this,
and someone shouted out from the darkness at the back
of the crowd that they were warriors not slaves, and
they did not have to be taught how to fight.

"Fight my way," Corfe shouted back. "Just once,
fight my way, and if I don't bring you to victory, then
you may fight any way you please. But ask Marsch
and his Felimbri if my way is not the best."

The muttering died down. The men now knew of
the battles the original Cathedrallers had fought in the

south, the odds they had overcome. Corfe realized he was on trial. If he led these men to defeat, initially at any rate, then he would never be able to lead them with confidence again. They respected ability, not rank, and deeds rather than flowery declarations.

On the night before they moved out, he was summoned to meet the Queen Dowager again. He turned up at her chambers in his old, ragged uniform, aware of the whispers which followed him through the palace. Rumour was running like fire through the city: Torunn was about to be besieged as Aekir had been, the King was about to abandon the city to the enemy and pull the garrison south, a treaty was to be signed, a deal to be struck. Martellus was dead, he was victorious, he was a hostage of the Merduks. No one could tell fact from fiction, and already thousands were fleeing Torunn, lines of carriages and wagons and hand-carts and trudging people heading south. At Aekir there had been hope, even confidence, that as long as John Mogen led them and the walls stood they would prevail. Here, hope was fleeing with the mobs of refugees. It sickened Corfe to his stomach. He was beginning to wonder if anything of the world he knew would survive another winter.

ODELIA was alone when he was shown in, sitting by a brazier with the shadows high and dark on the walls about her.

"Lady."

Something scuttled away from the flame-light too quickly for him to make out, but the Queen Dowager did not stir. "You have been lucky, Colonel."

"Why is that, lady?"

"You have been almost forgotten about. Thus far, you have been overlooked."

Corfe frowned. "I don't know what you mean."

"I mean that my son the King has forgotten you in the . . . excitement of the present time. But someone else—Colonel Menin, or I should say now *General* Menin—has just been made aware of your existence. The sooner you are away from the city the better."

"I see," Corfe said. "Does he mean to make a fight of it?"

Odelia smiled unpleasantly. "I do not know. I am no longer privy to the workings of the government. My instincts tell me that the King is timid and his general is a buffoon. Menin's lackeys have been watching your men drilling. Tomorrow morning you will receive a new set of orders. You will be ordered to turn over your command to another, more . . . amenable officer who only today arrived from the south."

"Aras," Corfe hissed.

"The very same. According to him, you left your work there half done, and he had the lion's share of the fighting to do while you hot-footed it back to the bed of the Queen Dowager." Odelia's smile was like a scar across her face in the firelight.

"I left wounded with him, the dastard."

"I have had Passifal quarter them in an out-of-the-way place, don't worry. But you have to get into the field, Corfe, before they ruin you."

"We leave at dawn. Or sooner, with this."

"Dawn should be safe enough. But no fanfare. A discreet exit is called for, I think."

"When have you found me anything but discreet, lady?"

She laughed suddenly, like a girl. "Don't worry, Corfe. Just make sure when you come back you have laurel on your brow, and I will do the rest. I still have strings to pull, even in the High Command. But that is not why I asked you to come here. I have something for you." She threw aside a cloth to reveal a long, gleaming wooden box. Intrigued, but chafing at the waste of time, Corfe stepped closer.

"Well, open it!"

He did as he was bidden, and there, set in silk padding, was the shimmer of a long, bright-bladed sword.

"It's yours. Call it a lucky charm if you like. I've had it sitting here these six years."

Corfe lifted the sword. It was a heavy cavalry sabre, only slightly curved, double-edged for all that, with a plain basket hilt, the grip wire-bound ivory darkened with another man's sweat. An old sword which had seen use—there were several tiny nicks in the blade. Looking closer, he saw the serpentine gleam of pattern welding.

"It must be ancient," he said, wondering.

"It was John Mogen's."

"My God!"

"He called it *Hanoran*, which in old Normannic means 'The Answerer.' It was an heirloom of his house. He left it here before he went to take up the governorship of Aekir. You may as well have it." Her voice was off-hand, but her eyes bored into him, twin peridot glitters.

"Thank you, lady. It means much to me, to have this."

"He would have wanted you to have it. He would have wanted it to taste blood again in an able man's hands rather than lie here gathering dust in an old woman's chambers."

Corfe looked at her, and he smiled, the joy of the sword's light, deadly balance upon him. The hilt fitted his hand as though it had been made for him. On an impulse, he knelt before her and offered it to her.

"Lady, for what it is worth, know that you have one champion at least in this kingdom." He raised his dancing eyes. "And you are not so old."

She laughed again. "Gallantry, no less! I will make a courtier of you yet, Corfe." She rose, and indeed in that moment she looked young, a woman barely into her third decade, though she must have been almost twice that. She was beautiful, Corfe thought, and he admired her. One slim-fingered hand stroked his cheek.

"That is all, Colonel. I won't keep you from your barbarians a moment longer. You must, *must* leave at sunrise. Fight your battle, come back with Martellus and his men, and I guarantee they will not be able to touch you."

He nodded. The Answerer slid into his scabbard with hardly a click, though it was an inch too long. He took the battered sabre which he had carried from Aekir and tossed it into a corner with a clang. Then he bowed to her and left the room without a backward glance.

But Odelia the Queen Dowager retrieved his discarded sabre and, taking it, she placed it in the silk-lined box which had once housed Mogen's blade, and then set the box aside as gently as if some great treasure were stored therein.

•   •   •

THE grey hour before dawn, chill as a graveside. And in the broken hills which bordered the Western Road to the north of Torunn a small party of weary travellers paused to look down on the sprawl of the Torunnan capital in the distance. Torches burned along the walls like a snake of gems trailed across the sleeping land, and the River Torrin was wide and deep and iron-pale as the sky began to lighten over the Jafrar Mountains in the east.

Two monks, two Fimbrian soldiers and two half-dead mules, all stained with the mud of their wanderings. They stood silent as standing stones in the sunrise until the shorter of the two monks, his face hideously disfigured, went down on his knees and clasped his hands in prayer. "Thank God, oh thank God."

The soldiers were looking about them like foxes for whom the hunt is on, but the hills were empty but for wheeling kites. "You shall have your fire, then," one of them said to the monks. "I doubt the Merduks will venture so close to the walls."

"Why not continue into the city?" Avila protested. "It's barely a league. We can manage that, I'm sure."

"We'll wait until it's fully light," Siward retorted. "If you approach the gates now you're liable to be shot. Torunn is all but under siege, and the gate guards will be jumpy. I've not come this far to finish with a Torunnan ball in me."

There was no more argument, and indeed the two monks were hardly able to advance another step. They had walked all night. Joshelin and Siward unloaded the bundle of faggots which one of the mules bore and began busying themselves with flint and tinder, after throwing the flaccid wineskin to their charges. Albrec

and Avila squirted wine into their throats for want of
a better breakfast, and sat gazing down on the last Ramusian capital east of the Cimbric Mountains.

"The Saint must have been watching over us," Albrec said. His voice trembled. "What a penance this
has been, Avila. I have never known such weariness.
But it refines the soul. The blessed Saint—"

"There are horsemen approaching," Avila cried.

Joshelin and Siward kicked out the nascent campfire,
cursing, and threw themselves upon the ground, haul-
ing the exhausted mules down with them.

"Where away?"

"My God, it's an army!" Avila said. "There—a column of them. They must have come out of the city."

Even the crannied features of the two Fimbrians fell
with despair. "They are Merduks," Siward groaned.
"Torunn has already fallen." Grimly, he began loading
his arquebus while Joshelin worked furiously to light
the slow-match.

"They are in scarlet," Albrec said dully. "Sweet
Saints, to think we came this far, only to end like this."

It was indeed an army, a long, disciplined column
of heavily armoured cavalry over a thousand strong.
They bore a strange banner, black and scarlet, and
some sang as they rode in an unknown tongue which
nevertheless sounded harsh and savage to the two cowering monks. The horsemen's line of march would take
them within yards of the foursome, and beyond the
hollow in which they hid the country was wide open
for miles around. There was nowhere to run.

Albrec prayed fervently, his eyes tight shut, whilst
Avila sat dully resigned and the two Fimbrians looked
as though they meant to sell their lives dearly. The

head of the column was barely a cable's length away, and the two soldiers were gently cocking their weapons when they heard a voice shout out in unmistakable Normannic:

"Tell Ebro to keep his God-damned wing on the road! I won't have straggling, Andruw, you hear me? Blood of the Saint, this is not a blasted picnic!"

Albrec opened his eyes.

The lead horsemen reined in and halted the long column with one upraised hand. The monks had been seen. A knot of troopers cantered forward, the thin birthing sun flashing vermilion off their armour. Their banner billowed in the cold breeze, and Albrec saw that it seemed to represent a cathedral's spires. He stood up, whilst his three companions tried to pull him down again.

"Good morning!" he cried, his heart thumping a fusillade in his breast.

The leading rider walked his horse forward, staring. Then he doffed his barbaric helm. "Good morning." He was dark-haired, with deep-hollowed grey eyes. He reminded Albrec of the two Fimbrians behind him. Hard, formidable, full of natural authority. A young man, but with a middle-aged stare. Beside him was another hewn out of the same wood, but with a certain gaiety about him that even the outlandish armour could not dim. In the early light the pair looked like two warriors of ancient legend come to life.

"Who are you?" Albrec asked, quavering.

"Corfe Cear-Inaf, colonel in the Torunnan army. This is my command." The man's eyes widened slightly as the rest of Albrec's companions finally stood up. "Would you folk happen to be Fimbrians, at all?"

"We two are," Joshelin said proudly. He held his arquebus as though he had not yet decided whether or not to fire it. "From the twenty-sixth tercio of Marshal Barbius's command, detached."

The cavalry colonel blinked, then turned to his comrade. "Get them going again, Andruw. I'll catch up." He dismounted and held out a hand to Joshelin, whilst behind him the long column of horsemen began moving once more. Hundreds of soldiers, all superbly mounted, weirdly armoured, many with tattooed faces. If they were Torunnan troops, they were certainly like no soldiers Albrec had ever seen or heard of before.

"Where is Barbius?" this Colonel Corfe Cear-Inaf demanded of Joshelin even as he gripped his hand.

"Why would you want to know?" the Fimbrian countered.

"I wish to help him."

ELEVEN

"AND these pair are from Charibon, you say?" Colonel Corfe Cear-Inaf asked Joshelin. "They are clerics, then. What are you two, emissaries from the Pontiff?"

"Not quite," Avila told him dryly. "Charibon's reputation for hospitality is vastly exaggerated. We decided to seek our earthly salvation elsewhere."

"They're heretics, like you Torunnans," Joshelin said impatiently. "Come bearing some papers for the other holy man you have stashed away here. Now I've told you, Torunnan, the marshal and the army were a week away from the dyke when we left them, headed south-east towards the coast. But listen—they go not just to link up with your Martellus. The marshal also means to assault the flank of the Merduk army coming up from the Kardian Gulf."

"They have a high sense of their own prowess, if

they think they can assault an army that size and live," Corfe said shortly. His eyes bored into the Fimbrian before him. "And a high sense of duty, also. I salute them for it."

Joshelin shrugged fractionally, as if suicidal courage were part of the normal make-up of any Fimbrian soldier.

"You cannot catch up with them before they make contact with the enemy," he said. "I take it your mission is to preserve the dyke's garrison."

"Yes."

"With thirteen hundreds?"

"I also have a high sense of duty, it seems."

The two soldiers looked at one another, and the glimmer of a smile went between them. Joshelin unbent a little.

"You are cavalry, so mayhap you will move swift enough to be of use," he admitted grudgingly. "What are your men? Not Torunnans."

"They are tribesmen from the Cimbrics."

"And you trust them?"

"Insofar as I trust any man. We have shed blood together."

"You know your own business, I am sure. What of the Torunnan King? Is your command all he is sending out?"

"Yes. The King is very . . . preoccupied at present. He prefers to stand siege in Torunn and await the Merduk assault here."

"Then he is a fool."

Albrec and Avila caught their breath, awaiting some outburst in reply to this comment, but Corfe only said, "I know. But we will bleed for him nonetheless."

"That is as it should be. We are merely soldiers."

The long column of horsemen had passed them by, the rearguard a dark bristle in the distance. Corfe raised his eyes to it, and then straightened, mounting his restive destrier. "I must be on my way. Good luck to you on your errand, priests. If you meet Macrobius, tell him that Corfe sends greetings, and that he does not forget the retreat from Aekir."

"You know Macrobius?" Albrec asked wonderingly.

"I travelled with him, you might say. A long time ago."

"What manner of man is he?"

"A good man. A humble one—or at least he was when I knew him. The Merduks cut out his eyes. But men change, like everything else. I can't answer for him now."

He turned to ride away, but Joshelin halted him. "Colonel!"

"Yes?"

"It may be that Barbius will not be so easy to find, nor Martellus either. Let me ride with you, and I will set you upon the right road at least."

Corfe looked him up and down. "Can you ride?"

"I can stay on a horse, if that's what is needed."

"All right, then. Get up behind me. We'll find you a mount from the spares. Good day, Fathers."

The warhorse leapt off into a canter with Corfe upright in the saddle, Joshelin clinging on behind him, as elegant as a bouncing sack. Siward followed his comrade's departure with thin lips, and it was with real disgust in his voice that he turned back to the two monks who were his charges.

"Well, let's get you down into the city. I may as well see it out to the end."

THE antechambers of the new Pontifical palace were large, bare halls of cold marble and stuccoed ceilings. Little gilt chairs stood in rows, seeming too frail to bear anyone, and the new Macrobian Knights Militant stood guard like graven mages, gleaming with iron and bronze. Someone had unearthed a few score sets of antique half-armour from a forgotten arsenal, and the Knights looked like paladins from another age.

The antechambers were busy, teeming with clerics and minor nobles and messengers. Macrobius, whom Himerius in Charibon labelled a heresiarch, was spiritual leader of three of the great Ramusian kingdoms of the west, and even in time of war the business of the Church—this new version of it, at any rate—must go on. Bishops had to be reconsecrated in the new order, replacements had to be found for those who remained faithful to the Himerian Church, and the palace complex was full of office-seekers and supplicants whose contributions to the Church's coffers had to be rewarded. A new Inceptine order was being organized, and in fact all the trappings and facets of the old Church were here being duplicated at high speed, so that the Macrobians might be considered worthy rivals to the unenlightened of Charibon. Albrec, Avila and Siward stood amid the crowds and stared. The Merduks were baying at the gates, and still men haggled here, seeking novitiates for second sons, exemptions from tithes, tenancy of Church lands.

"Life goes on, it seems," said Avila, not without bitterness. He had been the most worldly of clerics, and an aristocrat to boot, but he surveyed the worldly strivings of the New Church with much the same weary amazement as Albrec.

"We must see the Pontiff," they told a harried Antillian who was trying to organize the throng.

"Yes, yes, no doubt," and he walked on self-importantly, dripping disdain.

The two monks stood like a couple of lost vagabonds, and indeed that is what they were—disfigured, ragged and filthy. Albrec hobbled after the Antillian. "No, you don't understand, Brother—it is of the utmost urgency that we see the Pontiff today, at once!" He tugged at the cleric's well-tailored habit like a child harassing its mother.

The Antillian snatched himself away from the diminutive tramp. "Guards! Eject this person!"

Two Knights Militant strode forward, towering over the pleading Albrec. One seized him roughly by the shoulder. "Come, you. Beggars wait at the door."

But then there was a blur of dark movement, a whistle of air, and the Knight was smashed off his feet by the swing of Siward's arquebus butt. The Fimbrian dropped the weapon, whipped out his short sword, and the second Knight found its glittering point in his nostril.

"These priests will see the Pontiff," Siward said evenly. "Today. Now."

The hubbub in the antechamber died away, and there was a silence, all eyes on the ugly tableau unfolding before them. More Knights came striding up the hall, swords unsheathed, and for a moment it looked as though Siward would be cut down where he stood, but then Avila spoke up in a clear, ringing aristocratic voice:

"We are monks from Charibon, bearing important documents for the eyes of Macrobius himself! Our protector is a renowned Fimbrian officer. Any mistreatment of him will be seen as an act of war by the electorates!"

The Knights had frozen as soon as the word "Fimbrian" came out of Avila's mouth. The Antillian's jaw dropped, and he stammered:

"Put up your swords! There will be no blood shed in this place. Is this true?"

"As true as the nose on his face," Avila drawled, nodding at the sweating Knight who had two feet of steel poised at the aforementioned feature.

"I will have to see my superior," the Antillian muttered. "Put up your swords, I tell you!"

Weapons were sheathed, and the hall began to glimmer with talk, speculation, surmise. Avila clapped the narrow-eyed Siward on the shoulder.

"My friend, that was as good as a play. I'm only sorry you did not have the opportunity to spill his entrails on the marble." Siward said nothing, but picked up his arquebus, kicking aside the other, still-senseless Knight as he did so. No one dared interfere.

An Inceptine appeared, heavy-jowled and glabrous. "I am Monsignor Alembord, head of His Holiness's household. Perhaps you will be so good as to explain yourselves."

"We did not travel here through blizzards and wolves and marauding armies to bandy words with a lackey!" Avila cried. He was obviously enjoying himself. "Admit us to His Holiness's presence at once. We bear tidings that must be heard by the Pontiff alone. Thwart us at your peril!"

"For God's sake, Avila," Albrec murmured, helping the Knight Siward had knocked down to his feet.

Monsignor Alembord seemed torn between alarm and fury. "Wait here," he snapped at last, and jogged off with the unfortunate Antillian in tow.

"You should have been a passion-player, Avila," Albrec told his friend wearily.

"I'm sick of being abused, especially by fat insects like that Inceptine. It's time to stop sneaking around. Things need to be stirred up a little. Ramusio's beard, do they think they tore down the Church only to build a doppelganger in its place? Wait until the Pontiff sees the tale you carry, Albrec. If he's a decent man, as that fellow Corfe seemed to think he is, then by the blood of God we'll make sure he shakes the world with it."

PART TWO

INTO THE STORM

You must never drive your enemy into despair. For that such a strait doth multiply his force, and increase his courage, which was before broken and cast down. Neither is there any better help for men that are out of heart, toiled and spent, than to hope for no favour at all.

Rabelais

TWELVE

IT was the thunder of the distant guns that drew them.
It muttered beyond the horizon like the anger of
some subterranean god. Artillery, by battery, and the
rolling crackle of arquebus fire. Morin dismounted and
laid his ear to the ground, listening to the unseen engagement. When he straightened there was a look of
something like wonder on his face.

"Many, many men, and many big guns," he said.
"And horses, thousands of horses. War echoes through
the earth."

"But who is it?" Andruw asked. "Martellus or Barbius? Or both?"

The other members of the party, Corfe included,
looked at Joshelin. The grizzled Fimbrian sat upon a
restive Torunnan destrier looking tired and irritable. He
was not a natural-born horseman, to put it mildly.

"It will be the marshal," he said. "We have not gone

far enough north to intercept Martellus. We must be forty leagues from the dyke still. I would wager that Martellus's host is two or three days' march away."

The little knot of horsemen were half a mile in advance of the main body, though both Ebro and Marsch were detached for now, leading squadrons out on the flanks and destroying any Merduk skirmishers they came across. Corfe intended the approach of his men to remain a secret. As at Staed, if he could not have numbers on his side, he'd best have surprise.

"How far, Morin?" Corfe asked his interpreter.

"A league, not more."

Thirty minutes, perhaps, if he were not to wind the horses for a charge. He would have to leave at least one squadron with the mules . . . Corfe's mind raced through the calculations, adding up the risks and probabilities. He needed to make a reconnaissance, of course, but that would eat up valuable time. A reconnaissance in force, then? Too cumbersome, and it would throw away surprise. With his numbers, he needed to pitch into the Merduk flank or rear for preference. A head-on charge into a large army's front would simply be throwing his men's lives away.

"I'm going forward," he said abruptly. "Morin, Cerne, come with me. Andruw, take over the command. If we're not back in two hours, consider us dead."

THE roar of battle grew as they advanced. It ebbed and flowed, dying away sometimes and rising up again in a furious barrage of noise that seemed to make the very grass quiver. The three horsemen began to see stragglers running singly or in small groups about the slopes of the hills ahead, Merduks by their armour. Every army shed men as it advanced, like a dog shedding hair. Men grew footsore or exhausted or bloody-minded, and even the most diligent provost guard could not keep them all in the ranks.

Finally they rode up the side of one last bluff, and found themselves looking down like spectators in a theatre upon the awesome spectacle of a great battle.

The lines stretched for perhaps two miles, though their length was obscured by toiling clouds of powder smoke. A Fimbrian army was at bay there, fighting for its life. Corfe could see the fearsome bristle of a pike phalanx, eight men deep, and on its flanks thin formations of arquebusiers. But there were other western troops present also. Torunnan cuirassiers, perhaps three hundred of them, and several thousand sword-and-buckler men and arquebusiers intermingled, struggling against immense odds to extend their flanks. So Martellus was here. The dyke garrison must have marched more quickly than Joshelin had given it credit for. They had joined up with the Fimbrians, and for the first time in history were fighting shoulder to shoulder with their ancient foes. So few of them. Martellus had lost over half his command.

The Merduk host they were pitted against was vast. At least thirty or forty thousand men were hammering against the western lines, and Corfe could see more coming down from the south-east, fresh formations on flank marches which would encircle the western troops. The battle to their front was no more than a holding action. When the Merduks had their flanking units in place they would attack from all sides at once and nothing, not Fimbrian valour nor Torunnan stubbornness, would be able to resist them.

Look for a thin place, a weakness. Somewhere to strike which would lever open the enemy lines and sow the greatest confusion possible. Corfe thought he saw it. A long ridge ran to the left rear of the western battle-line, part of the outlying chain of hills which came trailing down from the south-western heights of the Thurian Mountains. The North More, men called them. Already, Merduk regiments were on the ridge's lower slopes, but the crest was empty. They had moved down from the summit to get within arquebus range, and there was nothing but emptiness behind them. Why should they look to their rear? They did not fear the arrival of Torunnan reinforcements. They were so intent on annihilating Martellus and Barbius that they had left themselves vulnerable. A strong blow would break open the trap there, might even roll up the enemy right flank. That was the place. That was what he must do.

"Back to the command," he told his two companions, and they set off at a full gallop for the column.

A hasty council of war during which Corfe outlined to Andruw, Ebro, Marsch, Joshelin and Morin his plan. Morin had become very quiet, but his eyes were shining. Clearly, he was in favour of attacking. Marsch was as imperturbable as always—Corfe might have been ordering him to go and buy a loaf of bread—and Joshelin obviously approved of anything which might help his countrymen. But Andruw and Ebro both looked troubled. It was Andruw who spoke up.

"You're sure about this, Corfe? I mean, we've faced long odds before, but this . . ."

"I'm sure, Haptman," Corfe told him. Time was wasting, and men were dying. He was chafing to be off. "Gentlemen, to your commands. I will lead the column. No trumpets, no damn shouting or cheering until I have you all in position and you hear Cerne give the order to charge. You have five minutes, then we move on my order."

The Cathedrallers were on the move less than ten minutes later. They shook out into three parallel columns, each over four hundred men strong. Corfe, Cerne and Morin made a little arrow of riders at their head. The monumental, earth-trembling roar of the battle ahead was rising to a climax. Corfe hoped he would not find the western forces completely swept away when they reached the top of the ridge. There would be nothing for it then but a headlong retreat to Torunn, the inevitable brutality of another siege. Defeat, utter and final. He found himself mouthing childish prayers he had not uttered in decades as his horse ascended the north-west slope of the ridge which hid the battlefield from view. He had never felt so alive, so *aware*, in his entire life.

They were still fighting, but they had their right flank hopelessly encircled. A dozen Fimbrian pike tercios there had gone into square and were completely surrounded, a sea of the enemy breaking against the grim pike points and falling back, the Fimbrian formation as perfect as though it were practising drill on a parade ground. In the centre, the Fimbrians and Torunnans were close to being overwhelmed. Their line had given ground, like a bow bending, and was now concave.

Soon, it would break, and the western armies would be split in two. Only on the left, scarcely half a mile from where Corfe's men were forming up on the ridge, was there any hope.

The Merduks on the left still had not manned the crest of the hill, and the Cathedrallers spread out along it in battle-line, four horses deep. Corfe could see some of the enemy below pointing at the newly arrived cavalry on the hilltop, but they would also see the Merduk armour they wore. He had a few minutes on his side.

The Cathedrallers were in position. A line of horsemen six hundred yards long, four ranks deep, completely silent, spectators of the vast carnage in the valley below them. Their scarlet armour gleamed in the thin sunlight, their banner flapped in the raw wind. Some of the enemy were becoming worried now about the motionless cavalry on the hill. A few hundred men had spread out into skirmish-line to counter any move round the Merduk right flank.

Corfe cantered over to Andruw and put out his hand. "Good luck, Haptman. If we don't meet again, it's been an honour serving with you."

At that, Andruw grinned, gripping Corfe's iron gauntlet in his own. "We have seen some sights, Corfe, haven't we?"

Corfe took up the position he had assigned for himself in the middle of the front rank. He turned to his trumpeter. "Cerne, sound me the charge."

Cerne, a heavily tattooed savage who would gladly have died for his colonel, raised his horn to his lips and blew the five-note hunting call of his own hills. Corfe drew out John Mogen's sword, and it flashed like a quiver of summer lightning above his head. Then

he kicked his mount into motion, whilst around him
the line began to move, the ground shook at the thunder of over five thousand hooves, and the battle-paean
of the tribes issued from a thousand throats.

THE Merduks in the valley looked up, and the Torunnans and Fimbrians who were fighting their
desperate battle for survival saw a long line of cavalry
come raging down from the hilltop like a scarlet ava-
lanche. One thousand two hundred heavy horses carrying men in red iron, their lances a limbless forest
against the sky, and that terrible, barbaric battle-hymn
roaring down with them.

They sped into a gallop, their lines separating out,
and the wicked lances came down from the vertical.
The Merduk skirmishers took one look at that looming
juggernaut, and began to run.

The first rank of the Cathedrallers rode them down,
spearing them through their spines and galloping on.
Half a dozen of the horsemen went down, their mounts
tripping on the broken ground, but they closed the gaps
and kept coming. The main Merduk formations below
frantically tried to change their facings to meet this
new, unlooked-for enemy clad in their own armour but
glowing red as fresh blood and singing in some barbaric tongue. A regiment of *Hraibadar* arquebusiers
stood to fire a volley, but the approaching maelstrom
was too much for some of them to bear, and they ran
also. Their formation was scrambled, even as the first
rank of the Cathedrallers smashed into them.

The big horses rode down the Merduks as though
they were a line of rabbits, and the terrible lances of
the riders speared scores in the first clash. Horses went

down, cart-wheeling, screaming, crushing friend and
foe alike, but the charge's momentum was too powerful to stop. They rode on, and behind them came the
second rank, and the third, and the fourth. More horses
falling, brought down by the corpses underfoot, their
riders flung through the air to be trampled by the ranks
behind them. Corfe lost sixty men in the first thirty
seconds, but the Merduks died by the shrieking hundred.

The entire Merduk right wing recoiled, the Cathedrallers ploughing through it in a cataclysm of slaughter.
The Merduks were crushed together so tightly that men
in the centre of the press could not even raise their
arms, and scores were trampled to death in Torunnan
mud. The entire enemy battle-line shuddered backwards as officers tried to pull their men out of the disaster and reorganize them. But the Cathedrallers kept
coming. Most of their lances were lost or broken now,
and the tribesmen had swept out their swords and were
cutting down the enemy like scythemen harvesting
corn. Nothing could withstand the sheer impact of
those hundreds of tons of flesh and muscle and steel,
but they were slowing down. The sheer numbers of the
enemy were bringing the charge to a halt, and while
the horsemen had speared and hacked and crushed a
path into the very heart of the Merduk right wing, they
were now becoming surrounded as reserve regiments
were rushed up around them.

Corfe could feel blood stiffening on his face. His
horse's neck was black with it, and the Answerer was
shining vermilion to the hilt. This was the first time
since Ormann Dyke that he had met Merduks on the
battlefield, and for a few minutes he had forgotten he

was an officer, the commander of an army. He had
ridden into the enemy with the fury of an avenging
angel, screaming wordlessly, his battle-cry the silent
reiteration of his dead wife's name ringing through his
mind like an agonizing accusation. Men had quailed
before the naked murder on his face, and always in the
charge he had been the foremost, desiring only to kill,
forgetting strategy and tactics and the responsibilities
of command. But now the battle-lust was fading, and
he was seeing clearly again.

He pulled his mount out of the front line and looked
around, panting, gauging the situation. He glimpsed the
fresh enemy forces manoeuvring off to his left, and
knew that his men had shot their bolt.

Cerne was still beside him, a bloody apparition of
war, his eyes a maniacal glitter under his helm. "Stay
by me," Corfe told him, and forged through the murderous press of men and horses off to the right.

Black-clad infantry here, pikes outlined against the
sky. His men had broken through to the Fimbrian line.
Something tugged at Corfe's shoulder, and he instantly
raised his sword to strike but found Joshelin at his side.
The veteran Fimbrian had a look in his eyes not unlike
that in Cerne's, and a wild gaiety about him.

"I'll get them to pull back," he shouted over the
road. "I'll talk to them. They'll take it from me. But
you have to get your men up the hill, or they'll be
overwhelmed!"

Corfe nodded. Joshelin gave him a crisp Fimbrian
salute, and then rode off into the heart of his countrymen's lines.

This was the hardest part, the worst manoeuvre to
undertake in war—a fighting withdrawal. Did the Fim-

brians have enough left in them to cover it? And where
was Martellus?

"Colonel!" a voice shouted, and Corfe wheeled
round. Joshelin was there, leading his horse, and with
him a red-sashed moustached Fimbrian.

"I am Marshall Barbius," the man said. "How many
are you?"

"Thirteen hundreds."

"That's all? You've made quite a dent."

Corfe leaned over in the saddle. He had received a
heavy slash from a Merduk tulwar which had not penetrated his armour but which nonetheless was stiffening
his entire torso. He hissed with pain as he shook the
marshal's hand.

"You must get your men out," he told him. "Where
is Martellus? I will save as many of you as I can."

"Martellus is dead," Barbius told him without emo-
tion. "My right is encircled and the centre too closely
engaged to break away. But I have given orders for
the left wing to follow you out. We will cover your
retreat."

"How?"

"Why, by attacking, of course."

The man was serious. Corfe did not know whether
to admire or despise him.

"You must escape with me," he told Barbius, but the
marshal shook his head.

"My place is here. What is your name?"

"Corfe Cear-Inaf."

"Then look after my men, Corfe. Joshelin, you go
with him."

"Sir—"

"Obey orders, soldier. You must go now, Colonel. I will not be able to hold them for long."

Corfe nodded. "God go with you," he said, knowing Barbius would not survive. The marshal turned without another word and strode back to his embattled line. Joshelin passed a hand over his face, eyes closed.

"Sound me the retreat," Corfe ordered his trumpeter.

Cerne gaped at him a moment, and then put the horn to his lips and blew. High and clear over the clamour of war came the hunting call of the Cimbrics, this time announcing the kill. Corfe wondered how many of his men could hear it.

THE battle opened out. The Merduk right wing, badly mauled by Corfe's charge, was reorganizing. Freed from its clutches for the moment was a motley formation of some six or seven thousand men, Torunnans and Fimbrians, who began to withdraw up the hill behind them, whilst what was left of the Cathedrallers formed a line to cover their retreat. Corfe kicked his exhausted horse into a canter and regained the hilltop, watching the battle unfold below.

A thousand surrounded Fimbrians out on the right were tying up ten times their number of the enemy and building a wall of dead around their pike square. Here on the left the western forces were in full retreat, the Torunnans running in a formless mob, the Fimbrians withdrawing in orderly fashion, by tercio. Their arquebusiers continued to fire aimed volleys at any of the enemy who ventured too close. But Corfe was concentrating on the centre, that howling, murderous chaos into which Barbius had disappeared. The Fimbrians there—hardly two thousand of them—dressed their lines, and began to advance.

Andruw joined him on the hilltop, reeking with blood, his horse earless where he had made too low a sword-swing. He did not speak, but sat and watched with Corfe as around the two of them the remnants of the Ormann Dyke garrison and Barbius's left wing streamed past.

"In the name of God," Andruw said in a shocked gasp as he saw the Fimbrians in the centre deliberately assault the main body of the Merduk host, thirty, forty thousand strong.

Their lines of pikes seemed inhuman, unstoppable. They actually pushed the enemy back, and began carving a swathe of slaughter deep in the Merduk centre. The enemy formations there recoiled from the machine-like efficiency of the Fimbrians. But it could not last. Already, the Merduks were flooding round the flanks and rear of the pikemen.

"Let's get out of here," Corfe said, his voice heavy and thick. "We can't waste the time they're buying us."

He kicked his horse into motion again. The animal could barely manage a trot. Around him his command was reforming. He saw Marsch there, and Morin haranguing the excited tribesmen, in some cases physically pulling at them to get them to retreat. They wanted to stay and fight, and Corfe could readily understand why. For a moment he wished that he, too, were down there in the valley with Barbius, making a glorious end. Easier to fight than to think. Better to fight than remember. But he had his job to do, and he had men depending on him. How many now? he wondered. How many left? He felt a weary disgust, but masked it as he always did. A black-garbed Fimbrian, his uniform in tatters under his armour, stood before him and saluted him.

"Yes?"

"Formio, sir, Barbius's adjutant. His orders are—were—to place myself and my men at your disposal. May I ask what your intentions are, sir?"

The Fimbrian was young, younger even than Corfe. He spoke stiffly, as if expecting to be given offence. Corfe found himself smiling at him.

"My intentions? My intentions, Formio, are to get us the hell out of here."

THIRTEEN

THEY had forgotten that he had been blinded. His ravaged face was a shock which rendered them dumb. He wore the simple brown robe of an Antillian, a single ring and a fine Saint's symbol of silver and black wood. A dozen Knights Militant, watchful, hard-faced men, ringed the walls of his chamber. There had been rumours of assassination attempts.

"Holy Father," Alembord said, bowing deep to kiss the ring, "those whom I told you of are here."

The High Pontiff Macrobius nodded and then spoke in a quavering voice, that of an old, tired man. "Strangers, introduce yourselves. And no ceremony, I beg. I hear your errand is most urgent."

Albrec it was who spoke up. Siward was eyeing balefully the surrounding Knights, and Avila seemed taken aback, almost disgruntled.

"Holiness, we are monks fleeing Charibon, under the

protection of a Fimbrian soldier. Our names are un-important, but what we bear may seal the fate of nations."

There was a long pause. Macrobius waited patiently, but Alembord snapped at last: "Well?"

"Forgive me, Monsignor, but what I have to say is for the Pontiff's ears alone."

"Merciful heavens, who exactly do you think you are? Holiness, let me take care of these upstarts. They are clearly eccentric adventurers, perhaps even in the pay of the Himerians. I will get the truth out of them."

Macrobius shook his head with the first touch of asperity they had seen in him.

"Step forward, young man—the one who spoke to me."

Albrec did so. As he came close to the Pontiff he heard the slight metallic grate of swords being gently loosened in sheaths as the Knights tensed. He moved slowly and deliberately until he was two feet from the Pontiff's face.

And here Macrobius reached out and laid his hands on Albrec's features, his old fingers feather-light as he traced his eyes, cheeks, lips—and the gaping hole which had been his nose.

"Your voice . . . I thought there was something amiss. What happened, my son?"

"Frostbite, Holiness, in the Cimbrics. We would have died had the Fimbrians not found us. As it was, we did not come away untouched."

"A disfigurement can be a heavy trial," Macrobius said with his blind smile. "But cruelty to the flesh can also refine the spirit. I see more now than I ever did when I had two eyes and sat in a palace in Aekir. Tell me your errand."

Taking a breath, Albrec told him in a low tone of the ancient document he had found in the bowels of Charibon, a biography of the Blessed St Ramusio written by one of his contemporaries, Honorius of Neyr. In it Honorius stated that Ramusio had not been assumed into heaven in the twilight of his life as the Church had taught for over four centuries, but had set off alone to proselytize among the heathen Merduks of the east and had become revered among them as Ahrimuz, the Prophet. The two great religions of the world, which had battled each other for centuries and piled up a million dead in their names, were the handiwork of one man. The Saint and the Prophet were one.

The expression of an eyeless man is hard to read. As Macrobius leaned back again Albrec could not be sure if he were shocked, angry, or merely bewildered.

"How do I know you are not an agent of Himerius, come here to sow the seeds of heresy and discord in the foundations of our New Church?" Macrobius asked gently.

Albrec sagged. "Holiness, I know it sounds like the merest madness, but I have the document here, and it is genuine. I know. I was a librarian in Charibon. This is the work of Honorius himself, written in the first century and hidden away by the Founding Fathers of the Church to suit their own ends. This is the truth, Holiness."

"These tidings, if they are indeed the truth, could tear up the world. I am an old blind man, Pontiff or no. Why should I act on your convictions? The world is in enough turmoil as it is."

"Holy Father," Albrec said hesitantly, "we met a man on the Western Road, a soldier who was going out to fight the Merduks, though he knew he was hopelessly outnumbered. He did not know if he would be coming back, but he went out anyway because it was his duty. And he knew you. He told us you were a good man, a humble one, and he bade me tell you to remember the retreat from Aekir."

"What was his name?" Macrobius asked, suddenly eager.

"Corfe, a colonel of cavalry."

Macrobius was silent for a long time, his face bent into his breast. A hush fell in the chamber, and Albrec wondered if he had fallen asleep. How could one tell, when he had no eyes or eyelids to shut? Finally, however, the Pontiff stirred. He rubbed his temples with his fingertips, raised his head, and said, "Monsignor Alembord!" in a voice that was startlingly clear and strong. Alembord actually flinched.

"Yes, Holiness?"

"Find suitable quarters for these travellers. They have journeyed a long way, bearing a heavy burden. And assemble the best scribes, scholars and copyists in the capital. I want them all gathered here tomorrow by noon, and quarters cleared in the palace for them also."

Alembord's mouth opened and closed like that of a landed fish for a few seconds, then he said, "It shall be done at once," and shot a look of pure hatred at Albrec. The little noseless monk felt a wave of relief flood over him, leaving him drained and exhausted.

"Corfe saved my life when it was not worth saving," Macrobius said quietly. "It was God's will that it be so, and it is God's will that you have come here to present me with this last task. What is your name?"

"Albrec, your Holiness."

"You shall be a bishop in the New Church, Albrec, and you are to have unhindered access to me any time you need it. Introduce your companions to me."

Albrec did so. "I knew your father," said Macrobius to Avila. "He was a rake and a spendthrift, but he had a heart as big as a mountain. He would never pay his tithes without a grumble, but no peasant on his lands ever wanted for anything. I honour his memory."

Avila kissed the Pontiff's ring, speechless.

"And I meet a Fimbrian at last," Macrobius went on. "You have my thanks, Siward of Gaderia, for preserving my brothers-in-faith. You have done the world as great a service as any ever performed on a battlefield. So it is true that a Fimbrian army marches to the aid of poor, embattled Torunna."

"It is true," Siward told him. "But only through the efforts of your friend Corfe will any of my people survive. Small thanks do we receive for shedding our blood on your battlefields."

"You have my thanks, for what it is worth."

Siward bowed, and managed to muster up some courtesy in return. "For myself, it is enough."

Macrobius nodded. "The audience is over. Monsignor Alembord will show you to your quarters. We will sup together tonight. Albrec, you shall sit by me and tell me what transpires in Charibon. It is time I concerned myself with the turning world again. For now, I must retire. I feel the need to pray as I never have before."

A young Inceptine came forward to help the Pontiff out of his chair and through a door in the rear of the chamber. The three travellers were left with Monsignor Alembord and the surrounding Knights.

"Your platitudes may have convinced *him*," Alembord told Albrec in a venomous whisper, "but I am not so simple. You had best watch your step, *Brother* Albrec."

THERE had been rumours flying about the capital for the past two days, travelling faster than any courier. A great battle had been fought up north, it was said, and Martellus was destroyed. The Merduk light cavalry which of late had been patrolling almost to the very walls had withdrawn, and the land to the north was uneasily quiet, scouting parties reporting it utterly deserted by man and beast. What this tense hush presaged no one could say, but the wall sentries had been doubled on the orders of the King himself.

The gates of Torunn were closed, and Andruw and his men had to cajole and threaten for fully a quarter of an hour in the pouring rain before the guards would admit them to the city. Their horses clopped noisily through the gloom of the barbican with the gore of the North More battle still upon them, ten riders looking like warriors out of some primitive bloodstained myth.

The haptman of the gatehouse accosted them on the street below the walls, demanding to know their names and their errand. Andruw fixed him with a weary eye. "I bear dispatches for the High Command. Where do they meet these days?"

"The west wing of the palace," the haptman said. "Whose command are you with? I've never seen your like. That's Merduk armour your men wear."

"Very observant of you. I'm with Colonel Corfe

Cear-Inaf's command. He's a day's march behind me
with seven thousand men, two thousand of them Fimbrians."

The haptman's face lit up. "Is Martellus with him?
Has he got through?"

"Martellus is dead, so is the Fimbrian marshal. The
greater part of their armies lie slain up on the North
More. Now are you satisfied?"

The officious haptman nodded, horrified. He stepped
aside to let the sombre cavalcade pass.

Andruw was kept waiting half an hour in an antechamber despite the urgency of his errand. His normally sunny outlook was soured by grief and
exhaustion. The North More had been a victory of
sorts, he knew—Corfe had saved part of an army from
destruction and was bringing it to the capital. But the
rest, including men Andruw had served with along the
Searil River, friends and comrades, had been wiped
out. And he could not get out of his mind the vision
of the Fimbrian pike phalanx advancing to its doom.
It was the most admirable and terrible thing he had
ever seen.

At last the door opened and he was admitted to the
council room. A score of tall beeswax candles burned
in sconces, and there was a trio of lit braziers glowing
along one wall. A long table dominated the chamber.
It was piled with maps and papers, quills and inkwells.
At one end sat King Lofantyr in a fur cloak, his chin
resting on one ring-glittering hand. A dozen other men
were present also, some sitting, others standing, all in
the resplendent finery of the Torunnan court. They
looked up as Andruw entered, and he saw the distaste
on more than one face as they took in his squalid con-

dition. He bowed, the mud-stained dispatch Corfe had dashed off with a saddle for a desk clenched in one fist.

"Your Majesty, sirs, Haptman Andruw Cear-Adurhal, bearing dispatches from Colonel Corfe Cear-Inaf."

Andruw distinctly heard someone say "Who?" as he laid the dispatch before his monarch and retreated, bowing again. A series of chuckles rustled through the gathering.

"Is it true Martellus is dead?" Lofantyr said suddenly, quelling the buzz of talk that had arisen. He made no move to read the crumpled scroll.

"Yes, sire. We came too late. He and the Fimbrians were already heavily engaged."

"Fimbrians!" a voice barked. Andruw recognized the broad form of Colonel Mcnin, now a general, and the commander of Torunn's garrison.

"On whose orders did Colonel Cear-Inaf take his command north?" Lofantyr demanded querulously. Andruw blinked, shifting his feet.

"Why, on yours, sire. I saw the Royal seal myself."

Lofantyr's face twisted. He whispered something which might have been "*Damned* woman." And then: "Are you aware, Haptman, that your commanding officer was sent orders to turn over his command to Colonel Aras the morning your men left for the north?"

"No, sire. We received no such orders, but we did move out before dawn. Your courier must have missed us." God almighty, Andruw thought.

"And you arrived too late to save Martellus and his men, you say," Menin accused Andruw.

"We saved some five thousands, sir. They will be here in one, perhaps two days."

"Why were you late, Haptman? Was not this mission deserving of some urgency?"

Andruw flushed, remembering the breakneck forced marches, the bone-numbing weariness of men and horses, tribesmen tumbling asleep from their saddles.

"No one could have gone any faster, General. We did our best. And"—his voice rose, and he looked Menin in the eye—"We were only thirteen hundreds, at the end of the day. Had Corfe been given more men, he might have saved the whole damned army, and Martellus might yet be alive to serve his country!"

"By God's blood, you insolent puppy!" General Menin raged. "Do you know who you are talking to, sir? Do you know?"

"Enough," the King said sharply. "Bickering amongst ourselves will lead us nowhere. I am sure that the full facts of this disaster will become known in time. Haptman, what in God's name are you wearing? And how do you come to present yourself before this council in such a state of filth? Have you no inkling of respect for your superiors?"

Andruw's blood was up, but he bit on his tongue to silence himself. He saw the drift of things. They needed a scapegoat, someone to off-load the burden of their own incompetence and cowardice upon. Corfe had not saved part of an army, he had lost the rest. They would twist the facts to suit themselves. Lord God, he thought. They would wrangle at the very gates of hell.

"My apologies, sire. I thought my news warranted great haste. I am come straight from the field."

"Ay, but whose field, I wonder?" a voice said mockingly.

Andruw turned to see the dapper form of Colonel Aras. He bowed, very slightly. "Sir. I am happy to see you well after your . . . endeavours, in the south of the kingdom."

"I'm sure you are, Haptman. I brought thirty of your wounded savages north with me when I had finished thrashing the rebels there. Your commander really should take better care of his men. I'm sure I shall."

Andruw stared at him, and something in his eye made Aras cough and bury his nose in a wine goblet.

After that he was ignored, left to stand there in his bloody armour as the council debated the news he had brought. No one dismissed him, and he seemed to have been forgotten. His hauberk pressed down on his shoulders. The heat of the chamber seemed stifling after the chill air out of doors, and his head began to swim. Someone nudged him and he gave a start just as his knees had begun to buckle.

"Here, drink this, Haptman," a voice said, and a glass of dark liquid was pressed into his hand. He gulped it down, feeling the good wine warm his innards. His benefactor was a young officer in the blue of the artillery. He looked vaguely familiar. Perhaps they had been at gunnery school together. His mind was too fogged to remember.

"Come into a corner. They won't miss you."

He followed the officer to the far corner of the spacious chamber, and there set down his helm, unbuckled his sword baldric and with the other soldier's help levered off his breast and back plates. Feeling more nearly human, he accepted another glass. By this time there was a group of four or five other officers clustered about him, and the droning voices at the council table went on and on over their shoulders.

"What was it like?" the artilleryman asked him. "The battle, I mean. The city's been running with talk for days. They say you slew twenty thousand Merduks up there."

"This Corfe—what manner of man is he?" another asked.

"They say he is John Mogen come again," a third said in a low voice.

Andruw rubbed his eyes. He had never really sat back and considered Corfe before, the kind of man he was, the things he had done. But he saw something in the eyes of these young officers, something which startled him. It was a kind of awe, a reflected glory. At a time when all hope for the future was being ground down into the winter mud, and the once-great Torunnan military was decimated, cowering behind walls, this one man had raised an army out of thin air and with it had fought to a standstill the invincible Merduk horde.

"He's a man like any other," Andruw said at last. "The greatest friend I have."

"By God, I'd give my right arm to serve under him," one of the young men said earnestly. "He's the only officer we have who's *doing* anything."

"They say he's the Queen Dowager's bedmate," another said.

"*They* don't know what they're talking about," Andruw growled. "He's the best officer in the army, but those stuffed fools over there cannot see it. They pule and prate about precedent and decorum. They'll be huddled over a brazier arguing when the Merduks are setting light to the palace itself."

Some of the young officers looked over their shoulders nervously. The stuffed fools were barely ten yards away on the other side of the chamber.

"We'll stand siege here soon," the artilleryman said. "Then there will be glory enough for all."

"But no one to make songs about it once the walls are breached and your wives and sisters are carried off to Merduk harems," Andruw said savagely. "The enemy needs to be beaten in the field, and Corfe is the only man in the kingdom who might be able to do it."

"I fancy half the army are beginning to think so too," the artilleryman said in a whisper. "It's common knowledge that he beat the rebels down south singlehanded, and Aras did nothing but a little mopping up. It doesn't do to say so, although—"

He broke off as Andruw was called back to the council table by his King.

"Be so good as to inform us of the strengths of the Merduk army your command encountered," the King said with a wave of his hand.

"At least forty thousand, sire, but our impressions were that it was but the van of the whole. More formations were coming up as we pulled out. I should not be surprised if the final number were double that."

A stir of talk, disbelief, or rather an unwillingness to believe.

"And how badly mauled was the enemy by the battle?"

"We did not see the end of the Fimbrians, sire—we left them still fighting, though surrounded. I would wager the Merduk general has lost perhaps a quarter of his strength. Fimbrian pikemen die hard."

"You sound almost as though you admire these mercenaries."

"I never saw men die better, sire, not even at the dyke."

"Ah! So you were at the dyke. We had forgotten." Several officers in the room seemed to warm to Andruw somewhat. He received a few approving nods.

"Corfe was at the dyke also, sire. He led the defence of the eastern barbican."

"The first place to fall," Aras murmured.

Andruw stepped forward until he had Aras penned against the long table. "I should be very sorry, sir, to hear anyone impugn the good name of my commanding officer. I feel I would have to ask for satisfaction in such a case." His eyes blazed, and Aras looked away. "Of course, Haptman, of course . . ."

The King seemed to have missed the exchange. "Gentlemen," he said, "with the addition of these men salvaged from Martellus's command, we will have almost forty thousand available to defend the capital, though it means denuding our southern fiefs of troops. Thanks to the work of Colonel Aras, however, the rebellious provinces of the south are once again recalled to their ancient allegiance, and I think we need not fear for our rear in the struggle to come."

Aras graciously accepted the mutter of approbation from the assembled officers.

"All bridges over the River Torrin, right up to the mountains, have been destroyed. The geography of our beloved country favours the defender. Our rivers are our walls."

Like the Ostian and the Searil rivers, Andruw thought, both of which had failed to hold back the Mer-

duk advance. Now that Northern Torunna had been
evacuated, the Merduks might even send an army
through the Torrin Gap and take Charibon if they
chose, or cross the Torian Plains and assault Almark,
even Perigraine. Those places were under the sway of
the Himerian Church, however, and Andruw did not
think that the men present would shed many tears if
Charibon were sacked, or Almark—now rumoured to
be Church-ruled—invaded. With the present religious
schism dividing the Ramusian kingdoms, there could
be no question of them presenting a united front to the
invaders. Corfe was right: if the enemy were not
crushed before Torunn, he would be able to send columns across half of Normannia. And if the Torunnan
army allowed itself to be bottled up in the capital, besieged as Aekir had been besieged, then it would take
itself out of the reckoning entirely. Almark and Perigraine were not great military powers. They could not
withstand the Merduk and the troops of the Prophet
would conquer the continent as far west as the Mal-
vennor Mountains.

A palace courtier entered, interrupting Lofantyr's
rosy predictions of Merduk disaster. He bent and whispered in the King's ear, and his sovereign shot up out
of his seat, an outraged look on his face. "Tell her—"
he began, but the doors of the chamber were thrown
open, and the Queen Dowager entered with two of her
ladies-in-waiting. Every man present bowed deeply,
save for her son, who was furious.

"Lady, it is not appropriate that you be present here
at this time," he grated.

"Nonsense, Lofantyr," his mother said with a winning smile, waving a folded fan. "I've sat in on meetings of the High Command all my life. Is that not true, General Menin?"

Menin bowed again and murmured something incomprehensible.

"In any case, Lofantyr, you left something behind when you visited me in my apartments the other day. I wished to make sure you received it." She held out a scroll heavy with the scarlet wax of the Royal seal.

Lofantyr took it as gingerly as if he expected it to bite him. His eyes were narrow with suspicion. As he opened and read the document his face flushed red.

"From whence did this come?"

"Come now, my sovereign, it bears your own seal— one which I no longer possess. Pray read it out to this august company. I'm sure they are with child to hear the good news it contains."

"Another time, perhaps."

"*Read it!*" Her voice cracked like a gunshot, the authority in it making every man there wince. Lofantyr seemed to shrink.

"It . . . it is a general's commission, for one Corfe Cear-Inaf, confirming him second-in-command of Martellus's army or, if Martellus no longer lives, he is appointed sole commander."

Andruw thumped his gauntleted fist into his palm with delight, and behind him several of the junior officers cried "Bravo!" as if they were watching a play. The Queen Dowager glided over to Colonel Aras, who looked as though he had just swallowed a bolus of foul-tasting medicine. "I hope you are not too disappointed, Colonel. I know how much you looked forward to commanding those red-clad barbarians."

"No . . . no, not at all. Delighted, happy to . . ." He trailed off in confusion. Odelia's concentrated regard was hard to bear.

"This is a mistake," King Lofantyr managed, regaining his poise. "I sealed no such orders."

"And yct they exist. Countermanding them is tantamount to breaking one's word, my son. You are a busy man—you have merely misremembered that you issued them. I am sure the recollection will come to you. In time. Gentlemen, I will leave you to your high strategies. I, a poor, incompetent woman, am obviously out of my arena here. Haptman Cear-Adurhal, pray stop by my chambers before you return to your command."

Andruw bowed wordlessly, his face shining. The other men there followed suit as the poor, incompetent woman made a regal exit.

FOURTEEN

THEY met him with a salvo of guns, Torunn's walls
erupting in smoke and flame as the army came into
view over the horizon. The exhausted men lifted their
heads at the sound, and saw a thousand-strong guard
of honour in rank on rank waiting to welcome them
into the city. Corfe reined in, bemused, to regard the
spectacle as his enlarged command continued to trudge
past him. Torunnan sword-and-buckler men, arquebusiers and Fimbrian pikemen. His own Cathed-rallers
out on the wings and bringing up the rear.

Marsch and Ebro joined him.

"Why do they fire guns at us?" Marsch wanted to
know. "Is it a warning?"

"It's a salute," Ebro informed him. "They're hon-
ouring us."

"About time someone did," another voice said as a
fourth horseman joined them. This was Colonel Ran-

afast, the only officer of any rank to have survived from the dyke garrison. He was an emaciated-looking hawkish man who had commanded the dyke's cavalry, only a score of which were now left to him. He had known Corfe as an obscure ensign, Martellus's aide, but he showed no resentment at his former subordinate's elevation.

The streets of the capital were lined with people. Corfe could hear their cheers from here, a mile away. They had turned out the populace to welcome his men. For their sake, he was glad of it—their morale needed the boost—but for himself, he would sooner have curled up in a cloak and stolen some sleep out here in the mud. He knew that the pantomimes would begin again the moment he was in the capital, and his soul was sick at the thought.

"Riders approaching," Marsch said. "It is Andruw, I think. Yes, that is him. I know that smile of his."

Andruw halted before them, breathing hard, and threw Corfe a salute.

"Greetings, General. I have orders to show you and your officers to a special set of quarters in the palace. There's to be a banquet tonight in your honour."

"What the hell are you talking about, Andruw?" Corfe demanded. "And what is this *general* horseshit?"

"It's not a jest, Corfe. The Queen Dowager swung it for you. You're now commander of this lot." Andruw gestured at the long muddy column of men that was marching past. "She's a wonder, that woman. Remind me never to cross her. Bearded Lofantyr in his own council chamber, bold as you please. What a king she'd have made, had she been born a man!"

General. He had not really believed she would do it.

General of a half-wrecked army. He could take little joy in it. A certain grim satisfaction perhaps, but that was all.

The Fimbrians were marching past now, and one detached himself to salute the group of riders.

"Colonel Corfe?" Formio, the Fimbrian adjutant, asked.

"General now, by the Saint!" Andruw chortled.

"Shut up, Andruw. Yes?"

"Are we to enter the city with your men? I shall understand if political ramifications dictate otherwise."

"What? No, by God, you'll march in along with the rest of us. I'll find quarters for every last one of you, in the palace itself if needs be. And if they refuse us, I'll damn well sack the place."

The men around Corfe fell silent. His anger subdued them. He had been like this ever since the battle.

"My thanks, General. And my congratulations on your promotion."

"What do you intend to do, Formio? You and your men."

"That is for you to decide."

"I don't follow you."

"The marshal's last order was to put ourselves at your disposal. Until I hear differently from the electorates, we are under your personal orders, not those of the Torunnan Crown. Good day, General." And the Fimbrian resumed his place in the long disciplined column of pikemen.

"A good man," Marsch said approvingly. "These Fimbrians know their trade. It will be a fine thing to fight beside them again. They are strangely ignorant of horses, however."

"Corfe," Andruw said, "they're waiting for you down there. The Queen Dowager set this up: the salute, the triumphal entry, everything. If the population get behind you, then the King himself cannot touch you. It's all part of the game."

Corfe smiled at last. "A great game. Is that what it is? All right, Andruw, lead on. I'll wave and grin and look general-like, but at the end of it I want a bath, a flagon of good wine and a bed."

"Preferably with something in it," Ranafast said, with feeling.

At that, the group crackled with laughter, and they followed the marching line of their army down to the cheering crowds that awaited them.

THE celebratory nature of it stuck in Corfe's throat, though. The banquet that evening was attended by a mere six hundred guests—officers of the Torunnan army and their ladies, the nobility, rich men of no rank but with bottomless purses. It swept over him in a haze of candlelight and laughter. The wine was running freely, and the courses came and went in a blur of liveried attendants and silver trays. His own stomach was closed, and he was desperately tired, so he drank glass after glass of wine—the finest Gaderian—and sat in his court dress with the new silver general's braid at his shoulders.

It was a hollow feast. The King was not present, having pleaded some indisposition—hardly surprisingly—but Corfe sat at the right hand of the Queen Dowager as she managed small-talk with their neighbours and contrived to make Corfe feel part of conversations he contributed no word to. Everyone seemed

intent on becoming roaring drunk and the din of the
massed diners was unbelievable, though Corfe's own
ears were still ringing from the thunder of the North
More battle. His ribs, too, ached from the sword blow
they had taken during the fighting.

Andruw was in tearing spirits, flirting outrageously
with two pretty duke's daughters who sat opposite, and
tossing back the good wine like a man unaware of what
he was doing. Marsch was there also, utterly ill-at-ease
and answering everyone in monosyllables. He seemed
staring sober, though the sweat was streaming down
his face and he had tugged his lace collar awry. Two
seats down from him was Ensign Ebro, who was already drunk and leering and regaling his neighbours
with gory tales of slaughtering Merduks. And the Fimbrian, Formio, sat like a mourner at a wake, drinking
water, being carefully polite. The diners around him—
a bluff Torunnan staff officer and a minor noble and
their wives—were obviously plying him with questions. He did not seem particularly responsive. His eyes
met Corfe's, and he nodded unsmilingly.

Martellus and the greater part of the Ormann Dyke
garrison, the finest army left to the country, lay dead
and unburied to the north. The wolves would be feast-
ing on their bodies, a mid-winter windfall. Laid beside
them, close as brothers, were three thousand of Formio's countrymen and his commander. And the city
celebrated as though a victory had been won, a crisis
averted. Corfe had never felt such a fraud in his life.
But he was not an idealistic fool. Once he might have
torn off this general's braid and raged at the crowd.
Before Aekir, perhaps. But now he knew better. He
had rank and he would use it. And he had a command

with which something might yet be accomplished.

He thought he fathomed the frenzied gaiety of the assembled diners. It was a last fling, a defiance of the gathering dark. He had seen its like before. In Aekir, as the Merduks began to surround the city, many noblemen had staged banquets such as this, and seen out the night in torrents of wine, processions of dancing girls. And in the morning they had taken up their stations on the walls. What had Corfe done, the day the siege began? Oh, yes. That night was the last time he had slept in the same bed as his wife. The last time he had made love to her. After that there was no more time left. She had brought him his meals as he paced the battlements, snatched previous minutes with him. Until the end.

"You're drunk, Corfe!" Andruw cried gaily. "Lady"—this to the Queen Dowager—"you'd best keep one eye on the general. I know his fondness for wine."

He was indeed drunk. Silent, brooding drunk. There was no joy left for him in wine; it merely brought the pain of the past floating in front of his eyes, all new and raw and glistening again. He felt the Queen Dowager's knee press against his under the table. "Are you all right, General?" she whispered.

"Never better, lady," he told her. "A fine gathering, indeed. I must thank you for it—for everything."

He turned his head and met her eyes, those perilous green depths, like sunlight on a shallow sea. So beautiful, and she had done so much for him. Why? What payment would be required of him in the end?

"You must excuse me, lady. I am unwell," he said thickly.

She did not seem surprised, and clapped her hands
for the serving attendants. "The general is taken poorly.
See him to his quarters."

HE rid himself of their ministrations as soon as he
was out of the hall, and staggered on alone
through the dimly lit palace, the sound of the banquet
a golden roar behind him. His shoulder brushed the
wall as he wove along. It was cold out here after the
stuffiness of the close-packed crowd, and his head
cleared a little. Why the hell had he drunk such a lot
of the damned stuff? There was so much to do tomorrow, no time to nurse a blasted hangover.

His mind was too blurred to hear the soft footfalls
behind him.

The parade ground before the palace. He stepped out
into the star-bright night and stood looking up at the
wheeling glitter of the sky. There were rows of massively designed buildings on both sides of the square,
but most of their windows were dark. His men were
quartered within, tribesmen and Torunnans and Fimbrians. No revelry there. They were too tired. They had
seen too much. He would give them a few days to rest
and refit, and then he would have to begin hammering
these disparate elements into an organic whole, a close-
knit organization.

Footsteps behind him, louder. He turned. "Andruw?"

And saw a dark shape lunging, the quicksilver flash
of the knife. He twisted aside, and instead of slashing
his throat it sliced open his right shoulder. The pain lit
up his mind, burning away the wine fumes. He threw
himself backwards as the blade came hissing towards
his face, tripped and fell heavily on to his back. His

attacker came at him again, and Corfe managed to
plant a boot in his midriff and kick him away. He
rolled, his cracked ribs screaming at him, his right arm
weakening as the blood streamed out black in the star-
light. But before he regained his feet another shape
appeared. It piled silently into his attacker. There was
a flurry of movement, too fast to follow in the darkness, and a grisly crack of bone. A body fell to the
cobbles of the parade ground and the newcomer bent
over him.

"General, are you much hurt?"

He was helped to his feet, his arm dangling stiff and
useless. "Formio! By the Saint, that was timely. Let
me have a look at the bastard."

They dragged the body inside and examined it. It
wore a black woollen mask with slits for eyes and nose.
Ripping it off they saw the swarthy face below, eyes
wide with surprise. An easterner, perhaps Merduk. His
neck was broken.

"I'll see the guard is turned out," the Fimbrian said.
"There may be more of them. This man was a professional."

"How did you come to be here?" Corfe asked. He
felt light-headed with loss of blood and the singing
adrenalin of the struggle.

"I followed you. I am not a great lover of formal
dinners either, and I wanted to talk . . ." He trailed off,
seeming almost embarrassed.

"Lucky for me. He'd have cut my throat, else. An
assassin, by God. The Sultan has a long arm."

"If it was the Sultan. Not all your enemies are beyond the walls. Come, we need to get that shoulder
dressed."

• • •

THE inevitable uproar as the guard turned out and the palace was scoured room by room for other assassins. The Queen Dowager was informed and at once had Corfe conveyed to her personal apartments, but those at the banquet feasted on into the night, unaware of the goings-on.

"I should be at your side permanently," Odelia told Corfe as the wound in his shoulder closed under her hands and the faint ozone smell of the Dweomer filled the room. "That way you would get into less trouble. Where have you stowed the body?"

"Formio had it thrown into the river."

"A pity. I should like to have examined it. A Merduk, you say?"

"An easterner of some sort or other. Lady, I wish we had a dozen folk with your skills in the army. Our wounded would bless their names." Corfe moved his right arm experimentally and found it slightly stiff, but otherwise hale. A tiny scar remained, that was all, though the assassin's knife had laid bare the bone.

"You would have trouble finding them," she said. "The Dweomer-folk grow fewer every year. It is a decade since we even had a true mage at court here in Torunna. Golophin of Hebrion is the only one I know of who remains in the public eye. The rest have gone into hiding."

"But not you."

"I am a queen. Allowances are made for my . . . eccentricities." She kissed him on the lips and when she drew back he saw to his surprise that the amazing eyes were alight with tears which would not fall.

"Was it the Sultan's doing, you think?" he asked gruffly, looking away.

"Who is to know? The assassins are killers for hire, for all that they come from the east. Their employers can be Merduk or Ramusian. They must only be rich."

"As rich as a king, perhaps?"

"Perhaps. The world is a dangerous place for those whose star is on the rise. There are men in this country who would see it in ashes ere they would let a commoner save it."

"John Mogen was of low birth."

"Yes. Yes, he was. And he never let anyone forget it!" She smiled.

"You knew him well?"

"I knew him. You might say I sponsored him in much the same way as I am sponsoring you."

"So that is your role in the world. The raising up of generals."

"The redemption of this kingdom," she corrected him shortly, "by any means available."

"I am glad to have it explained to me," he said, with a terseness to match hers.

She rose to go. "I am a woman as well as a queen, though, Corfe. I sought military brilliance, and I found it. I do not seek to love or be loved, if that is what is worrying you."

"I am relieved to hear it," he said. And he cursed himself as she left the room with the hurt plain to see on her face.

FIFTEEN

"BY the beard of the Prophet, who *were* they? Clad in our own armour, galloping out of nowhere and then disappearing again. Can anyone tell me, or are you all struck dumb?"

Aurungzeb the Golden, Conqueror of Aekir, Sultan of Ostrabar, raged at the huddle of advisors and officers who remained kneeling on the beautifully worked carpet before him. The walls of the great tent shuddered in the wind, and the dividing curtains billowed like rearing snakes.

"Well?"

A man in gorgeously lacquered iron half-armour spoke up. "We have spies out by the score at the moment, my Sultan. At this time, all we have are rumours picked up from captured infidels. They say this cavalry is something new, not even Torunnan. A band of mercenary savages from the Cimbric Mountains to the west led by a disgraced Torunnan officer. They are few though, very few, and we damaged them badly as they withdrew. They are not something we should be unduly concerned about, a . . . a unique phenomenon, a freak. It merely shows the desperation of the foe, when he must resort to hiring barbarians as well as the accursed Fimbrians."

"Well then." Aurungzeb appeared somewhat mollified. "It may be that you are correct, Shahr Johor. But I do not want any more surprises such as the last. Had it not been for those scarlet-clad fiends, we'd have destroyed the entire dyke garrison, and the Fimbrians as well."

"Our patrols have been redoubled, dread sovereign. All Torunnan forces are now within the walls of their capital. There is little doubt that they will stand siege there and then we will be free to send forces through the Torrin Gap to Charibon, that nest of disbelief. Thus we will have destroyed both centres of the heinous Ramusian faith. The Ramusian Aekir is but a memory— soon it shall be so with Charibon and its black-robed priests."

Aurungzeb nodded, his eyes bright and thoughtful in his heavily bearded face. "Well said, Shahr Johor. Though they have a Pontiff in Torunn now also, the one we missed in Aekir, he is no friend to Charibon. Such is the squalid state of the Ramusians' faith that they fight amongst themselves even as the sons of the Prophet knock on their walls."

"It is God's will," Shahr Johor said, bowing his head.

"And the Prophet's, may he live for ever."

An especially violent gust of wind made the entire

massive fabric of the tent twitch and tremble. Aurungzeb's face darkened again. "This storm . . . Batak!"

A young man in a coral-coloured robe stepped out
of the shadows. "My Sultan?"

"Can't you do anything about this cursed storm? We
are losing time, and horses."

Batak spread his hands eloquently. "It is beyond my
powers at present, lord. Weatherworking is an arcane
discipline. Even my master—"

"Yes, yes. Orkh would have had this snow melted
in a trice and the wind made gentle as an old man's
fart. But Orkh is off chasing rainbows. See what you
can do."

Batak bowed low and withdrew.

"That is all," Aurungzeb said. "I must commune
with my God. You may all leave. Akran!" This to the
tall, skeletal vizier who stood like a starved golem in
one corner. "See I am not disturbed for one hour."

"Yes, lord. At once." The vizier banged his staff on
the floor of the tent. Back in the palace it would have
rung impressively against marble, but here it produced
only a dull thump. Such were the indignities of following his Sultan into the field. The officers and ministers
took the hint, rose, bowed and backed out of the tent
into the baying blizzard outside, the vizier following
with a resigned look on his face.

Aurungzeb stirred and glanced around. He looked
now like a hirsute but mischievous boy.

"Ahara," he called softly. "Light of my heart, they
are gone. Come out now, my little sweetmeat. Your
master calls."

A slim shape filmy with gauze emerged from the
curtained rear of the tent, and knelt before him with

head lowered. He raised her by the chin and peeled away the veil which hid her features. A pale face, grey eyes, dark lips touched with rouge. He wiped it off them. "You do not need paint, my sweet. Not you. Perfection brooks no improvement."

He clapped his large, hairy-knuckled hands. "Music, there! The slow dance from Kurasan!"

From an adjoining, closed-off portion of the tent came the sudden chimes and pluckings of musicians, somewhat ragged at first and then growing in speed and harmony.

"Dance for me. Dance for your weary master and make him forget the cares of the turning world."

Aurungzeb threw himself down on a pile of silken cushions and commenced to suck on a tall water-pipe whilst his concubine paused for a second, and then began to move as slowly as a willow in a summer breeze.

Heria's mind blanked out when she danced. She liked it. The exercise kept her supple and fit. It was the aftermath she did not care for, even now. Especially now. She had listened in on the report of Shahr Johor as she listened to everything that went on in the tent of the Sultan. Her command of the Merduk language was perfect, though she still pretended to have only a rudimentary grasp of it. She had hidden her grief at the news of the dyke's fall, and her heart had soared at the account of the recent battle and the last-minute intervention of the mysterious and terrible red horsemen. Debased and soiled though she might be, she was still Torunnan. The man whose life she had shared until the fall of Aekir had been a Torunnan soldier, and it was no more possible that she should forget it than that the sun should one day forget to set.

The pace of the dance quickened. Aurungzeb, intent on the whirling movement of her white limbs, puffed out smoke in swift little clouds. At last it ended, and Heria froze in position, arms above her head, breathing fast. The Sultan threw aside the stem of his water-pipe and rose.

"Here. To me."

She stood close to him. His beard tickled her nose. She was tall, and he had not far to bend to nuzzle the hollow of her collar bone. His hands twitched aside her gauzy coverings. "You are a queen among women," he murmured. "Magnificent." He stripped her naked whilst she stood unmoving. His fingers brushed her nipples, erect and painfully sensitive.

"My Sultan," she began hurriedly as his hands wandered down her body. She had been depilated, after the fashion of the harem, and her skin was smooth as alabaster. His fingers became more urgent. She forced herself not to flinch as they explored her.

"My Sultan, I am with child."

He went very still, straightened. His eyes glowed.

"Are you sure?"

"Yes, lord. A woman knows these things. The Chamberlain of the Harem confirms it."

"Name of the Prophet, a child. A son. And you danced before me!" He was outraged, furious. He raised a hand to strike and then thought better of it. Instead he brought it down to rest on her taut belly. "My child—my son. I have never had a son that lived. Miserable girls, yes, but this—this shall be a boy."

"It may not be, my lord."

"It must be! He was conceived in war, at a time of

victory. All the omens are favourable. I shall have Batak examine you. He shall see. An heir, at long last!
You must dance no more. You must keep to your bed.
Ah, my flower of the west! I knew your coming would
be luck to me! I shall make you first wife, if it is a
boy—it will be a boy." He started to laugh, and
crushed her in a bearish embrace, releasing her an instant later. "No, no—no more of that. Like porcelain
you shall be treated, like the rarest glass. Put on your
clothes! I must have the eunuchs find something more
fitting for the mother of my son, not these damn slave-
girl silks. And maids—you shall have servants and a
pavilion of your own—" He stopped. He felt her over
as if she were some rare and delicate vase that might
be shattered in a moment. "How long? How far grown
is he?"

"Not far, lord. Two months, perhaps."

"Two months! My son's heart has been beating these
two months! I shall burn a wagonload of incense.
Prayers shall be said in every temple of the east. Ha,
ha, ha! A son!"

A son, Heria thought. Yes, it would be a boy—she
knew that, somehow. What would her Corfe have
thought of that? She bearing a son to some eastern
tyrant, a child of rape. Corfe had always wanted children.

The tears burned her eyes. "You weep, my dove, my
precious beauty?" Aurungzeb asked with concern.

"I weep with joy, my lord, that I have the honour
of bearing the Sultan's child."

Why was she still alive? Why had she not found
some way to end herself? But she knew the answer.
Human nature can bear many things, unimaginable

things. The body eats, sleeps, excretes and lives, even while the mind prays for oblivion. And in time the mind adapts itself, and the insupportable becomes the everyday. Heria wanted to live, and she wanted her child to be born. It was his son, but it would be hers also, something of her own. She would love it as though it were Corfe's, and her life might yet become worth something after all. She hoped that her husband's ghost would understand.

SIXTEEN

URBINO, Duke of Imerdon, was a tall, lean, cadaverous man with the look of an ascetic about him. He dressed habitually in black, and had done so since the death of his wife twenty-three years earlier. He was the most powerful nobleman in Hebrion, besides the King himself, but he was entirely unrelated— by blood at least—to the Royal House of Hibrusids. Imerdon had once been an outlying fief of the Fimbrian Electorate of Amarlaine, but the Fimbrians had relinquished their claims upon it decades ago, after the last battle of the Habrir River (which they had won). Few knew precisely why the Fimbrians had given up the duchy, the cities of Pontifidad and Himerio, all the land right up to the Merimer River, but it was rumoured that one of their then-endless civil wars had necessitated the removal of the garrison and its deployment elsewhere. The commander of the retreating garrison had not been able to resist giving the Hebrians a bloody nose one last time, hence the senseless battle of the Habrir.

The native nobility of the duchy had sworn fealty to the Hebrian monarch, whose kingdom was well-nigh doubled by Imerdon's acquisition, and successive rulers of the province had intermarried with the Royal House. But though the Duke of Imerdon and his family were well respected, and indeed immensely powerful, they tended to be seen as outsiders, foreigners. Imerdon's folk were of the same stock as those of Hebrion proper, but the long Fimbrian domination—almost five centuries—had rendered them slightly different from their western cousins. Many of them dressed in black for preference, like the men of the electorates, and they were generally a more disciplined and religious people who looked upon the excesses of gaudy old Abrusio with fascinated distaste. Their duke had remained aloof from the horrific war which had wrecked the kingdom's capital city, though he had given free passage to the Himerian Knights Militant as they fled the country after their defeat. It was said that though he followed his king into heresy, considering it his duty, he did so reluctantly, and his sympathies lay yet with the Himerian Church.

The duke now sat in a covered carriage in upper Abrusio, not far from the Royal palace. If he pulled back the leather curtains of the vehicle he could count the cannonballs still embedded in the walls.

"My lord," one of his retainers said outside the curtain. "The lady is here."

"Help her in then," the duke said.

The lady Jemilla climbed in beside him. He thumped

the roof of the carriage with one bony beringed fist,
and they trundled off.

"I hope I see you well, lady," he said courteously.

"I am blooming, thank you, sir," she replied. A few
minutes of silence, as if each waited for the other to
speak, until at last the duke said: "I take it your mission
was successful."

"Completely. I delivered the petition yesterday. The
Astaran woman and the mage are no doubt pondering
its implications even as we speak."

Urbino nodded, his face expressionless. Jemilla was
dressed in sober grey, the garb of a respectable noble
matron, and no hint of paint or rouge had touched her
face. She knew that different tactics were called for in
dealing with the austere Duke of Imerdon. One hint of
impropriety or wantonness, and he would drop her like
a dead rat.

The duke appeared ill-at-ease, uncomfortable. He
was obviously not fond of clandestine assignations and
midnight conspiracies, and yet he was the key and cor-
nerstone of all Jemilla's schemes, and his signature at
the head of the petition she had delivered to Isolla one
of her greatest coups. If this man, this cold-livered,
utterly respectable aristocrat, acknowledged the valid-
ity of her claims, then the rest would follow suit. Duke
Urbino was famous for his fastidiousness, his dislike
of intrigue. Only his sense of duty and honour had
prompted him to meet Jemilla, and a rising unease with
regard to the condition of the monarchy in Hebrion.
And she had convinced him. Abeleyn was incapable
of ruling, was barely alive. And the government of the
country had been usurped by three commoners, one of
whom was a wizard. And she bore the King's heir. If

the kingdom were not to become some outrageous oligarchy headed by men of low blood, then it was up to him, the most powerful nobleman remaining in Hebrion, to do something. His fellow lords agreed, and their letters had been arriving on his table for the past sennight. Jemilla had been very busy since her escape from semi-imprisonment in the palace. She had met the head of almost every noble house in Hebrion.

They were cowed, of course, terrified at the thought of sharing the fate of Sastro di Carrera and Astolvo di Sequero. Abeleyn's kingship had been restored in a welter of fire and blood, the Carreras and the Sequeros rendered impotent by the slaughter of their retainers and the execution of their leaders. If anything further was to be done, it had to be done constitutionally. Where the sword had failed, the pen might yet succeed.

"This council of nobles we have envisioned, it makes me uneasy, I have to say," Urbino said. "There is a certain lack of precedent. . . . The traditional platform of the nobles is the House Conclave, held yearly in this city, with the King as chairman and arbiter. I do not like something which smacks so of . . . *innovation.*"

"The King, my lord, is in no condition to chair anything," Jemilla told him, "and the House Conclave is legally unable to debate any motion not tabled by the King himself." A blue-blooded talking-shop was what that outmoded institution represented, Jemilla thought. She wanted something different, something with teeth.

"I see. And since the King cannot or will not appear, we are justified in setting up an entirely new institution to deal with this unique situation. . . . Still—"

"The other noble families have already indicated

their support, lord," Jemilla broke in swiftly. "But they await your word, as the foremost among them. They will not move without you." Play on his pride, she thought. It's his one vice—vanity. The cold-blooded old lizard.

Urbino did in fact seem visibly gratified by her words. "I cannot pretend you are mistaken," he said with a trace of smugness. "Do you think it wise, however, to convene this, this council in Abrusio itself?"

"Why not? It shows we have no fear of the King's forces, it brings the issues we are debating out into the open, and if the King should, by the grace of God, recover, then we will be at hand to bear witness and rejoice."

Urbino looked thoughtful. "If what you tell me of his injuries is accurate, then I fear there will be no recovery, not even with that Dweomer-crow Golophin lurking around." He sighed. "He was an able young man. Impulsive maybe, hot-headed at times, and sadly lacking in piety, but a worthy ruler for all that."

"Indeed," said Jemilla with the right mixture of regret and sorrow. "But the good of the kingdom cannot be neglected, despite our grief and our devotion to its nominal head. The house of the Hibrusids, lord, is virtually extinct. Abeleyn's reluctance to marry was a clever instrument of policy, but it has redounded against him in the end."

"The Astaran princess—" Urbino began.

"—is becoming a visiting dignitary, no more. She should, naturally, be accorded the respect due to her rank, but to suggest that her one-time betrothal to our dying sovereign renders her the right to govern this kingdom is absurd. Hebrion would become nothing more than a satellite of Astarac. Besides, she is a woman of low wit and mean understanding—I have met her, as you know—and she is hardly able to govern her own servants, let alone a powerful nation."

"Of course, of course . . ." Urbino trailed off.

What a dithering, vacillating old fool he is, Jemilla thought, for all his blue blood. Great God, would that I had been a man!

"And the Hibrusid house is not truly extinct," she went on smoothly. "I bear in my womb, my lord, the last scion of Abeleyn's line. What the kingdom needs is a strong caretaker who will watch over this unhappy realm until my son enters his majority. I cannot think of a more honourable task, or a more prestigious role. And may I say, confidentially, that the heads of the noble families with whom I have already been in contact seem to be in unanimity. There is only one obvious candidate for the position."

Urbino's chin had sunk on to his breast, but there was a light in his eye. She knew he was weighing up the risks to his own person on the one hand, and the dazzling prospect of the regency on the other. And the risks could be minimized if they proceeded as she planned. A proper show of loyalty to the Crown. Public and decorous proceedings open to all. Once the true nature of the King's condition became widely known, the commoners would clamour for someone to fill Abeleyn's shoes. A kingdom without a king—unthinkable!

"It may be that I have a certain standing," Urbino conceded, "but it is also possible that I am not the closest in . . . blood, to the monarch."

"That is true," Jemilla admitted in her turn. The fact was that if it came to blood, he was not close at all.

"But according to my enquiries there are only two other candidates for the position with better claims of blood, and who have not been tainted by the late rebellion. One is the eldest Sequero boy, son of the executed Astolvo, and the other is Lord Murad of Galiapeno, the King's cousin."

"Well, what of their claims?" Urbino demanded somewhat petulantly, no doubt envisioning the loss of the regency.

Jemilla let him squirm for a second before replying. "Both men are dead, or as good as. They were members of an ill-fated naval expedition into the west. Nothing has been heard of them in over six months, and we can safely assume that they are out of the running." A momentary pang as she thought of Richard Hawkwood, also lost in the west. A man she thought she might once have loved, though a commoner. His child in her womb, not Abeleyn's, but she was the only person living who knew.

"This is not a race, lady," Urbino snapped, but he looked relieved.

"Of course, my lord. Forgive me. I am only a woman, and these matters confuse my mind. The fairer sex can in no way fully understand the dictates and glories of honour, that goes without saying." And thank God for it, she thought.

The duke bowed his head as if in gracious forbearance. She could have killed him, then and there, for his pompous stupidity. But it was also why she had chosen him.

"So," the duke went on more affably. "When will this council convene, and where?"

"This very week, on St Milo's day—he is the patron

of rulers—and it shall be in the halls of the old Inceptine monastery. They have been empty since the end of the rebellion, and it will be a long time, I fear, before Hebrion has another prelate or another religious order to steer her in spiritual affairs. It is fitting that the council convene there, and the adjoining abbey will be convenient for those who wish to seek counsel in prayer. Though to be frank, my lord, I need some help refurbishing the place. It suffered grievously during the final assaults."

"I shall have my steward send you a score of domestics," Urbino said. His thin face darkened. "They say that is where he was struck down, you know, just outside the abbey walls."

"Do they? They say so many things. Now, my lord, I must test your forbearance with a further request. In order that this council be conducted with proper pomp and ceremony, and its participants welcomed with the dignity becoming their stations, I am afraid that certain sums are required. The other lords have agreed to contribute to a central fund which I have begun to administer through a trusted friend, Antonio Feramond. I hesitate to ask, but—"

"Think no more on it. My money man will call on you tomorrow and make out a writ for any sum you deem necessary. We cannot stint when it comes to upholding the dignity of our offices."

"Indeed not. I am greatly indebted to you, my lord, as all Hebrion one day will be. It is inspiring to see that there are still men of resolution and decision in this realm. I honour you for it." Blind fool. Perhaps a third of the collected monies would go towards prettifying the prelatial palace and laying in a larder of

dainties and a cellar of wine for these high-bred buf-
foons. The remainder would be distributed in bribes
across the city. A significant sum would ensure the
cheering presence of a crowd of citizens to welcome
the assembled nobles to Abrusio and the rest would
persuade several officers in the city garrison to look
the other way. It was how life operated in this venal
world. Antonio Feramond was Jemilla's steward, and
she held enough secrets over his head to warrant his
unswerving devotion to her. He was also an extortion-
ist and money-lender of some repute in what was left
of the Lower City, and had a gang of verminous thugs
at his beck and call. If anyone knew which palms to
grease it was he.

"And now, my lord, I am afraid I must leave you,"
Jemilla told Urbino with a proper show of deference.
"I have errands to run on my own behalf. You would
not believe the price of silk in the bazaars these days,
what with the war in the east."

"You are still living in the palace, I trust?"

"In the guest wing, my lord."

"Pray send my greetings and best wishes to the lady
Isolla and the mage Golophin. One must remain civilized in these matters, mustn't one?"

Civilized, she repeated to herself as her barouche
sped her away. The spectacle of the recent blood-
letting has gelded the lot of them. And they call themselves men!

Weakness she despised in all things and all people,
but especially in those hypocrites who professed to be
strong. Men of power whose spines were made of
willow-wand. She idly went over in her mind the men
she had found to be different. Those whom she might

have respected. Abeleyn, yes, once he had grown a
little. And Richard, her lost mariner. They were both
gone, but there was a third. Golophin. He, she thought,
could well be the most formidable of the three. A worthy adversary.

Naturally enough, she did not take her fellow fe-
male, the lady Isolla, into account.

ACROSS the breadth of the Old World, the wide
kingdoms of the Ramusians. Beleaguered Torunn
bristled with troops like the fortress it had become, and
the city was deep in snow. The blizzards had whirled
farther down into the lowlands than they had in decades, and rime lay even on the shores of the Kardian
Sea.

Afternoon in Hebrion was dark evening here. Albrec, Avila and the High Pontiff (or one of them), Macrobius, sat around one end of a massive rectangular
hardwood table which was littered with papers. Fine
candles burned by the dozen to illuminate their reading
matter. Down at the far end of the table were gathered
half a dozen other clerics, most in Antillian brown, but
two, Monsignor Alembord and Osmer of Rone, in the
black of Inceptines. The room was silent as they prayed
together. Finally Macrobius raised his head.

"Mercadius of Orfor, I ask you again: are you sure?"

An old gnomish Antillian monk started. Before him
on the table was the battered, stained and bloodied document which Albrec and Avila had brought from Charibon. His hands trembled over it as though he were
warming them at its pages.

"Holy Father, I say once more I am as sure as it is
possible to be. It is Honorius's original hand, of that

there is no doubt. We have nothing scribed by him here, but in Charibon once I saw an original of his *Revelations*. The hand is one and the same."

Albrec spoke up. "I too saw that copy. Mercadius is correct."

The glabrous face of Monsignor Alembord went even paler. "Holy Saint! But that does not confirm anything, surely. Honorius was mad. This document is the product of a mind unhinged."

"Have you read it?" Mercadius asked him.

"You know I have not!"

"Then I say to you, Monsignor Alembord, that this text was not written by a madman. It is measured, succinct and luminously clear. And intensely moving."

"You cannot expect me to believe that our own Blessed Saint and that abomination, the so-called Prophet Ahrimuz, are one and the same!"

"I wonder," Avila said lazily. "Has it ever occurred to you, Alembord? Ramusio, Ahrimuz. The names. There is a certain similarity, don't you think?"

Alembord was sweating. "Holy Father," he appealed to Macrobius, "I remained faithful to you when the usurper set himself up in Charibon. I never doubted, and still do not, that you are the one true head of the Church. But this gibberish—this vile identification of our faith's very founder with the evil one of the east—I cannot stomach. It is rank heresy, an affront to the Church and your holy office."

Macrobius was impassive. "It is said—by St Bonneval, I believe—that the truth, when it is uttered, has a resonance not unlike that of a soundless bell. Those who can hear it recognize it at once, while for others there is only silence. I believe the document is genuine, and that, terrible though it may be, it tells the truth. God help us."

A stillness in the room as his words sank in. It was broken at last by Albrec—Albrec a bishop, clad in the rich robes of one of the Church's hierarchy.

"This revelation is more important than the outcome of any war. The Merduks are our brothers-in-faith, and the hostility between them and the Ramusian race is founded on a lie."

"What must we do, then? Go out proselytizing among the enemy?" Avila asked lightly.

"Yes. That is precisely what we must do."

Shock was written over all their faces, save for that of the blind Pontiff. "Would you be a martyr, Albrec?" Avila asked.

The little monk retorted somewhat testily, "That is beside the point. This message is the nub of the matter. The Torunnan King must be informed at once, as must the Merduk Sultan."

"Sweet Saint's blood!" Osmer of Rone exclaimed. "You are serious."

"Of course I'm serious! Do you think it is mere chance that this revelation has come here, now, at this time? We may have an opportunity to halt the course of this awful war. It is the hand of God at work. There is no element of chance involved."

"The Merduks fight for the joy of conquest, not religion only," Osmer observed. "A common faith is not enough to settle all wars, as we Ramusians know only too well."

"Nevertheless, the attempt must be made."

"They'll crucify you on a gibbet as they did the Inceptines of Aekir," Alembord said. "Holy Father, if we assume that this is true, that our faith is founded on a lie, then at least let us keep it to ourselves for now. The Ramusian kingdoms are divided as it is. This message would cripple them utterly, and it will split down the middle the New Church itself. The only beneficiaries of such a course would be the Himerians."

"The Himerian Church, as it has been called, has a right to know also," Albrec told him. "An embassy must be sent to Charibon. This news will eventually be proclaimed from the rooftops, Brothers. The Blessed Saint himself would wish it so."

"The Blessed Saint, who died a Merduk prophet in some barbaric yurt city of the east," Osmer muttered. "Brothers, my very soul quakes, my faith flickers like a candle in the wind. What will the lowly and the uneducated of the Ramusian world make of such tidings? Maybe they will turn away from the Church altogether, seeing it as a hoarder and propagator of lies. And who could blame them?"

"This is the New Church," Albrec said implacably. "We have turned our face from the scheming and politicking of the old. Our job now is to tell the truth, no matter what the consequences."

"Noble words," Alembord sneered. "But the world is a messy place, Bishop Albrec. Ideals must yield to reality."

Albrec brought his fingerless fist thumping down on the table, startling them all. "Horseshit! It is attitudes such as that which have corrupted our faith and landed us in this quandary to begin with! It is no longer our purpose in this world to obfuscate and deal in semantics. We have had five centuries of it, and it has brought us to the brink of disaster."

"So we'll don the grey garb of the Friars Mendicant and preach the new message throughout the world, becoming an order of evangelists and missionaries, no less!" Alembord shouted back.

"Enough!" Macrobius broke in. "You forget yourselves. I will have decorum in my presence, is that clear?"

Hasty assent. They glimpsed for a moment the powerful authoritarian figure Macrobius had been before Aekir fell.

"I will talk to the king," the Pontiff went on. "Eventually. I will impress upon him the pre-eminent importance of our findings. Do not forget that we are here at the sufferance of the Torunnan sovereign and, high ideals or no, we must think carefully ere we cross his wishes. And I cannot believe he will look upon these revelations favourably. Albrec, Mercadius, you will continue your researches. I want every shred of evidence you can muster to support this work of Honorius. Brothers, this thing goes out into the world soon, and once out it can never be recalled. Be aware always of the gravity of your knowledge. This is not a subject for gossip or idle speculation. The fate of the continent is in our hands—and I mean no exaggeration. The wrong thing said in a moment of carelessness could have the most severe consequences. I enjoin you all to silence whilst I meditate on my meeting with the King."

They bowed where they sat, and several made the Sign of the Saint at their breasts. This Pontiff was not the humble, vague man they had known hitherto. He sat upright and commanding in his seat, his head moving left and right. Had he possessed eyes, they would have been glaring at his fellow clerics.

"A Papal bull is the proper way to announce this thing, but I no longer have regiments of Knights Militant to ensure its swift dissemination among the kingdoms. We must rely on King Lofantyr for that, and I will not have him given information which is already extant in the tittle-tattle of the palace servitors. There must be discretion—for now. Albrec, your impulses do you credit, but Monsignor Alembord has a very valid point. If we are not to sow chaos among the faithful and fatally undermine the New Church, then we must be careful. So very careful . . ." Macrobius sagged. His brief assertion of authority seemed to have drained him. "I would that this cup had been passed to another, as I am sure you all do, but God in his wisdom has chosen us. We cannot change our fates. Brothers, join me in prayer now, and let us forget our differences. We must ask the Blessed Saint for his guidance."

The room went quiet as they joined hands in meditation. But there was no prayer in Albrec's mind. The Pontiff was wrong. This was not something to be announced by decree, to be carefully released to the faithful. It had to explode like some apocalyptic shell upon the world. And the Merduks—they had to be given their chance to accept or deny it also, and as soon as possible. If martyrdom lay along that road, then so be it, but it was the only road Albrec could see himself taking.

And at last he did pray, the tears running down his face.

SEVENTEEN

THE talking-shop is open for business, Corfe thought wearily.

The long table was almost obliterated by the scattered papers upon it, and spread out over them was a large-scale map of Northern Torunna, all the land from the capital up to Aekir itself. Little wooden counters coloured either red or blue were dotted about the map. Nearly all the blue were crowded into the black square that represented Torunn, whilst the reds were ranged over the region between the River Torrin and the Searil. Ormann Dyke had a red counter upon it. It pained Corfe to even look at it.

Men were sitting down both sides of the table, the King at its head. To Lofantyr's right was General Menin, commander of the Torunn garrison and the senior officer present. To his left was Colonel Aras, pleased and self-important at being seated so close to the King. Further down the table was white-haired Passifal, the Quartermaster-General, and a quartet of others whom Corfe had been introduced to at the start of the meeting. The man in sober civilian clothing was Count Fournier of Marn, head of Torunn's city council. He looked like a clerk, a lover of quills and parchment and footnotes. He was rumoured to be the Torunnan spy-master, with a secret treasury to finance the comings and goings of his faceless subordinates. Opposite him were two more robust specimens: Colonel Rusio, commander of the artillery, and Colonel Willem, head of cavalry. Their military titles were largely traditional. In fact they were Menin's second- and third-in-commands. Both were iron-grey, middle-aged men with sixty years in the army between them, and court rumour had it that both were as outraged as the King at the upstart from Aekir's sudden promotion over their heads.

Seated to their left was a big, grey-bearded man dressed in oil-cured leather whose face was deeply tanned despite the season, his eyes mere blue glitters under lids which seemed perpetually half closed against a phantom gale. This was Berza, admiral of His Majesty's fleet. He was not a native Torunnan, having been born in Gabrion, that cradle of seafarers, but he had been twenty years in the Torunnan service and only a slightly odd accent betrayed his origins.

Corfe sat at the bottom of the table, flanked by Andruw—a colonel now, promoted on Corfe's own authority—the Fimbrian commander Formio, and Ranafast, once leader of Ormann Dyke's mounted arm. Marsch, whom Corfe had also promoted, should have been present, but he had begged off. There were too

many things to do, and he had never been much of a
one for talking. Besides, he had added, he served
Corfe, not the King of Torunna. In his place sat Morin,
obviously fascinated by this glimpse into the military
politicking of Torunna. The tribesman had insisted on
wearing his chainmail hauberk to the meeting, though
he had been prevailed upon to leave his weapons behind. Clearly, he still distrusted all Torunnans, save for
his general.

Two hours they had been here, listening to report
after report, speculation piled upon speculation. They
had heard lists of troops, equipment, horses, details of
billeting, minor infractions of discipline, loss of weapons. And they had been saying nothing of any real use,
Corfe thought. What was more, hardly a word had been
said about the attempt on his life the previous night.
The King had uttered some vague banalities about "that
unfortunate incident," and there had been mutters
around the table condemning the Merduks for resorting
to such treacheries, but no discussion about palace se-
curity, or even speculation as to how the assassin had
penetrated the palace. Clearly, it was not a subject the
King wanted aired.

But now, finally, they were getting to more relevant
matters. The deployment of the Merduk forces. Corfe's
flagging interest waxed again.

"Intelligence suggests," Fournier was droning on, his
voice as dry as his appearance suggested, "that the two
main Merduk armies are in the process of combining.
They are somewhere in this area"—he used a wooden
pointer to indicate a position on the map some ten
leagues north-east of the capital—"and their total
strength is estimated at one hundred and fifty to two

hundred thousand men. This, gentlemen, is after leaving one substantial detachment at the dyke, and another down on the coast to guard their supply base. Nalbenic transports are ferrying stores across the Kardian, building up a sizeable supply dump there—exactly where, we are not yet sure. They are provisioning for a siege, obviously. I would guess that within a week, perhaps two, we will have their van encamped within sight of the walls."

"Let them encamp all they like," General Menin growled. "They can't encircle the city, not so long as we control the river. And Berza here can see off any river-borne assault."

"What of our fleet, Admiral?" Lofantyr asked the sea-dog. "What is its condition?"

Berza had a voice as deep as a wine cask, coarsened to a bass burr by years of shouting orders over the wind. "At present, sire, the great ships are at anchor along the city wharves, taking on powder and shot. I have a squadron of lightly armed caravels down at the mouth of the Torrin, to warn us lest the Nalbeni try to fight their way upriver. Work on the two booms is almost complete. When they are ready, it will be virtually impossible for any vessel to force the passage of the Torrin."

"Excellent, Admiral."

"But sire," Berza went on, "I must put it to you again that the booms, whilst admirable for defence, curtail our own offensive movements. The Merduks cannot sail upriver, but equally the fleet cannot sail down to the sea. My ships will be little more than floating batteries once the city is besieged."

"And as such they will make a valuable contribution

to Torunn's defences," the King said crisply. "Their broadsides will command the approaches to the walls, doubling our fire-power."

Berza subsided, but he seemed discontented.

Corfe could remain silent no longer. "Sire, with respect, would it not be better to keep our fleet free to manoeuvre? Count Fournier says the enemy is building a large supply dump on the coast. What if the fleet were to sally out and destroy it? The Merduks would have no choice but to retreat in order to preserve their lines of communication. We might throw them clear back to the Searil, and Torunn would be spared a siege."

The King looked intensely annoyed. "I quite understand your fear of sieges, General," he said. "Your *record* in such engagements is known to all. However, the strategy of the army and the fleet has already been decided upon. Your comments are noted."

If it's decided already, then why are we here? What are we talking about? Corfe wondered furiously. The gibe about sieges had cut deep. He was the only man of the Aekir garrison to have survived, and he had done so by running away, fleeing along the Western Road in company with the rest of the civilian refugees whilst Mogen's lieutenant, Sibastion Lejer, had led a last, hopeless stand west of the burning city. A senseless gesture. He might have brought eight or nine thousand men intact out of the wreck of Aekir, but he had chosen to die gloriously instead. Corfe did not admire a commander with a death wish. Not when it condemned the men under his command along with himself. *Honour!* This was war, not some vast tournament where points were awarded for quixotic gestures.

Admiral Berza met his eyes and made a small, hope-less gesture with one brown-skinned hand. So at least Corfe knew he was not alone in his thinking.

"With the addition of the forces which General Cear-Inaf recently brought into the capital," Fournier was saying, "we have some thirty-five thousand men available for Torunn's defence, not counting the sailors of the fleet. That is ample for our purposes. The Merduk armies will be broken before our walls. There will be no need to worry about supply bases then. Our main concerns will be the harrying of the defeated enemy, and the possibility of regaining Ormann Dyke. Aekir, I venture to say, sire, may well be lost for ever, but there is a good chance we can win back the land up to the Searil."

"We quite agree," the King said. "Now what concerns us today, gentlemen, is the organization of a field army which might be sent out after the Merduks are repulsed from the walls. General Menin."

The corpulent general preened his magnificent moustache as he spoke. Perspiration gleamed on his bald scalp. "There are a few points which must be cleared up first, sire. The troops General Cear-Inaf commands must be integrated into the army, and that officer must be given a command more fitting his abilities." Menin did not look down the table. "Adjutant Formio, I assume your men are at our disposal."

The Fimbrian, dapper and composed in his sable uniform, frowned slightly. "That depends on what exactly you mean."

"What I mean? What I mean, sir, is that your command is now under the aegis of the Torunnan crown. That is what I mean!"

"I must disagree. My marshal's final orders were to place the command at the disposal of the officer who . . . came to our assistance. I take my orders from General Cear-Inaf, until I hear differently from my superiors in the electorates."

Admiral Berza barked with laughter whilst Menin's face grew purple. "Do you bandy words with me, sir? General Cear-Inaf is subject to the orders of the High Command, and the troops under him will be deployed as the High Command sees fit."

The Fimbrian was unperturbed. "We will not serve under anyone else," he said flatly.

The entire table, Corfe included, was taken aback by the statement. In the silence, Morin spoke up. "We tribesmen, also, will fight under no other." He smiled, happy to have added his mote of discord.

"God's blood, what is this?" Menin raged. "A Goddamned mutiny?"

Old Ranafast, the hawk-faced survivor of the dyke's garrison, had a predatory grin on his face. "I fear it could well be so, General. You see, I think I may say the same for the remnants of my own comrades. As far as I can make out, this High Command was going to abandon us as a lost cause whilst it sat safe behind these walls. Had it not been for Corfe—acting entirely on his own initiative—I would not be here, nor would five thousand of Martellus's troops. The men are aware of this. They will not forget it."

No one spoke. Menin appeared decidedly uneasy, and King Lofantyr was rubbing his chin with one hand, his gaze fixed on the papers before him.

"This . . . devotion is quite touching," he said at last. "And laudable, to a degree. But it is hardly conducive

to good discipline. Soldiers cannot pick and choose
their officers, especially in time of war. They must
obey orders. Do you not agree, General Cear-Inaf?"

"Yes, of course, sire." Corfe knew what was coming,
and he dreaded it. Lofantyr was not going to back away
or smooth things over. The fool was going to assert
the authority of the crown, and damn the consequences.
His ego was too fragile to allow him to do otherwise.

"Then do as I say, General. Relinquish your command and submit yourself to the orders of your superiors."

There it was, naked as a blade. No room for compromise or face-saving. Corfe hesitated. He felt there
was a fork in the road before him, and what he said
next would set him irrevocably on one path or the
other. There would be no turning back. Every man in
the room was looking at him. They knew also.

"Sire," he said thickly, "I am your loyal subject—I
always have been. I am yours to command." Lofantyr
began to beam. "But I have a responsibility to my men
also. They have followed me faithfully, faced fearful
odds, and seen their comrades fall around them whilst
they did my bidding. Sire, I cannot betray their trust."

"Obey my orders," Lofantyr whispered. His face had
gone pale as bone.

"No."

Audible gasps around the table. Old Passifal, who
had helped Corfe equip his men when no one else
would, covered his face with his hands. Andruw, Formio and Morin were as rigid as statues, but Andruw's
foot was tap-tap-tapping under the table as though it
did not belong to him.

"*No*? You dare to say that word to your *King*?"

Lofantyr seemed torn between outrage and something akin to puzzlement. "General, do you understand me aright? Do you comprehend what I am saying?"

"I do, sire. And I cannot comply."

"General Menin, explain to Cear-Inaf the meaning of the words 'duty' and 'fealty,' if you will." The King's voice was shaking. Menin looked as though he would rather have been left out of it. The colour was leaking from his cheeks.

"General, you have been given a direct order by your King," he said, his gruff voice almost soft. "Come now. Remember your duty."

His duty.

Duty had robbed him of his wife, his home, anything he had ever valued—even his honour. In return, he had been given the ability to inspire men, and lead them to victory. More than that: he had earned their trust. And he would not give that up. He would die first, because there was nothing else left for him in life.

"They are my men," he said. "And by God, no one but me will command them." And as he spoke, he realized that he had uttered a kind of inalienable truth. Something he would never compromise to the least degree.

"You are hereby stripped of your rank," the King said in a strangled voice. His eyes gleamed with outrage and a wild kind of triumph. "We formally expel you from the ranks of our officers. As a private soldier, you will be placed under arrest for high treason and await court martial at our pleasure."

Corfe made no answer. He could not speak.

"I think not," a voice said. The King spluttered.

"What? Who—?"

Andruw grinned madly. "Arrest him, sire, and you must arrest us all. The men won't stand for it, and I won't be able to answer for their actions."

"You pitiful barbarian rabble!" Lofantyr shouted, outraged. "We'll slap them in irons and send them back to the galleys whence they came!"

"If you do, you will have two thousand Fimbrians storming this palace within the hour," Formio said calmly.

The men at the King's end of the table were stunned. "I—I don't believe you," Lofantyr managed.

"My race has never been known for idle boasting, my lord King. You have my word on it."

"By God," the King hissed, "I'll have your heads on pikes before the day is out, you treacherous dogs. Guards! *Guards!*"

Admiral Berza leaned across his neighbour and grasped the King's wrist. "Sire," he said earnestly, "do not do this thing."

The doors of the chamber burst open and a dozen Torunnan troopers rushed in, swords drawn.

"Arrest these men!" the King screamed, tugging his hand free of Berza's grip and gesturing wildly with it.

The guards paused. Around the table were the highest ranking officers and officials in the kingdom. They were all silent. At last General Menin said: "Return to your posts. The King is taken poorly." And when they stood, unsure, he barked like a parade-ground sergeant-major. *"Obey my orders, damn it!"*

They left. The doors closed.

"Sweet blood of the Blessed Saint!" the King exclaimed, leaping to his feet. "A conspiracy!"

"Shut up and sit down!" Menin yelled in the same

voice. He might have been addressing a wayward re-
cruit. Beside him, Colonel Aras was aghast, though the
others present seemed more embarrassed than anything
else.

Lofantyr sat down. He looked as though he might
burst into tears.

"Forgive me, sire," Menin said in a lower voice. His
once ruddy face was the colour of parchment, as if he
was realizing what he had just done. "This has gone
quite far enough. I do not want the rank-and-file privy
to our . . . disagreements. I am thinking of your dignity,
the standing of the crown itself, and the good of the
army. We cannot precipitate a war amongst ourselves,
not at this time." Sweat set his bald pate gleaming. "I
am sure General Cear-Inaf will agree." He looked at
Corfe, and his eyes were pleading.

"I agree, yes," Corfe said. His heart was thumping
as though he were in the midst of battle. "Men say
things in the heat of the moment which they would
never otherwise contemplate. I must apologize, sire, for
both myself and my officers."

There was a long unbearable silence. The King's
breathing steadied. He cleared his throat. "Your apologies are accepted." He sounded as hoarse as a crow.
"We are unwell, and will retire. General Menin, you
will conduct the meeting in our absence."

He rose, and staggered like a drunken man. They all
stood, and bowed as he wove his way to the door.

"Guards!" Menin called. "See the King to his chamber, and fetch the Royal physician to him. He is—he
is unwell."

The door closed, and they resumed their seats. None
of them could meet one another's eyes. They were like

children who have caught their father in adultery.

"Thank you, General," Corfe said finally.

Menin glared at his subordinate. "What else was I to do? Condone a civil war? The lad is young, unsure of himself. And we shamed him."

The lad was scarcely younger than Corfe, but no one pointed this out.

"Been hidden behind his mother's skirts too long," Admiral Berza said bluntly. "You did right, Menin. It's common knowledge that General Cear-Inaf's troops could wipe the floor with the rest of the army combined."

Menin cleared his throat thunderously. "Gentlemen, we have business still to attend to here, matters which cannot be postponed. The deployment of the army—"

"Hold on a moment, Martin," Berza said, addressing General Menin by his rarely heard first name. "First I suggest we take advantage of His Majesty's . . . indisposition to air a few things. There's too much damned intrigue and bad feeling around this fucking table, and I'm well-nigh sick of it."

"Admiral!" Count Fournier exclaimed, shocked. "Remember where you are."

"Where I am? I'm in a meeting convened to discuss our response to a military invasion of our country, and for hours I've been forced to listen to a stream of administrative piddle and procedural horseshit. According to the King, all we have to do is sit with our thumbs up our arses and the enemy will obediently march into the muzzles of our guns. That, gentlemen, is a surrender of the initiative which could prove fatal to our cause."

"For a foreigner and a commoner, you are remarkably patriotic, Admiral," Fournier sneered.

Berza turned in his seat. His broad whiskered face was suffused with blood but he spoke casually. "Why you insignificant blue-veined son of a bitch, I've bled for Torunna more times than you've taken it up the arse from that painted pansy you call an aide."

Fournier's face went chalk-white.

"Call me out if you dare, you self-important little prick." The Admiral grinned maliciously. Corfe had to nudge Andruw, who was trying desperately not to let his mirth become audible.

"Gentlemen, gentlemen," General Menin said. "Enough of this. Admiral Berza, you will apologize to the count."

"In hell I will."

"You will ask his pardon or you will be expelled from this meeting and suspended from command."

"For what? Telling the truth?"

"Johann—" Menin growled.

"All right, all right. I apologize to the worthy gentleman for calling him a prick, and for insinuating that he is an unnatural bugger with a taste for pretty young men. Will that suffice?"

"It'll have to, I suppose. Count Fournier?"

"The good of my country comes before any personal antipathies," Fournier said, with a definite emphasis on the "my."

"Indeed. Now, gentlemen, the army," Menin went on. "We are, it seems, committed to a ... defensive posture, but that does not mean we cannot sortie out in force. It would be a pity to let the foe entrench and camp in peace before the walls. General Cear-Inaf, according to the battle plan the King and I have drawn

up, your command—it was to have gone to Colonel
Aras, of course, but circumstances change—will be our
chief sortie force, since it has a significant proportion
of heavy cavalry. Your men will be re-billeted within
easy distance of the North Gate and will hold themselves in a state of readiness should a sortie be called
for. In the general engagement that will no doubt follow the Merduk repulse from the walls, your men will
form the centre reserve of the army, and as such will
remain to the rear until called upon. I hope that is
clear."

Exceedingly clear. Corfe and Andruw glanced at one
another. They would bleed before the walls, wear the
Merduks down; and if the decisive battle were finally
fought, they would be safely in the rear. "All the work
and none of the glory," Andruw muttered. "Things
don't change."

"Perfectly clear, sir," Corfe said aloud.

"Is this strategy yours or the King's, Martin?" the
irrepressible Berza asked.

"It—it originated with His Majesty, but I have had
my hand in it as well."

"In other words he thought it up, and you had to
make the best of it."

"Admiral . . ." Menin glowered warningly. Berza
held up a hand.

"No, no, I quite understand. He is our King, but the
poor fellow doesn't know one end of a pike from the
other. We are outnumbered—what? Five, six to one?—
it makes sense that we rely on walls to equal the odds.
But no army ever won a war by letting itself become
besieged, Martin, you know that as well as I. We cannot win that way. It will be Aekir over again."

A gloom hung over the chamber, oppressing everyone. It was Formio who broke the silence. "Numbers mean nothing," he said. "It is the quality of the men that counts. And the leadership which directs them."

"Fimbrian wisdom has always come cheap," Fournier retorted. "If platitudes won wars there would never be any losers." Formio shrugged.

Finally, reluctantly, Menin cleared his throat and in an oddly savage tone of voice he said, "General Cear-Inaf, you were at Aekir, and again at Ormann Dyke. Perhaps,"—it evidently pained Menin to say it—"perhaps you could give us the benefit of your—ah, *unique*, experience."

All eyes were on him again, but there was not so much of hostility in them now. They are afraid, Corfe thought. They are finally facing the truth of things.

"Aekir was stronger than Torunn, and we had John Mogen—but Aekir fell," he said harshly. "Ormann Dyke was stronger than Aekir, and we had Martellus—but the dyke fell also. If Torunn is besieged, it will fall, and with it the rest of the kingdom. And if Torunna goes under, then so will Perigraine and Almark. That is reality, not speculation."

"Then what would you have us do?" Menin asked quietly.

"Take to the field with the men we have. It is the last thing the enemy expects. And we must do it at once, try to defeat the foe piecemeal before the two Merduk armies have fully integrated. Shahr Baraz lost many of his best men before the dyke and much of the remaining enemy strength will be the peasant levy, the *Minhraib*. We seek them out, hit them hard, and the odds will be substantially reduced. The Merduk always

encamp the *Minhraib* separately from the *Ferinai* and
the *Hraibadar*—the elite troops. I would undertake to
lead out two thirds of the garrison and take on the
Minhraib. At the same time, Admiral Berza should assault this coastal supply base of theirs and destroy it,
then put the fleet to patrolling the Kardian so that there
will be no more amphibious flanking manoeuvres such
as the one which lost us the dyke. With the bulk of his
levies destroyed or scattered, his supply lines threatened and the weather worsening, I think Aurungzeb
will be forced to withdraw."

"There is almost a foot of snow out there," Colonel
Aras pointed out. "Would you have us seek battle in a
blizzard?"

"Yes. It will help hide our numbers, and increase
confusion. And the foe will not be expecting it."

Silence again. General Menin was studying Corfe's
face as if he thought he might read the future from it.
"You take a lot upon yourself, General," he said.

"You asked me for my opinion. I gave it."

"Foolhardy madness," Count Fournier decided.

"I agree," Aras said. "Attack a foe many times our
strength in the middle of a snowstorm? It is a recipe
for disaster. And the King will never consent to it."

"His mother would," Berza rumbled. "But she has
more balls than most of us here."

"It may have escaped your notice, General Cear-
Inaf," Menin said, "but I am the senior officer here,
not you. If this strategy were agreed upon, I would
command." Corfe said nothing.

"Enough then," Menin continued. "I must speak to
the King. Gentlemen, this meeting is at an end. We
will reconvene when His Majesty is . . . recovered and

I have put this new strategy to him. I am sure you all have a lot to do."

"Shall I leave off work on the river booms?" Berza demanded.

"For the moment, yes. We may as well keep our options open. Gentlemen, good day." Menin rose, and everyone else with him. The assembled officers collected their papers and made for the door. Corfe and his group of subordinates remained behind whilst their superiors exited.

Admiral Berza came over and clapped Corfe on the shoulder.

"You spoke up well. I'd have done the same, had they tried to take me away from my ships. But they hate you now, you know. They can't stand having the error of their ways pointed out to them. Even Martin Menin, and he's a good friend."

Corfe managed a smile. "I know."

"Aye. In some ways, palace corridors are the deadliest battlefields of all. But from what I hear, you're quite the hero to the common soldiers. Keep their loyalty, and you may just survive." Berza winked, and then left in his turn.

EIGHTEEN

ALL morning the brightly liveried cavalcades had been trekking into the city. Crowds of commoners turned out to cheer them as they trotted and trundled across the blackened Lower City and began following the paved expanse of the Royal way into Upper Abrusio and the twin towering edifices of the palace and the monastery.

They were magnificently turned out, the horses richly caparisoned, the closed carriages gay with paint and banners, the gonfalons and fanions of the noble houses of the kingdom snapping and flaming out overhead like brilliantly plumaged birds. Their procession stretched for the better part of a mile, from the Eastern Gate clear across to the foot of Abrusio Hill. Above them, the abbey and the monastery of the Inceptines were hung with flags in welcome, patches of newly mortared stone bright against their weathered old walls.

In the courtyard before the abbey ranks of servitors waited and a dozen trumpeters stood ready to blare out a salute when the nobles drew near.

Jemilla sat watching from an open carriage, well wrapped up against the flurries of sleet that were rattling in from the Hebros. Beside her sat her steward, Antonio Feramond. He was red-nosed and sniffling and had his collar turned up against the raw wind.

"There—there, do you see? That bloodless, pompous old fool. There he sits, the very picture of the gracious host, looking like the cat who caught the mouse."

Jemilla spat. She was talking of Urbino, Duke of Imerdon, who sat on a patient white destrier at the entrance to the great courtyard, ready to welcome his fellow nobles to the council.

Well, one could not have everything. Those with an inkling of intelligence would know who had brought this about. But it galled Jemilla that she was to have no part in the proceedings until Urbino produced her and the child she bore like a cony from a conjuror's hat. She would act the dutiful noble-woman, grieving for the King who had been her lover, whilst behind the scenes she would pull the strings that made Urbino dance.

"The venison was brought in this morning, was it not?" she demanded of the miserable Antonio.

"Yes, madam. A score of plump does, well hung, too. But had I known these blue-bloods were going to flood the city with their retainers I'd have ordered a dozen more."

"Don't worry about the hangers-on. Bread, beer and cheese is good enough for them."

"At least we did not pay for the wine. That saved us a pretty penny," Antonio said smugly. Though the monastery and abbey had been looted in the aftermath of the late war, the Inceptine cellars had escaped damage. There was enough wine in them to float a fleet of carracks. Antonio had also made himself a pretty penny by selling a few tuns of it to an enterprising Macassian ship's captain. He thought this was his secret, and Jemilla did not intend to disabuse him of the fact until she deemed it useful to do so.

"How stand our funds at the moment?" she asked him.

"We have fifteen hundred and twelve gold crowns left over, madam. The duke was very generous. We'll make a profit from the affair, never fear."

Short-sighted fool. He thought in terms of profit and loss, while Jemilla's eye was set much higher. One day soon she'd have the entire Hebrian treasury at her disposal. Let them have their pomp and panoply, for now.

A commotion at the western side of the courtyard drew her attention. A knot of riders trotting into view.

"Who in the world—?"

Foremost among them was a noble lady riding sidesaddle. She was hooded and cloaked against the inclement weather, but Jemilla knew her at once. That Astaran bitch, Isolla. What did she think she was doing here? And beside her a man in a broad-brimmed hat that buckled and tugged in the wind. He wore a patch over one eye and seemed a mere skeleton under his fur-trimmed riding robes. Jemilla's mouth opened as she recognized Golophin. Behind the pair were four heavily armed knights bearing the livery of Astarac, and then four more in the colours of Hebrion. The

group of riders joined Duke Urbino in the centre of the
square. Even from this distance, Jemilla could see that
the duke was taken aback. Golophin swept off his hat
and bowed in the saddle, his head as bald as an egg-
shell. Isolla offered the bemused duke her hand to kiss.

"Madam," Antonio began. "Who—?"

"Shut up, you fool. Let me think."

The head of the nobles' procession entered the
square, and there was a deafening flourish of trumpets.
Isolla and Urbino greeted the arriving noblemen together, the Astaran princess throwing back her hood to
reveal an intricately braided head of auburn hair set
with diamond-headed pins.

Jemilla had been outmanoeuvred, upstaged. But as
she turned the thing over in her mind she realized that
it did not matter. The council would run its course, a
regency would be voted into existence. Let the odd pair
have their triumph; it would mean little enough in the
end.

THE council assembled in what had once been the
refectory of the monastery. The broken windows
had been replaced—though plain glass was now in-
stalled where once there had been ancient and beautiful
stained-glass windows—and the huge chamber had
been swept clean, the walls replastered and the banners
of the nobles hung along the massively beamed vault
of the ceiling. Two fireplaces, each large enough to
accommodate a spit-turned bullock, had been cleaned
out and blazed with welcome flame. The long refectory
table had survived and stood where it always had.
Crafted of iron-hard teak from Calmar, the only marks
it bore of the recent fighting were a few arquebus balls

buried deep in the timber. High-backed chairs, ornate as small thrones, were ranged along it, and the nobility of the kingdom took its seats amid a buzz and hubbub of animated talk, whilst serving attendants set decanters of wine and platters of sweetmeats at intervals along the table and lit the dozens of thick beeswax candles which stood in clusters everywhere.

Along the walls, scribes sat at little desks prepared to take down every word spoken by the assembled dignitaries, and a trio of brawny servitors manhandled extra chairs to accommodate the unexpected additions to the throng. The seating had been nicely arranged in order of precedence and rank, but the arrival of Isolla and Golophin had thrown these out and things were being hastily rejuggled. The larger throne at the table's head would remain empty, of course, to represent the absent King and, a princess being as lofty in rank as a duke, Isolla would be sitting opposite Urbino in the next two places. Golophin declared himself happy with a well-padded chair by the fire. He had a decanter and glass brought to him there and sat sipping and watching the crowd with evident enjoyment.

It took an hour for the notables to finish greeting each other, find their places and assume their seats. During that time Jemilla appeared and had another comfortable chair brought in so that she could sit opposite Golophin at the fire. He offered her wine but she demurred graciously, citing her pregnancy. They sat staring into the flames, for all the world like an old married couple, whilst the clamour died around them into an orderly silence.

A grey-clad Friar Mendicant appeared by the empty King's place, and raised his hands.

"My lords, noble lady, a moment of prayer, if you please, for our poor afflicted King. May he soon recover his senses and rule over us with the justice and compassion that was his wont."

Those present bowed their heads. Golophin leaned forward and whispered to Jemilla:

"Your idea, I suppose."

"You won't object to a prayer for the King's health, surely, Golophin."

"Poor and afflicted. I'll bet you just wish."

The cleric withdrew. Duke Urbino stood up. For a second he seemed at a loss for words. Then he met Jemilla's eye, and his spine seemed to stiffen.

"Gentlemen, my worthy cousins, gracious lady, we are gathered here on a mission of paramount importance for the future of the kingdom of Hebrion . . ."

"A good choice," Golophin told Jemilla. "Respectable, but dense. No doubt you've got him close to thinking he's his own man."

"Any man who thinks he's his own man is a fool. Even you, Golophin. You hold fast to Abeleyn although he's as good as a corpse. Why not give your loyalty to his son? What principles would that compromise? He would wish it so, were he alive."

"He is alive. He is alive and my King. And he is my friend."

"If he were dead—truly dead—would you recognize his son as the heir to the throne?"

Golophin was silent a long time whilst the Duke of Imerdon rambled on in his portentous, pompous way and the rest of the assembly listened with grave attention to his platitudes.

"If it were his son," he said finally.

Jemilla felt a cold hand about her heart. "You need not concern yourself on that score. Abeleyn himself was convinced. Besides, there have been no others in my bed."

"Palace guards do not count, then."

"I had to gain my freedom. I used the only tool I had." It seemed suddenly very warm here by the fire with the old wizard's bird-bright eye intent upon her.

Golophin's eye left her as he drank more wine. Jemilla's face did not show the relief she felt. This man must go, she thought. He is too knowing, too damned shrewd by half. I can fool the rest, but not him—not for ever.

"Do not trouble to talk to me of the King's heir, lady," the wizard said, wiping his mouth. "We know who will rule in Hebrion if that prating fool up there is appointed regent, or if your brat is finally brought into the world and survives to his majority. If it is indeed Abeleyn's child in your belly, then I would be the first to recognize the infant's claims, but I would sooner stick my head in a she-wolf's den than let you have any say in the child's rearing."

"It is well that we understand each other," she said.

"Yes. Honesty is often refreshing, don't you find? Have a taste of this superb wine. You look somewhat peaked, and one glass will not hurt the child any."

He poured her some, and they both raised their glasses, looked at each other, and clinked the glasses together.

"To the King," Golophin said.

"To the King. And his heir."

•   •   •

WELL?" Golophin asked Isolla. "What did you make of it?"

They were in the King's private chambers, sharing a late supper of pheasant stuffed with truffles and basil—one of Golophin's favourites. The weather had worsened, and hail rattled at the tall windows.

"The Hebrian nobility is even more long-winded than that of Astarac," Isolla replied. "They must have talked for seven or eight hours, and they barely got beyond introductions."

"They're feeling their way. Our presence unsettled them. After Jemilla left I made a point of ostentatiously taking down their names. Let them fear a pogrom. It will concentrate their minds wonderfully."

"That Jemilla; you were talking to her for a long time. One might have thought you were old friends."

"Let us say that we understand one another. In many ways she is an admirable woman. She might have made Abeleyn a worthy queen, were she not so . . . ambitious."

"She'd rather be king."

Golophin laughed. "There you have hit the nail on the head. But she is not of the calibre of Odelia of Torunna, another scheming and ambitious woman. Jemilla wants to rule, and damn the consequences. She would lay the kingdom waste if it would put her on a throne."

"Is she that highly born? I was not aware."

"Oh, no. She is a noblewoman, and she married well, but her blood is not of such a vintage that it would ever enable her to rule constitutionally, even if she had been a man. But she has brains. She will rule through others."

"Urbino of Imerdon."

"Quite."

"How are you going to stop them, Golophin? They'll begin discussing the regency tomorrow."

"We can't stop them, lady," Golophin said quietly.

Isolla was startled. "So what are we to do?"

The old wizard sat back from the table and laid aside his napkin. "Jemilla has planned well. In the absence of the King, a quorum of the nobility is allowed to make decisions of state. It has precedent, my legal minds tell me. The decrees of the council will have the full force of law."

"But we have the army and the fleet behind us."

"What would you have me do, lady? Stage a coup? Rovero and Mercado would never agree to it. The city has suffered enough, and it would make us no better than Jemilla. No. There is another way, though. Only one thing can take the wind out of their sails now."

"And that is?"

"The King himself."

"Then we are finished. That's impossible. Isn't it, Golophin?"

"I—I'm not entirely sure. I must do some reading on the matter. I will tell you later. Later tonight, perhaps. Could you meet me in the King's bedchamber by, say, the fifth hour of the night?"

"Of course. Have your powers come back then?"

The old mage grimaced. "They are not a migrating flock, Isolla. They do not fly away and return overnight. There is some recuperation, certainly. Whether it will be enough is another matter."

"Do you think you could heal him? It would be the answer to everything."

"Not quite everything, but it would make life . . . better, yes."

Isolla regarded her companion closely. Although he was still rail-thin, his face did not have quite the skull-like look about it which had so startled her at their first meeting. She wondered what had happened to his eye. She had not asked, and Golophin had ventured no explanation. It wept tears of black blood from under the patch sometimes, and he carried a stained handkerchief to blot them away.

"My thanks for the fowl, lady," he said. "I must retire to my books for a while." He rose. There had never been any ceremony between them after the first few days.

"Are you—are you in pain, Golophin?"

His quirkish smile, warm and yet gently mocking. "Aren't we all, in this unhappy world? Until later, Isolla."

GOLOPHIN had a tower out in the hills, a discreet run-down place where he could attend to his researches in peace. Once he might have spirited himself there in a matter of moments, but nowadays it took two hours on a fast-stepping mule. The door, invisible to the naked eye, opened on a word of command and he wearily climbed the circling steps to the uppermost room. From there he could look out of the wide bay windows across twenty leagues of Hebrion, a kingdom asleep under the stars, the sea a faint glimmer on the horizon, and to his right the black bulk of the Hebros Mountains blotting out the sky. The witching hour, some called it. Dweomer worked best at night, which did nothing for the reputations of those who practised it. Something to do with the interfering energy of the sun, perhaps. There had been a paper presented to the guild about it a few years back, he remembered. Who—? Ah yes, Bardolin, his former apprentice.

And where are you now, Bard? Golophin wondered. Did you ever find that land in the west, or are your bones fifty fathoms deep in green water?

He closed his remaining eye. Mind-rhyming was one of his disciplines, and the one least affected by all that had come to pass lately. He let his thought drift free, gossamer thin, frail as shadow, and sent it drifting over the sea. It touched upon a few hard-working night fishermen in a winter ketch, flicked around the massive, formless intelligence of a whale, and ranged farther yet, out into the empty seas of the west.

No good. His power was still ragged and convalescent. It could not focus or observe with any accuracy. Even when he had been whole, his gyrfalcon familiar had always been necessary for that. He began to withdraw, to call back his glimmering mindscrap.

Who might you be?

He staggered physically. Something like the glare of a bonfire passed over him, the massive, all-seeing regard of an immensely powerful mind.

Ah, there I have you. Hebrion! Now there is synchronicity in action. Not many of you left, are there? The continent is dark as a grave. They have almost done us all to death.

Golophin was frozen, a specimen turned this way and that for inspection. He tried to send a probing feeler towards the mind that held him, but it was rebuffed. Amusement.

Not yet, not yet! You'll know me soon enough. What

*are you doing scanning the empty west this night? Ah,
I see. He lives, you know. He is not happy, but he will
come to it in time. I have great plans for your friend
Bardolin.*

And then a feeble spark of someone else, hurled
across the darkling ocean.

Golophin! Help me, in the name of God—

And nothing. Golophin fell to his knees. Something
huge and dark seemed to blot out the stars beyond the
tower window for an instant, and then it was gone and
the cold night air was empty and silent.

"Lord God," he croaked. He spun a cantrip to light
up the midnight room, but it guttered and flared out in
seconds. He knelt in the darkness, gasping, until finally
he mustered the strength to fumble for flint and tinder
and light a candle. His hands were shaking and he
skinned a knuckle with the flint.

And it smote him.

A bolt of mind energy so intense that it manifested
physically. He was tossed across the room. The power
crackled through him, contorting his limbs, ripping a
shriek out of his throat. He rose in the air and the
chamber grew bright as day as the excess poured out
of him in a discharge like the effulgence of a captured
sun. He blazed like a torch for ten seconds, writhing
in an extremity of pain he had never before experienced or imagined. His robes burned away to ash and
the candle was shrivelled into a pool of steaming wax.
The heavy wood furniture of the room smouldered.

Then it left him, and he fell with a crack of bones
to the floor.

NINETEEN

THE copyists had finished ahead of time, and the fruit of their round-the-clock labours sat on the table amid a jumbled pile of other gear. Albrec had had it bound in oilskin against the wet, but it was small enough to fit into the bosom of his robe if need be.

He ran his hands over his things again. Fur-lined boots, socks that stank of mutton fat, a pair of thick woollen habits, mittens, a heavy cloak and hood, and the capacious valise with the extra straps he had had a leatherworker add. Some store of dried and smoked food, a full wineskin, flint and tinder in a cork-lined metal box, and a bearskin bag that he was somehow supposed to sleep in. And the book, the precious copy of the even more precious original which he had carried from Charibon.

He dressed in the bulky winter travelling clothes, stuffed his valise with the rest and pulled the straps over his shoulder. Done, he thought. The baggage is ready, but is the resolve?

Torunn's streets were quiet as he left the palace. The succession of blizzards which had been battering the city of late had stalled, and there was icy stillness in their place, the creak of solid ice underfoot. But the stars were veiled in thick cloud, the night sky heavy with the promise of more snow.

Albrec negotiated three separate sets of sentries without incident, passing as a Papal courier, and crunched through the freezing snow towards the North Gate. They opened the postern for him, though one soldier wanted to hold the little monk until he could call on an officer for confirmation of Albrec's errand. But another, looking at the monk's ravaged face, prevailed upon his comrade to forbear.

"There's no harm in him," he said. "Go with God, Father, and for the Saint's sake watch out for those fucking Merduk cavalry, begging your pardon."

Albrec blessed the unsure group of gate guards, and moments later heard the deep boom as the heavy postern was shut behind him. He made the Sign of the Saint, sniffed the frigid night air through the twin holes which had been a nose, and began trudging north through the snow. Towards the winter camps of the enemy.

FROM the height of the palace Corfe could clearly see the tiny shape forging off into the hills, black against the snow. What poor soul might that be? he wondered. A courier without a horse? Unlikely. He considered sending down to the gate guards to find out, but thought better of it. He closed the balcony screen instead, and stepped back into the firelit dimness of the Queen Dowager's bedchamber.

"Well, General," Odelia said softly, "here we are."

"Here we are," he agreed.

She was in scarlet velvet beaded with pearls, a net of them in her golden hair. The green eyes seemed to have a light of their own in the darkened room.

"Won't you come and sit with me, at least?"

He joined her at the fire. Mulled wine here, untouched, a silver tray of cloying pastries.

"How is your shoulder?" she enquired.

"Good as new."

"I'm glad. The kingdom has need of that arm. No word on the investigation into the . . . incident?"

His mouth curved into a sardonic smile. "What investigation?"

"Quite. It was my son, you know."

Corfe gaped. "My God. You're sure?"

"Quite sure. He is learning, but not fast enough. His spies do not rival mine yet. The assassin was not one of the true brotherhood, but a sellsword from Ridawan. An apprentice. As well for you, I suppose, though even an adept of the Brotherhood of the Knife would have had trouble with both you and that Fimbrian acolyte of yours."

Corfe frowned, and she laughed. "Corfe, you have this rare gift with men. There's not a soldier in the garrison would not give an arm to ride by your side. Even that Fimbrian martinet is not immune. Do you think he'd have put the remnants of his men at the disposal of Menin or Aras, had they been his rescuers? Think again. And then his absurd offer to storm the palace. You have become a power in the world, General. From now on you will attract followers as a candle does moths."

"You are well-informed," Corfe told her.

"I make it my business to be, as you well know. The King has decided to adopt your suggested strategy, by the way."

"Has he?" Hope leapt in Corfe's heart.

"Yes, but only because Menin put it forward as his own. Lofantyr will be leading the army, and he and Menin will do their best to keep you out of any great victory."

"I don't care. As long as we win. That's all that matters."

She shook her head in mock wonder. "Such altruism! Even Mogen was not so selfless. Have you no lust for glory?"

He had asked that question himself once, when Ebro was worried about the odds they faced. He could answer it honestly now.

"No, lady. I have seen glory enough to turn my stomach."

"Have you, indeed?" The marvellous eyes looking him up and down, for ever gauging him. Then she rose, and stretched like a girl before him. "Well, you'll receive your orders in the morning, and the army will march the day after tomorrow. Right into the maw of another blizzard, no doubt." Her tone was off-hand, but he sensed a tenseness in her. The taut, velvet-clad abdomen was inches from his face. She set her hands on his shoulders, and it seemed the most natural thing in the world for him to encircle the slim waist with his arms, and lay his head on her, burying his face in the warm velvet. Her fingers ruffled his hair like those of a mother.

"My poor Corfe. You will never revel in your glory, will you?"

"It's bought with too much blood."

She knelt and kissed him on the lips. In a second, they seemed somehow to catch fire from one another. He tugged the gown down her shoulders and it fell to her hips, gripped it harder and rent the material so that it flowed down her thighs. A little explosion of dislodged pearls, her warm skin under his hands. She was entirely nude underneath the gown. He fumbled with his breeches, but she made a kind of sign in the air with her hand which left a momentary glimmer behind, and at once he was naked also. He laughed.

"The Dweomer certainly has its uses."

Afterwards they lay before the fire on a tangled mat of their discarded clothing. She rested her head on his chest whilst he stroked the small of her back, the delicate bumps of her spine. As always, the sadness hit him, the desolation of loss as he recalled Heria, and the times they had been like this. But for once he fought the feeling. He was tired of seeing only the shadow cast by every light. He esteemed this woman— there was no need to feel guilty about that. He *would* not feel guilty.

She raised her head and touched the tears on his face. "Time heals," she said gently. "A cliché, but true."

"I know. It seems endless, though. I don't want to forget her, yet I must."

"Not forget, Corfe. But she must not become a ghost to haunt you, either." She paused. "Tell me about her."

He found it incredibly hard to speak. His throat ached. His voice when it finally came out sounded harsh as a raven's.

"There is not much to tell. She was the daughter of a silk merchant in the city—Aekir, I mean—and she ran the business for him. As the junior officer of my regiment, I was colour-bearer, responsible for our banners, which were of silk, like the Merduks'. They needed replacing, so I was sent to this merchant's house, and there she was."

"And there she was," Odelia repeated quietly. "She never came out of Aekir, then?"

"No. I looked for her after the walls were overrun, deserted my post to try and find her, but our home was already behind the Merduk lines and that part of the city was burning. I was caught up in the flood of refugees, borne along the Western Road. I wanted to die, but did my best to live. I don't know why. I just hope it was quick, for her. I have pictures in my mind . . ." He could speak no longer. His body had become rigid in Odelia's arms. She felt the bottled-up sobs quiver through his frame, but he made not a sound and when she looked at his face at last she saw that he was dry-eyed again. There was a glitter in those eyes that chilled her, a light of pure hatred. But it faded, and he smiled at the concern on her face.

"I am glad of this," he said haltingly. "I am glad of you, lady. Time heals, perhaps, but you do also." And he pulled her closer.

She finally admitted it to herself. She was in love with him. The knowledge shook her, rendered her abruptly unsure of herself. She found herself hating the memory of his dead wife, envying a ghost for its hold on him. All her life, she had schemed and plotted and fucked to further her ambitions, to safeguard this kingdom. And she realized now that she would walk away from it—palace, kingdom, velvet robes and all—if he asked her to. She felt dizzied with fear and exhilaration in equal measure.

"Is there hope for us?" she asked him.

"I think so. If we hit them hard enough, quickly enough, and Berza's fleet does its job down on the coast, they *must* withdraw. We will have won time, and a little space. But even so, it will not be over. Come spring, we will see the decisive battle."

It was not what she had meant, but she was glad he had misunderstood her. It was near dawn, and he had come quite far enough for one night.

DAWN in Torunna was the sixth hour of the long winter night in Hebrion. Isolla paced the Royal bedchamber impatiently. Golophin was late, which was unlike him. If she opened the screens and peered out of the balcony she would be able to see the lights and merrymaking which had been going on throughout the night in the former monastery on the hilltop opposite the palace. A ball was being thrown there for the assembled nobility. It had been no great wrench on her part to turn down her invitation, but the faint, tinny clamour of the music penetrated even this room and intruded on her thoughts, irritating. She was beginning to doubt her role in this, and even found herself thinking nostalgically of the Astaran court, and especially her brother, Mark. What was she to do, send him a letter saying "I want to come home," for all the world like a child sent away to a strange school? Her pride would never let her recover. So she paced the room with her long, mannish stride, and thought.

The click of the secret doorway stopped her dead. The section of wall slid inwards, and Golophin appeared. He smiled at her. "My apologies for being late, lady."

"It doesn't matter." There was something different about him. Something—

"Golophin!" she cried. "Your eye, it's healed."

He raised a hand to his face. "So it is."

"Have you recovered your powers?"

He stood before her. He had changed. His bones had fleshed out and he stood somehow taller. He looked twenty years younger than when she had last seen him, scant hours ago. But something was amiss. She could have sworn that he was confused—no, more than that. He was *frightened*.

"Golophin, are you all right?"

"I suppose I am. Very much so. I am wholly restored, Isolla." Bale-fire clicked into life above his head, lighting the gloomy room. At the same time, every unlit candle in the chamber suddenly fizzled into flame.

"But that's wonderful!" Isolla exclaimed.

The old wizard shrugged. "It is. It is, indeed."

"What's wrong? You should be overjoyed. You will be able to heal the King. Our troubles are over."

"I don't know how it happened!" he shouted, shocking her.

"You don't? But . . . How is that possible?"

"I don't know, lady, and my ignorance is driving me mad. Something happened to me this night, but I can remember nothing of it."

"It's like a miracle."

"I don't believe in them," he said darkly. "Enough. This is not the time or place." He rubbed his eyes. "I must go to work at once, if this damn council of theirs is to be thwarted. They'll be voting on the regency tomorrow afternoon. Forgive me my bluntness, lady. I am somewhat out of order."

"It doesn't matter. Just heal him."

He nodded and sighed as if exhausted, though he was fairly crackling with energy. Even the wattles below his chin had tightened and disappeared. She longed to pose question after question, but remained mute. They repaired to the King's bedside. Golophin looked down on the unconscious, mutilated form, and seemed to calm. He glanced around. "What have we here to work with? Not a lot. We are in too much haste." He stroked the heavy wood of the bedposts. "It will do for now, I suppose." He turned to Isolla. "Lady, I need you to hold the King's hands. Whatever you see, whatever he does, you must not let them go. Am I clear?"

"Perfectly," she lied.

"Very well. Then let us draw up some chairs and begin."

She took Abeleyn's hands. They were hot and feverish, but the King's face was as still as that of a wax image. The sheets, though changed daily, were soaked with sweat. The King seemed to be burning away like a hearth of coals with a bellows feeding them.

Golophin closed his eyes and sat as motionless as his King. Nothing happened. A quarter of an hour went by. Isolla longed to change her posture, stretch her neck, but she dared not move. She had been prepared for lightnings, thunder, a blaze of theurgy or a chat-

tering of summoned demons—*something*. But there
was only the stifling room, the weird flicker of the
bale-fire, the wizard's composed face.

And then the creak of wood. She started as the bed
began to tremble and shake. The canopy overhead billowed like a ship's sail. It cracked and flapped, the
heavy drapes whipping her across the face, and then
the whole thing took off and tumbled end over end
across the room.

The bedposts, thick carved baulks of timber as wide
as her thigh, began shrinking. She gaped at them. They
were disappearing from the top down. It was like
watching the hugely accelerated work of termites. They
had been taller than a man—now they were dwindling
foot by foot as she watched.

At the same time, the sheet covering Abeleyn shifted
and moved. Isolla stifled a cry as something began to
grow under there. It was the stumps of the King's legs.
They were lengthening, pushing up their covering. She
glanced at the wizard. His face had not changed, but
sweat had set it ashine and his eyes were rolling frantically behind their closed lids.

Two feet poked out at the end of the sheet that covered the King's body. Isolla jumped in horror. They
were human, perfectly shaped down to the very toe-
nails, but they were made of dark wood. And they
twitched with life.

The King groaned, and for the first time the wizard
spoke.

"Abeleyn," he said quietly, but low though his voice
was it made the very furniture in the room shake.

"Abeleyn. My King."

The man in the bed growled like a beast. His hands,

hitherto limp, clenched tightly upon Isolla's, squeezing out the blood until her fingers were white. She bit her lip on the pain, determined not to cry out.

Then the King's body arched up in the bed, his wooden heels drumming on the mattress, his spine bent back like a fully drawn bow. His sweating hands were slipping free. In panic, Isolla threw herself on top of him. Convulsions battered her up and down. One hard knee came up and stove in a rib. The King shrieked, and she wept with the pain.

The convulsions died, and he was quiet again. Isolla's face was buried in his neck. She could not move. His hands loosed their awful grip and disengaged gently from hers.

"What in the world?" the King said.

She raised her head, peered into his face. His eyes were open, and he smiled at her, looking utterly bewildered and at the same time amused.

"Issy Long-nose," he said, and laughed. "What *are* you doing?"

TWENTY

ALL morning, the army had been marching out of the North Gate of Torunn. The line of men and horses and ox-drawn field artillery and baggage wagons and pack mules seemed endless. They had trodden the new snow down into the mud and carved a dark line across the hills north of the capital. On the flanks of the column patrolled restless squadrons of heavy Torunnan cuirassiers. The column's head was already out of sight three miles away. Over thirty thousand men were on the march, the last field army left in the kingdom.

"There is a grandeur in war," Andruw said, blowing on his mittened hands. His metal gauntlets hung at his saddle bow.

"I never thought there were so many Torunnans in the world," Marsch admitted. "If we had known, we might not have fought you for so long."

"Numbers aren't everything," Corfe said.

"Any sign of our lot yet?" Andruw asked.

They were sitting on their horses on a knoll half a mile from the North Gate. They had been here an hour already, and still the stream of men went on.

"Shouldn't be long now," Corfe said. "Here comes the main baggage train. We're behind that."

A convoy of tall, heavy wagons drawn by mules and oxen. The baggage train held the spare ammunition and rations. Corfe had been given the job of guarding it, and the rear of the army. When the battle occurred, he and his men would be spectators rather than participants. Unless something went badly wrong.

"The best troops in the army, and we're guarding the wagons," Andruw said disgustedly. "What a prick that Menin is."

Corfe disagreed. "He did what he could. It's a miracle he persuaded the King to march out and fight at all. And besides"—he grinned at Andruw—"the rear is the post of honour. If the army's beaten, then it's we who have to cover the retreat."

"Post of honour my—"

"Here they come," Marsch interrupted.

Corfe's command began marching out of the gate behind the last of the wagons. The thousand-strong scarlet-armoured Cathedrallers were unmistakable, their stark banner flapping in the cold wind. Behind them came the black-clad, pike-wielding Fimbrians, marching in perfect time—two thousand of them, with Formio at their head. And finally, the last survivors of Ormann Dyke, five thousand arquebusiers and sword-and-buckler men under Ranafast. The command formed a column almost a mile long.

How would they fight together? There was a strong bond between them, Corfe knew. It came from the North More battle, when they had faced annihilation together. And they collectively despised the garrison soldiers of Torunn, most of whom had never fought in a single pitched battle. But they were certainly a disparate bunch. Wild mountain tribesmen, Fimbrian professionals and Torunnan veterans. They had had a chance to recover from their ordeal at the North More, and were rested, refitted and their morale was superb. If things went well, they would hardly need to fire a shot in the forthcoming contest. Corfe hoped it would be so, much though he would have liked to wield this new instrument of his in battle.

"Snow's starting again," Andruw noted gloomily. "God's teeth, will this winter never end? Bloody unnatural time of the year to be campaigning."

"Let's join the column," Corfe said, and the three riders cantered down the slope, kicking up a cloud of snow which the wind bore away like smoke behind them.

THE army marched a mere six miles that first day, the endless procession of men halting and starting again, the wagons getting stuck in the mud that lay beneath the snow, the heavy guns losing wheels, mules going lame. Corfe's men finally halted for the night three hours after the head of the column had pitched their tents. As far as the eye could see, the wink of campfires stretched over the hills and lit the sky from afar. It was good to be in the field again. Things were always simpler here.

Or so he thought. While he was at the horse-lines

with Marsch and Morin inspecting some lamed mounts, a courier brought him a message from the High Command. There was to be a strategy meeting that evening in the Royal tent, and his presence was required.

Resigned, he made his way through the vast firelit camp. Everywhere, men sat around their campfires heating their rations and drying their boots. A few flurries of snow had fallen during the day and it was getting colder. The mud was starting to harden underfoot, and the snow crunched.

The King's tent was a massive leather affair with half a dozen shivering sentries posted about it, their armour beginning to glister with frost. On his own authority, Corfe ordered them to build themselves a fire.

Inside the tent three braziers were glowing merrily. The King was there, dressed plainly in the leather gambeson that soldiers wore under their armour. With him were Count Fournier, General Menin, Colonels Aras and Rusio and seven or eight more junior officers whom Corfe did not recognize. Colonel Willem had been left in command of the five thousand or so men who remained in the capital.

"Ah, so we are all here. At last," the King said as Corfe came in. Lofantyr looked as though he had not slept in a week. There were grey hollows under his eyes and new lines of strain about his mouth. "Very well, Fournier, proceed." The King sat himself down in a canvas camp chair. Everyone else had to stand.

Fournier, rather ridiculous in antique half-armour that had not a scratch on it, cleared his throat and toyed unceasingly with a wooden pointer.

"Our scouts have just returned, sire, and they report

that the enemy is in three camps. The largest is some
four leagues to the north-west. They estimate there are
some eighty to ninety thousand men within it. It is not
fortified, and they have horse herds picketed around its
perimeter and patrols of light cavalry as well as the
regular sentries." Fournier cleared his throat again.
"The second camp is a league to the east of the first.
The scouts estimate that it holds some fifty thousand,
including *Ferinai* heavy cavalry and many arquebusiers. It is fortified with a ditch and palisade. The third
is farther yet to the north, perhaps another league from
the first two. Within it are the elephants, many more
cavalry and the main baggage train. It is believed that
the Sultan himself is in this third camp, and his—his
harem. Another forty or fifty thousand."

"Why does he split up his army so?" someone muttered.

"Flexibility," Corfe said. "If one camp is attacked,
the attacker will find columns from the other two on
his flanks."

Menin frowned at Corfe. "The general idea was that
we would attack their main camp and remain immune
to assaults from the other two. But we had not bar-
gained for the camps being so close together. Suddenly
this campaign looks a lot riskier than it did."

"You can still do it, if the assault is swift and powerful enough. To rouse the men of a large encampment,
get them into battle-line and then march them a league
will take at least two to three hours. In that time, given
a little luck, we could cripple the *Minhraib* contingent
of the Merduk army—the bulk of its troops. We would
then be in a position to deal with the other two armies
as they came up, or we could withdraw. In any case,

it would be wise to detach strong formations to the flanks, in case we're still heavily engaged when the Merduk reinforcements come up."

"Yes. Yes, of course," Menin said. "My thought exactly . . ." He trailed off, appearing old and apprehensive.

"Ninety thousand men in that first camp," someone said dubiously. "That's three times our strength. Who says they'll be an easy target?"

"Their camp is unfortified," Corfe pointed out. "They'll be keeping warm in their tents. Plus, they are nothing more than the peasant levy of Ostrabar, conscripts without firearms. So long as we retain the element of surprise, they should not prove too much trouble."

"I am relieved to hear it," the King said. He looked with obvious dislike at his youngest general. "You seem to have an answer for everything, General Cear-Inaf. I see we no longer have need of strategy conferences. All we do is consult you."

A series of titters throughout the tent. Corfe was impassive. He merely bowed to his monarch. "My apologies, sire, if I overstep my station. I worry only about the good of the army."

"Of course." The King stood up. "Gentlemen, regard this plan here. Fournier, will you oblige us, please?"

The count unrolled a page of parchment with a pattern of diagrams drawn upon it. They gathered closer to look.

"This is how the army will go into battle. General Menin, kindly explain."

"Yes, sire. Gentlemen, we shall be in four distinct commands. In the centre will be the main body, eighteen thousand men under His Majesty, myself and Colonel Rusio. Within this formation will be the field artillery—thirty guns under you, Rusio—and the cuirassiers—three thousand horsemen. His Majesty will lead the heavy horse personally.

"On the right flank of the main body will be a smaller formation, a flank guard to deal with the possibility of a Merduk assault from that quarter. This will be under Colonel Aras, and will number some five thousand, primarily arquebusiers. To the rear will be General Cear-Inaf's command, eight thousand men. These constitute our only reserve, and will also have the task of guarding the baggage train. Am I clear, gentlemen?"

"What about the left flank?" Corfe asked. "It's up in the air."

"We do not feel that the left flank is particularly threatened," the King told him. "The only threat from that quarter is from the baggage and headquarters camp of the enemy. We feel that the Merduk Sultan will not detach troops which are guarding his person until he knows exactly what the situation is. By that time we will have withdrawn. No, the only real threat is on the right, from the camp of the *Hraibadar* and the *Ferinai*. Aras, you have the position of honour. Hold it well."

"I will indeed, sire, to the last man, if needs be."

Corfe opened his mouth to protest, and then thought better of it. There was a possibility that the King was right, but he did not like it. Nor did he think it wise to have the heavy cavalry in the centre, where their mobility would be reduced and they would face the prospect of a charge into a tented camp: no job for horsemen. It would do no good to point it out, though.

"We move out in the morning," the King went on. "Two days' march will bring us to the environs of the enemy. We will go into battle-line somewhere out of view from their camp, and sweep down on them in one grand charge at dawn. As General Cear-Inaf has said, numbers will be less important in the confusion. We have an impenetrable screen of cavalry about us, so the enemy should remain unaware of our intentions until it is too late. We hit them hard, and then withdraw. Admiral Berza's fleet will be attacking their coastal bases at round about the same time. After this double-pronged attack, the Sultan will have to retreat to the Searil, and Ormann Dyke is almost indefensible if one is attacking from the south. We will have delivered Northern Torunna from the enemy. Gentlemen, are there any questions?"

"This battle will go down in history, sire!" Aras exclaimed. "We are lucky to have the chance to participate in it."

The King inclined his head graciously. Even Menin looked a little impatient at Aras's toadying.

"You are dismissed, gentlemen," the King said. "We will meet again the night before the ballet commences to finalize things. Until then, fare you well."

The assembled officers exited, bowing. General Menin caught Corfe outside the tent flap and grasped his arm. In a low voice he said, "A word with you, if you please, General."

They strolled through the camp together. Menin's face was a study in night-dark and firelight. He seemed deeply troubled.

"This is not to be bruited about," he said in a subdued tone. "But if I do not live through the battle, I wish you to take command of the army and lead the withdrawal."

Corfe froze in his tracks. "Are you serious?"

The older man produced a sealed scroll. "Here it is in writing. The King will object, of course, but there will be little time for objections. His first choice after me for the command is Aras, and he has already been promoted beyond his abilities. This army must survive, whatever happens. Get these men back to Torunn, Corfe."

Corfe took the scroll. "You pick an odd time to finally show confidence in me," he said, not without bitterness.

"The time for politics is past. The country needs a soldier to lead it now."

"You will survive, Menin. This is unnecessary."

"No, General. My death lies there to the north. I know I shall not be coming back. But you make sure that this army does!" He gripped Corfe's forearm with bruising force. His face was stark and livid. There was fear on it, but not for himself, Corfe was certain.

"I'll do what I can, if it should prove necessary," Corfe said haltingly.

"Thank you. And Corfe, your men may be in the rear, but they will have the hardest job in the days ahead, make no mistake about it." And he walked away without further ceremony.

"HERE," Andruw said, offering him the wineskin. "You look as though you could use a snort. What did they do, overwhelm you with their strategic brilliance?"

Corfe squeezed a stream of acrid army wine into his mouth. "Lord, Andruw, I needed that."

Seated about the campfire were most of his senior officers. He had asked them to await his return from the conference. They looked at him expectantly. In addition to Andruw, Marsch was there, and Morin beside him. Formio stood warming his hands at the flames next to Ranafast, and Ebro had paused in the process of whittling a stick to stare at his commanding officer. In the shadows beyond were many others. Corfe thought he saw Joshelin, the Fimbrian veteran, and Cerne, his trumpeter. His very heart warmed at the sight of them, doing away with some of the chill generated by Menin's words. With the loyalty of men such as these, he felt he could accomplish almost anything.

"We pitch into them in two days, lads," he said at last. "Ebro, give me your stick. Gather round, everyone. Here's how we're going to do it."

TWENTY-ONE

DAWN over Northern Torunna. In the Merduk camps the sentries were being changed and men were stirring the embers of their campfires in preparation for breakfast. Along the horse-lines thousands of animals were champing on hay and oats and generating a steam of damp warmth into the frigid air. Supply wagons came and went in sluggish convoys. Over the tented cities of the Merduks a haze of smoke and vapour rose skywards, visible for many miles despite the low cloud. The conical tents sprawled for hundreds of acres, and streets had been laid down between their rows, fashioned of corduroyed logs. Women and children were visible, and there were market places and bazaars in the midst of the encampments where canny traders which followed the armies had set up their stalls. The three vast winter camps of the Merduks were as peaceful looking as military settlements could possibly be. It was commonly known that the cowardly Torunnans were lurking behind the walls of their capital, preparing for the inevitable siege. There were no enemy formations for leagues around, apart from a few isolated bodies of cavalry. In a week or two the tent cities would be broken up and the armies would be on the move again, but for now the soldiers of the Sultan were more preoccupied with the problems of keeping warm and dry and well fed in the barbarous Torunnan winter.

Shahr Indun Johor, senior khedive of the Sultan's forces, had his headquarters tent in the midst of the encampments of the *Hraibadar* and the *Ferinai*, the elite of the army. Rank had its privileges, and he was dozing with his head between the breasts of his favourite concubine when his subadar, or head staff officer, poked his head around the heavy curtains of the tent.

"Shahr Johor." And again when there was no answer: "Shahr Johor!"

He stirred, a young, lean man, dark and quick as an otter. "What? What is it, Buraz?"

"It may be nothing, my Khedive. Some of the perimeter guards report gunfire coming from the west."

"I'll be a moment. See my horse is saddled." Shahr Johor threw aside his grumbling concubine and hauled on his breeches and tunic. He wrapped a sash about his middle, thrust a poniard in the folds and pulled on his heavy knee-high riding boots. Then he kissed his scented bed partner. "Later, my dove," he murmured, and strode out of the tent into the raw half-light of dawn.

Buraz awaited him with two saddled horses, their

breaths steaming in the cold. The two officers mounted and cantered off to the perimeter of the vast camp, scattering soldiers and camp followers as they clattered along the timbered road. He sat in the saddle, breathing hard, staring at the empty horizon. It was still so gloomy that he could see the glare of the *Minhraib*'s campfires against the cloudy sky, three miles away. Thin flakes of snow had begun to fall, and there was more in the lowering nimbus overhead.

"I hear nothing. Who reported this?"

A *Hraibadar* sergeant stepped forward, a veteran with a hard, seamed face and black eyes. "I did, my Khedive. It comes and goes. If you wait, you have my word, you will hear it."

They sat still, listening, whilst behind them the great camp and its tens of thousands of occupants came to life in the growing light. And at last Shahr Johor caught it. A distant, intermittent thunder rolling in from the west, the fainter crackle of what might have been volley fire.

"Artillery," Buraz said.

"Yes. And massed arquebusiers. There is a battle going on out there, Buraz."

"It may be only a raid, a skirmish."

They both listened again. The *Hraibadar* sergeant angrily called for silence and around the two officers hundreds of men stopped what they were doing and paused, listening also.

The faraway thunder intensified. Everyone could hear it now. It seemed to echo off the face of the very hills.

"That is no skirmish," Shahr Johor said. "It is a full-scale engagement, Buraz. The Unbelievers have attacked the *Minhraib* camp."

"Would they dare?" his subordinate asked incredulously.

"It would seem so. Get me a trumpeter. Sound the alarm. I want the army ready to move immediately. And send a courier off to the Sultan in the northern camp. We will chastise these infidels for their impertinence. I shall come down on their flank with the *Ferinai*. You follow with the infantry. Make haste, Buraz!"

THE *Minhraib* camp was a rough square, a mile and a half to a side. It lay on a gently undulating plain criss-crossed with small watercourses and dotted with copses of alder and willow where the ground was wet. To the east of it a small range of hills rose to perhaps four or five hundred feet, and on these heights a smaller camp of perhaps a thousand men had been pitched to dominate the ground below and safeguard communications with the other Merduk camp to the east. The main encampment was a huge sea of tents bisected by muddy roads, with corrals for the pack animals to the north. South-west of it, on a slight rise, was a long string of scattered woods, perhaps two miles from the first lines of tents. In these woods, the Torunnan army shook out from column into line of battle.

THREE great formations of men emerged from the woods as the sky lightened steadily above their heads. They were late. The approach to the enemy was meant to be made under cover of the pre-dawn dark-

ness, but it had, inevitably, taken longer than expected
to reform thirty thousand men in the dark, and now
they had two flat and open miles to march at the quick-
time before they would come to blows with the Merduks.

Out in front of the main body, batteries of galloper
guns under Colonel Rusio had dashed ahead and were
unlimbering a mile from the enemy lines. Soon the
little six-pounders were barking and smoking furiously,
generating bloody chaos in the camp, flattening tents,
shattering men.

Behind them the King's formation, eighteen thousand strong, advanced at the double. The battle-line
was on average six ranks deep, and it stretched for
almost two miles, a dark, bristling, clanging apocalypse
of heavily armoured men and horses. The earth shook
under their feet, and in the centre the heavy sable-clad
cuirassiers were ranged under the banners of the King
and his noble bodyguard.

Off to the east, perhaps a mile from the main body,
Colonel Aras's five thousand were advancing also,
their target the small Merduk camp on the hills. They
were to take the camp, and hold the heights against the
arrival of any enemy reinforcements. Aras's men were
lightly armoured, swift moving, and they trailed
streamers of smoke from the slow-match of their arquebusiers so that it looked as though they were burning a path across the land as they came.

And behind the main fighting line, another formation. Seven thousand foot and a thousand horse—
Corfe's men, in a deep body only some two thirds of
a mile long. He was stationed on the left of his line
with the Cathedrallers, the Fimbrians were on the right,

ten deep, and his dyke veterans were in the centre. Behind them, in the woods, were the hundreds of wagons which comprised the baggage train. Field surgeons and their assistants were busy amid the vehicles setting out their instruments, and crowds of wagoneers were frantically unpacking crates of shot, barrels of gunpowder. Scores of light galloper carts stood in their midst, ready to start the ferrying forward of ammunition and the ferrying backwards of casualties to the rear aid stations. A thousand men worked busily there, and Corfe had also left behind two hundred arquebusiers in case small bodies of the enemy should break through the front lines.

He halted his command when it was a mile from the Merduk camp. The roar of the artillery had begun to intensify. He could see the frenzied activity in the midst of the tented city, officers trying to get clotted crowds of men into battle-line only to have the artillery blow them apart as soon as they had dressed their ranks. The main Torunnan line advanced inexorably to the dull thunder of the infantry drums and a braying of army bugles. It looked as though nothing on earth would be able to stop it. Corfe felt a moment of pure, savage exultation, a fierce, dizzying joy at the sight of the advancing Torunnan army. If there was any glory in war, it was in spectacles such as this, neat lines of men advancing like chess pieces on the gameboard of the world. Once you took a closer look the glory died, and there was only the scarlet carnage, the agonizing misery of men dying and being maimed in their thousands.

The King's formation was passing through the galloper batteries now. The squat guns fired only on a flat

trajectory and thus were masked by their own troops
as the advance continued. The gunners leaned on their
pieces and cheered as their comrades passed by. Had
they no further orders? Corfe scowled. Thirty guns left
sitting idle. It was an incompetent oversight, and tech-
nically he outranked Colonel Rusio, the artillery commander. He reached in his saddlebag for pencil and
paper, scrawled a message and sent it off to the idle
batteries. A few minutes later, the gunners began lim-
bering their pieces and withdrawing up the slope towards Corfe's command. He could see Rusio in their
midst, shouting orders, helmless. The grey-haired officer looked furious. Too bad. Corfe would find him
something better to do than sit on his hands for the
remainder of the battle.

Farther away on the plain, the main Torunnan formation had halted a scant two hundred yards from the
Merduk camp, and the entire battle-line erupted with
smoke as the massed arquebusiers let off a volley. A
second later, the stuttering crackle of it could be heard.
Then there was a huge, formless roar as the line
charged, eighteen thousand men shouting their heads
off as they slammed into the Merduk camp at a run.

Corfe could see the wedge of three thousand heavy
cavalry, the King's banner at its head, forging ahead
of the rest. Horses going down already, no doubt tripping on downed tents and guy-ropes. The disorganized
unfortunates of the *Minhraib* had no chance. They presented a ragged line, which disintegrated into a howling mob, then a crowd of fleeing individuals. In
minutes, the Torunnans had smashed deep into the enemy encampment and were carrying all before them.
But now their own lines had become splintered and

disorganized. The fighting inside the complex of tents degenerated into a massive free-for-all, and in the thick of it the King and his cuirassiers rampaged like dreadful animated engines of slaughter. Lofantyr had courage, Corfe thought. You had to give him that.

Corfe looked at the right, where another, smaller struggle had begun on the eastern hills. Aras had his men advancing in a perfect line, firing as they went. The Merduks in the hill camp, outnumbered five to one, nevertheless rushed down to meet them. They had few or no firearms and so had to try and engage at close quarters. They were cut down in windrows by exact volleys, and the survivors, a beaten rabble, fled the field. Aras advanced his men up to the hilltops and arranged them for defence.

"I hope he digs in," Corfe muttered. He felt uneasy about the small size of Aras's force. Soon they would have to cover the withdrawal of the King's formation, and if the enemy came in any strength from the east they would have a hard time of it.

"Colonel Rusio reporting, *as ordered*," a voice spat. Corfe turned. Rusio and his guns had reached his position. The older officer was glaring at him, but there was no time to massage his ego.

"Take your guns over to Aras's position and make ready to repel an attack on the hills, Colonel," Corfe said briskly. "How much ammunition is left in your limbers?"

"Ten rounds per gun."

"Then I suggest you send galloper carts back to the baggage for resupply. You'll need every round you can muster in a little while."

"With respect, *sir*, we seem to be driving them beautifully. I was given no such orders in my briefing. I don't see why—"

"Do as you're damn well told!" Corfe snapped, his patience fraying. "This is an army, not a debating chamber. Go!"

Rusio, Corfe's elder by thirty years, glared venomously again, then spun his horse off without another word and began bellowing at his gun teams. Thirty guns, each pulled by eight horses, pounded off eastwards.

The Merduk camp was wreathed in a pall of smoke. Flames glowed sullenly at its base and tiny black figures flickered in mobs like throngs of ants. It would be utter chaos in there, Corfe thought, as bad for the attackers as the defenders. But chaos favoured the smaller army. It was easier to control eighteen thousand in that toiling hell than ninety thousand. So far, so good.

It was full daylight now, a dull morning low with cloud, the snow showers coming and going. The trained warhorses of the Cathedrallers were restless and sweating despite the cold; they could smell the stink of battle, and their blood was up. The men were much the same, and the ranks of horsemen buzzed with talk. In the centre of Corfe's line the dyke veterans had their arquebuses primed and ready, laid on the Y-shaped gunrests they had stabbed into the ground before them. And on the far right the black-armoured Fimbrians stood like raven statues, their pikes at the vertical.

Andruw cantered over and doffed his helm. "What's our job in all this, Corfe?" he asked. "To make notes?" He had to shout to be heard over the titanic din of battle.

"Hold your water, Andruw. This thing is only just begun."

Andruw joined his general in staring out at the left of the battlefield, to the west of the Merduk camp. Men were streaming away there, fleeing enemy trying to escape the murderous hell within the tent lines, tercios of Torunnans firing at their backs as they ran. But beyond them there was only a huge stretch of empty hill and moorland, completely deserted.

"You think they'll hit the left?" Andruw asked.

"Wouldn't you? We're killing conscripts at the moment. The professionals have yet to arrive. Aras will hold on the right I think, what with Rusio's guns and the terrain. But the left is another thing entirely. We have nothing there, Andruw, nothing. If the Sultan makes even a cursory reconnaissance, he'll realize that and he'll come roaring down on us there."

"And then?"

"And then—well, we'll have a fight on our hands."

"That's why you've kept us so far back. You think we'll have to move up to support the left."

"I hope not, but it's as well to be prepared."

"Aye. At any rate, the King is doing his job. Another hour and he'll have wiped half the Merduk army off the map."

"Getting into the fight is one thing, getting out is something else."

"Do I detect a note of envy, Corfe?" Andruw grinned.

"It's a glorious charge, but I wish he'd stop and take stock for a minute. The army is hopelessly disorganized in there. It'll take hours to reform them and withdraw." Corfe smiled. "All right, maybe I envy him his glory a little."

"Give him his due, he took them in there like a veteran. I'd best get back to my wing. Cheer up, Corfe! We're making history, after all." And he galloped off.

Corfe sat his restive horse another half an hour. The fighting in the *Minhraib* camp went on unabated, though it had spilled out on to the plain beyond the tents. He could see Torunnan arquebusiers and cuirassiers fighting intermingled, banners flashing bright through the smoke. Beyond the camp a great cloud of men took shape as the *Minhraib* abandoned the tent lines and strove to reform in the open ground to the north-west. Twenty, thirty thousand of them dressing their ranks unmolested whilst the Torunnans were embroiled in the terrible struggle within the camp. The enemy had taken huge losses, but he had the numbers to sustain them and he was bringing some order out of chaos at last. It was time to get out. The Merduk reinforcements would be on the march by now.

A courier emerged from the cauldron, beating his half-dead horse up the slope towards Corfe's line. Corfe cantered out to meet him. The man was a cuirassier. His mount was slashed in half a dozen places and his armour was a pitted mass of dents and scrapes. He saluted.

"Beg pardon, sir—" He fought for breath. "But the King, the King—"

"Take your time, trooper," Corfe said gently. "Cerne! Give this man some water."

His trumpeter handed the man his waterskin and the courier squirted half a pint into his smoke-parched mouth. He wiped his lips.

"Sir, the King wants your men in the camp right away. The enemy is fleeing before him but his own men are exhausted. He wants you to take up the pursuit. You must bring the entire reserve into the enemy camp and finish the buggers off—begging your pardon, sir."

Corfe blinked. "The King, you say?"

"Yes, sir, at once, sir. He says we'll bag the whole lot if only you make haste."

Just then a heavy fusillade of gun and artillery fire broke out on the right. Aras's men had opened up on an unseen enemy below them. Corfe called for Andruw.

"Have a courier sent to Aras. I want to know the strengths and dispositions of the enemy he's firing at, and his best estimate as to how long he can hold them. And Andruw, tell Marsch to take a squadron out on the left a mile or two. I want advance warning if they start coming in on us from there." Andruw saluted and sped off towards the ranks. Corfe fished out his pencil and grubby paper again and used the thigh-guard of his armour as a desk.

"What's your name, soldier?" he asked the battered courier.

"Holman, sir."

"Well, Holman, take a look at the land beyond the Merduk camp, to the north. What do you see?"

"Why, General, it's an army, another Merduk army forming. Looks like it's going to attack our lads in the tents!"

"It's not another army, it's the one you've been fighting, but so far you've only tackled the half of it. The other half has withdrawn and has been reorgan-

izing for the better part of an hour. Soon, it'll be ready
to charge back into its camp and retake it. And now
Merduk reinforcements have arrived on the right,
also. You must tell the King that his position is unten-
able. I cannot reinforce him—he must withdraw at
once. And I want you to take this to General Menin
first, Holman. It's absolutely vital this message gets
through. The army *must* withdraw, or it will be destroyed. Do you understand me, soldier?"

Holman was wide-eyed. "Yes, General."

"My command will cover the retreat for as long as
we can, but the main body has to fall back at once."

"Yes, sir." Holman was eager and appalled. Down
in the hellish mêlée of the Merduk camp no one had
noticed the Merduk thousands beyond preparing for a
counter-attack. Corfe did not envy the young man his
errand. The King would explode, but Menin would
probably see sense.

Holman thundered off, his tired mount rolling like a
ship on a heavy swell. At the same time Marsch and
his squadron set off north-westwards to keep an eye
on the left flank. Corfe slammed one gauntleted fist
into another. To sit here, doing nothing, galled him
beyond measure. He half wished he were a junior officer again, doing as he was told, in the thick of it.

The courier from Aras, a tribesman whose mount
was blowing foam, stamping and snorting. He handed
his general a scrap of paper, saluted awkwardly and
rejoined the ranks.

6–8000 to my front, all cavalry—the Ferinai *I
believe. A body of infantry visible several miles
behind. Artillery keeping them at a distance for*

*now. They are massing for general assault. Can
hold another hour or two, not more. Aras.*

"Lord God," Corfe said softly. The Merduk khedive
had been quick off the mark.

He kicked his mount into motion and cantered along
the battle-line until he reached the Fimbrians. His men
cheered as he passed and he waved a hand absently at
them, his mind turning furiously.

"Formio? Where are you?"

"Here, General." The slim Fimbrian officer stepped
out from the midst of his men. Like them, he bore a
pike. Only the sash about his middle differentiated him
from a private soldier.

"Take your men out to the hills in the east and reinforce Colonel Aras. He's up against heavy cavalry—
your pikes will keep them at bay. You have to buy us
time, Formio. You must hold that position until you
hear otherwise from me. Is that clear?"

"Perfectly, General."

"Good luck."

A series of shouted commands, a bugle call, and the
Fimbrians moved into march column and then stepped
off as smoothly as a great machine, every component
perfect. Corfe hated splitting his command, but Aras
would not be able to hold for long enough by himself.
He felt like a man trying frantically to repair a leak in
a dyke, but every time he plugged a hole in one place,
the water erupted out of another.

Andruw joined him again. "I have a feeling there's
hot work approaching," he said, almost merry. Action
always did that to him.

"They'll hit the left next," Corfe told him. "And if

they hit it hard, I'll have to commit the rest of the command. There are no more reserves."

"You think we've bitten off more than we can swallow?"

Corfe did not answer. He could feel time slipping away minute by minute as though it were his lifeblood ebbing from his veins. And with the passing of that time, the army's chances of survival grew ever slimmer.

TWENTY-TWO

AURUNGZEB had not ridden a horse any distance for longer than he cared to admit. His thighs were chafing and his buttocks felt like a pair of purple bruises. But he sat straight in the saddle, mindful of his station, and ignored the snow which was thickening in his beard.

"Blood of the Prophet!" he exclaimed, exasperated. "Can't they move any faster?"

Shahr Harran, his second khedive, sat a horse with more obvious ease beside him. "It takes time, Highness, to get an army on the march. These things always appear slow at first, but the Torunnans will be embroiled for hours yet. Our scouts report that they are fighting square in the midst of the *Minhraib* camp—they have their heavy cavalry engaged right among the tents, the fools. They will not escape us, never fear. And their left flank is still unguarded."

"What of those damned red-armoured horsemen everyone is so terrified of? Where are they?"

"To the enemy rear, my Sultan, in reserve. And they number scarcely a thousand. We are sending in twenty thousand Nalbenic horse-archers on their left and Shahr Johor should be assaulting their right with the *Ferinai* any time now. The Torunnans cannot escape. We will destroy their army utterly, and it is the last field army their kingdom can possibly muster."

"Oh, hold the damn thing straight, can't you?" the Sultan barked. This to the unfortunates who were striving to shield their lord from the spitting snow with a huge parasol, but the wind was wagging it like a kite above Aurungzeb's head. "I am sure you are right, Shahr Harran; it is just that lately I have had my khedives assure me of Torunnan annihilation many times, and always the accursed Ramusians seem to be able to salvage their armies with some last-minute trick. It must not happen this time."

"It will not. It cannot," Shahr Harran assured him.

The two riders were surrounded by hundreds of others in silvered mail—the Sultan's personal bodyguard. Beyond them a steady stream of lightly armoured cavalry trotted past endlessly. These were unarmoured, though well wrapped up against the cold. Their horses were light, high-stepping, delicate-looking creatures built for speed. The riders were dark men as fine boned as their steeds, armed with bows and with quivers of black-fletched arrows hanging from their pommels.

"Where is my intrepid infidel?" Aurungzeb asked in a lighter tone. "I must hear what he thinks of this array."

A small, dark figure on a mule rode to Aurungzeb's

side. He was dressed in the habit of a Ramusian monk and his face was hideously disfigured.

"Sultan?"

"Ah, priest. How does it feel to look upon the might of Ostrabar, and know it shall soon accomplish the spiritual liberation of your benighted nation? Spreak freely. I value the nonsense you spout. It reminds me how hopelessly misled you Ramusians are."

Albrec smiled strangely. "Not only the Ramusians, Sultan, but your own people too. Both peoples worship the same God and venerate the same man as his messenger. It is the pity of the world that you war on each other over an ancient misunderstanding. A lie. One day both Merduk and Ramusian will have to come to terms with this."

"Why you arrogant little—" Shahr Harran sputtered, but Aurungzeb held up a hand that flashed with rings.

"Now, Khedive, this maniac came to us in good faith, to show us the error of our ways. He is as good a jester as I have ever had." The Sultan laughed loudly. "Priest, you have spirit. It is a shame you are mad. Keep up your insane pronouncements and you may even live to see the spring, if you do not endeavour to escape first." And he laughed again.

Albrec bowed in the saddle. His feet had been lashed to his stirrups and the mule was connected by a leading rein to a nearby warrior's destrier. Escape was a possibility so remote as to be laughable. But he did not want to escape. He would not have chosen to be anywhere else. His ravaged face was impassive as he watched the mighty army that coursed endlessly past— and this, he had learned, was only one third of the whole, and not the greatest third at that. His heart

twisted in his breast at the thought of the slaughter that
would soon begin. Torunna could never hope to win
this awful war through force of arms alone. His mission among the Merduks was more important than
ever.

They had beaten him, the night he staggered into
their camp on the wings of the storm, and he had almost been slain out of hand. But some officer had been
intrigued by his appearance, thinking him perhaps a
turncoat who might have useful information, and he
had been sent to the Sultan's camp, and beaten again.
At last the Sultan himself had been curious to see this
strange traveller. Aurungzeb spoke Normannic well
enough to need no interpreter. Albrec wondered who
had taught him—some captured Ramusian or other, he
supposed. The Sultan had been first astonished and
then intensely amused when Albrec had told him of his
mission: to convince the Merduk peoples that their
Prophet was one and the same as the Ramusian's
Blessed Saint. He had called in a pair of Mullahs—
learned Merduk clerics—and Albrec had debated with
them all night, leaving them as astonished as the Sultan. For Albrec had read every scrap he could find
about the Merduks and their history, both at Charibon
and then in the smaller library in Torunn. He knew
Aurungzeb's pedigree and clan history better than the
Sultan did himself, and the monarch had been oddly
flattered by the knowledge. He had kept Albrec in light
chains in the Royal pavilion, for all the world like a
performing bear, and when the army's officers assembled for conferences, Albrec had been there and was
told to stand up and do his party piece for the amusement of his captors.

Many of the men he had spoken before had not been amused, however. What the Sultan considered a diverting madman, others deemed a blasphemer worthy of a lingering death. And still others said nothing, but looked troubled and confused as Albrec told of the Blessed Ramusio's coming into the eastern lands beyond the Jafrar, his teachings, his transformation into the Prophet who had enlightened the eastern tribes and brought to an end their petty internecine warfare, moulding them into the mighty hosts which threatened the world today.

There had been a woman present on one of these occasions, one of the Sultan's wives, dressed as richly as a queen, veiled, silent. Her eyes had never left Albrec's face as the little monk had gone through his sermon. The light-coloured eyes of a westerner. There was a despair in them, a sense of loss which wrenched at his heart. He seemed to remember seeing the same look in someone else's eyes once, but he could not for the life of him remember whose.

The distant roar of battle jerked his mind back to the present. The Sultan was talking to him again.

"So do you know who this general is who leads these red-clad horsemen, priest? My spies tell me nothing of use. I know that the Torunnan King is no phoenix, and his High Command are a bunch of old women, and yet against all expectations they have come out to fight us. Someone among them is a true warrior at least."

"I know little more than you, Sultan. I have met this general you speak of, though."

Aurungzeb twisted in the saddle, eyes alight with interest. "You have? What manner of man is he?"

"It was a brief meeting. He is—" Suddenly Albrec remembered. That look he had seen in a woman's eyes, above a veil. Now he knew who it reminded him of. "He is a singular man. There is a sadness to him, I think." He recalled the hard grey eyes of the officer named Corfe he had encountered outside Torunn, the line of scarlet, barbaric cavalry behind him, passing by like something out of legend.

"A sadness! What a fellow you are, priest. By all accounts he is their best general since Mogen, and a raging fury in the saddle. I should like to meet him. Perhaps I will order him to be kept alive after we have broken his army." And Aurungzeb chuckled to himself. "Listen to me! I am becoming like Shahr Baraz, chivalrous towards enemies."

"Magnanimity becomes a great ruler, Sultan," Albrec told him. "Only lesser men indulge their cruelty."

"What is that, one of your Saint's platitudes?"

"No. It is a saying of your Prophet."

ANOTHER courier, the snow freezing on his shoulders and matting his horse's mane. "I come from Marsch," he said, and pointed westwards to reinforce the statement.

"Well?" Corfe demanded.

"Many, many horsemen coming. Small horses, men with bows."

"How many? How far?"

The courier wrinkled his tattooed face. "Marsch tell me," he said, "as many as the King's army, or more, coming from the north-west. In one hour they will be here." His face relaxed. He was obviously relieved to have got it out without mishap.

"Men with bows," Andruw said thoughtfully. "Horse-archers. That'll be the Nalbenic contingent. And if they have as many as the King commands . . ."

"Eighteen, twenty thousand," Corfe said tonelessly.

"Damn it, Corfe, we're finished then. Menin and the King have started to reorganize down in the camp, but there's no way they can get their men out in an hour."

"Then we'll have to take them on ourselves," Corfe said flatly.

Andruw managed a rueful grin. "I know we're good at beating the odds, but don't you think we're pushing what luck we have left? We don't even have the Fimbrians now. Just the Cathedrallers and Ranafast's men. Six thousand."

"We've no choice. They have to be thrown back before they can come in on our left. If they do that, the entire army will be surrounded."

"How?" Andruw asked simply.

Corfe kicked his mount forward a few yards. He had learned many things about the nature of war in the last few months. It was like any other field of human endeavour: often appearance was as important as reality. And guile more important than brute strength.

Charge horse-archers with his heavy cavalry? Suicide. The enemy would simply fall back, shooting as they retreated. They would wear his men down with arrow fire and never let them come to grips. He had to pin them in place somehow, and then hit them hard at close quarters where the weight and armour of his men would make up for their lack of numbers. Fight fire with fire, he realized. Fire with fire. And he had five thousand veteran arquebusiers from Ormann Dyke under his command.

He scanned the huge battlefield before him. Down in the wreckage of the *Minhraib* camp the fighting was still going on, but it seemed to have abated somewhat. Both armies were trying to reorganize and he could see crowds of Torunnan troops being dressed back into disciplined lines. Fully half the tents in the vast camp seemed to have been flattened, and fires were burning everywhere, smoke hanging in great sodden grey banks. Beyond the camp, the *Minhraib* survivors had almost completed their own rebuilt battle-line. They would counter-attack soon. But that was not his problem right now. One thing at a time.

Over to the east, Aras and the Fimbrians were struggling to contain the Merduk flanking column. Formio had mingled his pikemen with Aras's arquebusiers and Rosio's guns. The position was enveloped in a pall of smoke which the flickering stabs of gunfire lit up red and yellow, but the westerners were holding. Corfe knew that Formio would not retreat a yard. The right flank was safe, for the time being.

So the left—the left was where disaster loomed most clearly. How to cripple this new threat with the few men he had remaining to him . . .

It came to him all at once. Guile, not force. And he knew exactly what he had to do. He jerked his horse round to face Andruw.

"We're moving out. I want Ranafast's men to lead the way, at the double. Andruw, you take the Cathedrallers off to their left. I'll explain as we go along."

TWENTY-THREE

A VAST cavalcade of horsemen, numerous as a locust swarm. There was no order in their ranks and as they trotted along they jostled one another and expanded and contracted with ever dip in the terrain. They had a frontage of half a mile, but as they advanced the rear ranks broke into a canter and began to move up to left and right, extending that yard by yard. By the time they had come within sight of the *Minhraib* camp and the battle that was tapering off there, they had expanded into a great arc, a shallow new-moon sickle which stretched almost half a league from tip to tip and whose coming seemed to make the frozen earth quake and quiver below their hooves. Twenty thousand of Nalbeni's finest men, come here in alliance with the Sultanate of Ostrabar to close the trap on the enemy and grind the Torunnans into the snow.

Corfe watched them from the trees, and could not

help but feel a kind of admiration. They were a magnificent sight. In these days of cannon and gunpowder they were like something out of the barbaric past, but he knew that their powerful compound bows had virtually the range of an arquebus, and were easier to reload. They had teeth in plenty.

Behind him, hidden in the line of trees which extended all the way to the rear of the Torunnan line, his Cathedrallers waited with growing impatience. The Nalbenic horsemen would sweep past them on their way to take the King's forces in the flank. He in turn would attack them in the rear, and hit them hard. But first they had to be halted. They had to meet the anvil before the hammer could fall.

And the anvil was in place, awaiting their arrival.

Clouds and spumes of powdery snow were blowing across the slopes of the hills. The sky had lightened a little, but the day had become much colder and Corfe's breath was wreathing a white filigree about the front of his helm. The blowing snow would cover the fume of four thousand coils of burning match. Ranafast and his men, in two ranks over a mile long, lying out there somewhere in the snow, waiting. Corfe's anvil.

He had found them a long reverse slope where they could lie hidden until the last moment, and the blowing snow had quickly broken up the stark blackness of their uniforms. It would be cold out there on the hard ground with the rime blowing in their faces, but they would have warm work soon enough. How long had the fighting been going on? It seemed to have lasted for ever, and yet Corfe's sword had not yet cleared its scabbard. That was part of the price of command: ordering other men to die while you watched.

Not for much longer, by God. Soon the enemy—

A huge tearing sound, like heavy fabric being ripped. Off to the right a wall of smoke rose. Ranafast's men had fired.

Corfe sat up in the saddle. His horse was dancing under him. He drew out Mogen's sword and held it upright. He could feel the eyes of his men on him in anticipation of the signal. It was like sitting with one's back to a bulging dam, waiting for it to burst.

The lead ranks of the Nalbenic horsemen looked as though they had simultaneously hit a tripwire. Ranafast had fired at point-blank range—less than a hundred yards. As Corfe watched, the second rank fired. He could faintly hear the commands in the brief moments between volleys: "Ready your pieces! Prime your pieces! Give fire!"

The enemy had been halted as if they had slammed into a stone wall. They milled there for a few deadly minutes with the heavy lead bullets snicking and ripping and slamming into them. Horses screaming, rearing, kicking, tumbling to the snow, men jerking as the heavy balls impacted, flying out of the saddle, shrieking, grasping at bloody holes. The press of animals was so great that the riders who were being decimated at the front could not retreat from the murderous fire. Showers of arrows were fired, but Ranafast's men were lying down and presented a minuscule target. The thousands of horsemen in the fore of the Nalbenic host were caught there like a beetle on a pin, the victim of their own numbers. In the space of a hundred heartbeats a veritable wall of writhing bodies built up, hundreds, thousands of them. It was one of the most ghastly things Corfe had ever seen. With a flash of intuition he realized he was looking at the death of cavalry—of all cavalry.

But it was not enough. The work had to be completed. The Nalbenic formation was beginning to become more fluid. They were backing away, rear ranks streaming in retreat so the wretches at the front could get clear of the withering barrage. Soon they would open out, find the ends of Ranafast's line and envelop him. They had to be packed together again, forced back upon the anvil.

Corfe brought down Mogen's sabre. *"Charge!"*

The hammer fell.

THE King of Torunna wiped the soot from his face and, grimacing, realized that his gauntlet had been dripping with blood. He was trembling with fatigue and his armour seemed twice its normal weight. He was mounted on his third horse of the day, his ankle so badly twisted by the headlong fall of the first that he could no longer walk. His crowned helm had given him an almighty headache and below it the sweat ran in streams. His throat was dry as sand, and his voice had become a croak.

Around him the remains of his three thousand cuirassiers clustered. Two thirds of them were dead or too injured to lift a sword, and nine tenths of them were afoot. They had been in the forefront of the attack all morning and had performed wonders. He was proud of them—he was secretly proud of himself. His first battle, his first charge, and he had acquitted himself as a king should, he thought.

The rest of the army was reforming, crowds of men being harangued into line by their surviving officers.

The *Minhraib* had withdrawn for the moment, and the camp was his, what was left of it. It was a dreary, smoking wasteland strewn with mounded corpses, collapsed tents and dead horses, shrouded in smoke. Here and there the wounded writhed and wailed, but there were not many of those. No quarter had been asked or given, and when a man on either side fell helpless he would find his throat cut soon after. There was a sputtering of arquebus fire where the perimeter tercios were still contending with the enemy out in the smoke, but for the most part the army had fallen back to reform and prepare for the final push. Now where were those damned reinforcements he had ordered?

Lofantyr could hear the glorious, sullen rumble of war continuing off to the right, where Aras and his men were fighting off the Merduk relief column. Nothing on the left as yet. Or was that arquebus fire he heard out there? No, it was too far away. An echo, no doubt. He had been right not to worry about the left flank. And they thought he was no strategist!

General Menin trudged wearily over, saluted. His sword arm was bloody to the elbow.

"Ah, General, what is the delay? Where is General Cear-Inaf and our reserve? The courier went out an hour ago."

An enormous clatter of musketry to their front, the roaring of a host of men in onset. The ranks of the Torunnans stiffened, and they strained to see through the murk and reek. Of the eighteen thousand the King had led into the camp, perhaps twelve thousand remained, but they had inflicted four or five times their own casualties on the enemy. Those twelve thousand were now arrayed in an untidy line a mile long. In some places the line was only two ranks deep, in others a veritable mob would gather, exhausted and injured men drawing together, taking reassurance out of the proximity of others. The army was spent, and it was hardly midafternoon on the longest day most of them had ever known.

"The courier returned a few minutes ago, sire."

"I see. And why did he not report to me?"

Menin leaned against the flank of the King's horse. He spoke quietly.

"Sire, Corfe is witholding the reserve. He fears for the left flank. Also, he informs me that the *Minhraib* are about to counter-attack." The general glanced northwards, to where the sound of battle was rising to a roar in the smoke. "In fact they may well be doing so already. He advises us to withdraw at once. I concur, and have already given the necessary orders."

"You have *what*? You exceed your authority, General. We are on the edge of a famous victory. One more push will see the day ours. We need Cear-Inaf's reserve here, now."

"Sire, listen to me. We have shot our bolt. According to General Cear-Inaf, thirty to forty thousand of the *Minhraib* have reformed on the northern edge of the camp and will be about our ears any minute. Aras is fighting for his life on the right, and Corfe *must* keep the reserve ready to face any new eventualities. We must fall back at once."

"By God, General—"

But his words were drowned. The clatter out in the smoke had risen to a crescendo, and men were appearing in ones and twos, running. Torunnan arquebusiers in confused flight, throwing away their weapons as they ran. And behind them the formless clamour of a great host of men, shouting.

"Too late," Menin said. "Here they come. Men! Prepare to repel an attack!"

The exhausted soldiers braced themselves.

"Sire, you should go to the rear," Menin urged Lofantyr. "I do not know if we can hold."

"What? Nonsense! I'll lead another charge. We'll see who—"

The western line erupted in a ragged volley as the lead elements of the enemy came thundering into view. Too soon—the Merduks were still out of range. But they were bowling forward, an unstoppable wave of armoured infantry under the bobbing horsetail standards. Tens of thousands of them.

The King's face paled at the sight. "My God! I did not think there were so many left," he croaked.

The two armies met in an appalling roar. It was hand-to-hand at once all down the line, the Torunnan arquebusiers unable to reload their weapons fast enough to keep the *Minhraib* at a distance.

Murderous, lunging chaos around the King as an entire enemy regiment homed in on the Royal standard. The more lightly armed Torunnans there were swept away by the fury of the Merduk onset, leaving the iron-clad cuirassiers standing alone like an island, swinging their heavy cavalry sabres to terrible effect. In moments the entire Torunnan battle-line had been thrown back. Menin and Lofantyr found themselves surrounded, cut off from the main body of the army.

Lofantyr's mind froze. He sat his terrified horse and watched as the Merduks flung themselves upon the ranks of his bodyguard with suicidal abandon. The

heavily armoured knights were slaughtering their attackers, but they were being overwhelmed. Three or
four of the enemy would throw themselves upon each
armoured Torunnan, bear him down to the ground under their bodies, then rip off his helm and slit his throat.

"We are finished," Menin said.

Lofantyr read the words on his lips, though the din
of battle suffocated the sound of his voice. Menin was
smiling. Panic rose like a cloud in Lofantyr's throat.
He would die? He, the King? It was impossible.

One of the enemy broke through the shrinking cuirassier cordon and dived at the King's horse. A tulwar
glittered and the animal screamed as it was hamstrung.
Menin decapitated the man, but the King was down.
The warhorse crashed, kicking, on to its side, trapping
Lofantyr's leg beneath it. He felt the bones wrench and
shatter, and screamed, but his shriek was lost in the
cacophony that surrounded him.

Menin was standing over him, hewing like a titan.
Bodies were falling everywhere, men squirming in the
snow and muck. An unbelievable tumult, a pitch of
savagery and slaughter Lofantyr had not believed men
could endure. He scrabbled feebly for the sword that
had been his father's, a Royal heirloom, but it was
gone. He felt no pain or fear, only a kind of crazed
incredulity. He could not believe this was happening.

He saw four Merduks bring Menin down, the old
general fighting to the last. They stabbed a poniard
through one of his eyes and finally quelled his strug-
gles. Where were the rest of the bodyguard? There was
no line now, only a few knots of men in a sea of the
enemy. The last of the cuirassiers were being torn
down like bears beset by hounds.

Someone ripped off Lofantyr's helm. He found himself looking into a man's face. A young man, the eyes dark and wild, foam at the corners of the mouth. Lofantyr tried to raise an arm, but someone was standing on his wrist. He saw the knife and tried to protest, but then the swift-stabbing blade came down and his life was over.

TWENTY-FOUR

O F the eighteen thousand Torunnans who had
charged into the enemy camp that morning, perhaps half made it back out again. They withdrew dog-
gedly, stubbornly, contesting every bloody foot of
ground. The word of the King's death had not yet
spread, and there was no panic despite the incessant
fearfulness of the *Minhraib* counter-attack. Field officers and junior officers took over, for the entire High
Command lay dead upon the field, and brought their
men out of the Merduk camp in a semblance of order.
The *Minhraib*—once more disorganized, but this time
by advance, not retreat—surged on regardless to the
edge of what had been their encampment, and were
astonished by the sight that met their eyes.

There on the high ground to their right, where they
had been promised the Nalbenic cavalry would support
them, they saw instead a steady unbroken line of five

thousand grim Torunnan arquebusiers. And behind them in silent rank on rank were the dread figures of the red horsemen who had wreaked such havoc at the North More, their lances stark against the sky, their armour glinting like freshly spilled blood.

The Merduk advance died. The men of the *Minhraib* had been fighting since dawn. They had acquitted themselves well and they knew it, but nearly forty thousand of their number lay dead behind them, and thousands more were scattered and leaderless over the field. The unexpected sight of these fresh Torunnan forces unnerved them. Where had the Nalbeni disappeared to? They had been promised that their counter-attack would be supported on the Torunnan left.

As if in answer, a lone horseman came galloping out of the ranks of the scarlet riders. He brought his horse to within three hundred yards of the *Minhraib* host and there halted. In his hand he bore a horsetail standard which was surmounted by the likeness of a galley prow. It was the standard of a Nalbenic general. He stabbed the thing into the ground contemptuously, his destrier prancing and snorting, and as he did the cavalry on the hill behind him began to sing some weird, unearthly chant, a barbaric battle-paean, a song of victory. Then the horseman wheeled and cantered back the way he had come.

The song was taken up by the ranks of the Torunnan arquebusiers, and in their throats it became something else, a word which they were repeating as though it had some kind of indefinable power. Five thousand voices roared it out over and over again.

Corfe.

•   •   •

THE gunfire died, and a tide of silence rolled over the tortured face of the hills. The winter afternoon was edging into a snow-flecked twilight. Two armies lay barely a league from one another, and between them sprawled the gutted wreck of what had once been a mighty encampment, the land about it littered with the dead. Two armies so badly mauled that as if by common agreement they ignored each other, and the shattered men which made them up strove to light fires and snatch some sleep upon the hard ground, hardly caring if the sun should ever rise on them again.

A single battered mule cart came trundling off the battlefield bearing a cloak-wrapped bundle. Besides its driver, four men on foot accompanied it. The four paused, doffed their helms and let it trundle into the Torunnan camp below, the wheels cracking the frozen snow like a salute of gunshots, whilst they stood amid the stiffened contortions of the dead and the first stars glimmered into life above their heads.

Corfe, Andruw, Marsch, Formio.

"Menin must have died defending him to the end," Andruw said. "That old bugger. He died well."

"He knew this day would be his last," Corfe said. "He told me so. He was a good man."

The foursome picked their way across the battlefield. There were other figures moving in the night, both Torunnan and Merduk. Men looking for lost comrades, brothers searching for the bodies of brothers. An unspoken truce reigned here as former enemies looked into the faces of the dead together.

Corfe halted and stared out at the falling darkness of the world. He was weary, more weary than he had ever been in his life before.

"How are your men, Formio?" he asked the Fimbrian.

"We lost only two hundred. Those *Ferinai* of theirs—they are soldiers indeed. I have never seen cavalry charge pikes like that, uphill, under artillery fire. Of course, they could not hope to break us, but they were willing enough."

"Nip and tuck, all the way," Andruw said. "Another quarter of an hour here or there, and we would have lost."

"We won, then?" Corfe asked the night air. "This is victory? Our King and all our nobility dead, a third of the men we brought out of Torunn lying stark upon the field? If this is victory, then it's too rich a dish for me."

"We survived," Marsch told him laconically. "That is a victory of sorts."

Corfe smiled. "I suppose so."

"What now?" Andruw asked. They looked at their general.

Corfe stared up at the stars. They were winking bright and clean, untouchable, uncaring. The world went on. Life continued, even with so much death hedging it around.

"We still have a queen," he said at last. "And a country worth fighting for . . ."

His words sounded hollow, even to himself. He seemed to feel the fragile paper of Menin's final order crinkling in the breast of his armour. Torunna's last army, what was left of it, was his to command. That was something. These men—these friends here with him—that was something too.

"Let's get back to camp," he said. "God knows, there's enough to do."

EPILOGUE

THE dregs of the winter gale blew themselves out in the white-chopped turmoil of the Gulf of Hebrion. Over the Western Ocean the sun rose in a bloodshot, storm-racked glory of cloud and at once the western sky seemed to catch fire from it, and the horizon kindled, brightening into saffron and green and blue, a majesty of morning.

And out of the west a ship came breasting the foam-tipped swells, scattering spindrift in rainbows of spray. Her sails were in tatters, her rigging flying free, and she bore the marks of storm and tempest all about her yards and hull, but she coursed on nevertheless, her wake straight as the flight of an arrow, her beakhead pointed towards the heart of Abrusio's harbour. The faded letters on her bow labelled her the *Gabrian Osprey*, and at her tiller there stood a gaunt man with a salt-grey beard, his clothes in rags, his skin burnt brown as mahogany by a foreign sun.

Richard Hawkwood had come home at last.